QUINTAIN

QUINTAIN

A NOVEL BY

R.E. HARRINGTON

G.P. PUTNAM'S SONS

NEW YORK

First American Edition.

Copyright © 1977 by R.E. Harrington

SBN: 399-11908-6

Library of Congress Catalog Card Number: 77-4598

PRINTED IN THE UNITED STATES OF AMERICA

For my children, Susan, Robert and John-o,
and
For Ben Kamsler, whose crystal ball is never cloudy.

Quintain (kwin't^{a}n), *n*. a dummy used as a
target in the medieval sport of tilting . . .

and

the name of a man . . .

QUINTAIN

Chapter 1

BROTHER FELIX stood at the window, naked, and looked out upon the spring-quickened landscape. Dropping abruptly away from the window was a narrow ravine, choked with budding brush and wild azalea in abandoned bloom. Beyond the ravine were the fresh-plowed fields of the monastery farm. He heard the groan of the trestle in the bell tower before he heard the first boom of the matin bell.

He took a leather strap from the wall, and let it hang between his legs. He closed his eyes briefly and inhaled the raw odor of the plowed fields laced with the bright-sweet smell of the azalea blossoms. He brought the strap up with a stiff motion of his arm. It snapped across his shoulder, the end striking him between his shoulder blades. The sky was charged with light now, its porcelain glaze unmarked save for the streak of a jet contrail. He began to time the stroke of the strap with the rhythm of the bell. By the time the bell finished tolling the call to matin prayers, his back was a network of bloody welts.

Brother Felix replaced the strap on its hook and, still naked, knelt on the rough stones to offer up his morning devotions. His fellow Brothers, on their way to the fields, looked in the courtyard window at Brother Felix as they silently passed along the walk, their worn sandals scraping the stones.

After his devotions Brother Felix rose stiffly and slipped his black cassock over his head. A worn leather satchel stood open on the stool by his bed. He folded the leather strap and placed it on top of the few articles of clothing already in the

7

satchel. He stepped to the window that faced the courtyard. The yard was empty. Through the other window the Farming Brothers could be seen spreading out into the fields. Somewhere in the distance a tractor engine coughed twice and came to life. Brother Felix stretched out on his back on the floor and inched his head under his bunk. He put his hands up to the underside of the wooden slabs that formed the bunk's only mattress, and tore free an oilskin package anchored there with adhesive tape. Before rising he inched his head into the clear and carefully looked at each window and listened. Then he rose, unfolded the stiff oilskin, and, using a rag to protect his hands, separated an object from the oilskin, carefully folded the oilskin, and put it in his valise. With the valise in one hand, he left the cell without looking back.

Brother-Abbott Gregory was still at his morning prayers when Brother Felix entered the old man's cell. Brother Gregory was always longer at his prayers than the others because, as Abbott, he felt it his duty to pray for each of the living Brothers and as many of those passed on as his brittle old mind could remember. Brother Felix slipped silently into the only chair in the cell and waited for the Abbott to finish.

Brother Gregory stirred, tried to rise, couldn't, and then rested with his palms against the floor. Brother Felix went to him and offered his arm, but Brother Gregory waved it off. "Mortification ... of ..." Brother Gregory said as he painfully got his feet under him, "the ... *flesh* ..." And he was up, swaying slightly as the blood returned to his legs, his breath wheezing through constricted nostrils. Brother Gregory lowered himself carefully into the chair and fastened his eyes on the other man's face. "So. You have prayed over this matter, my brother?"

"Yes. My decision is unchanged."

8

"The Way is hard," Brother Gregory said sternly. "Yet, a month is hardly a trial."

Something flared in Brother Felix's eyes. "I could take it as long as anyone."

Brother Gregory sighed. "Brother—it is not a competition. Well—perhaps it is for the better. Before you told me you were leaving I had my doubts. You were a stranger to me. You still are."

Brother Felix's laugh echoed harshly in the cell. "Brother, this is a *monastic* order."

The old man smiled. "Yes. Still, it would surprise you how well we come to know one another. Words are not necessary, perhaps even a barrier. A glance, a smile, the ... the emanation of a man's spiritual essence. All those ways. Yet, with you, I sensed a closing, a shutting off of yourself from us." Brother Gregory passed a trembling hand across his eyes. "Ah, well. That is not uncommon, I suppose. We didn't have enough time." He looked up into Felix's face. "I wish I had been of service to you, brother."

Felix smiled. "Believe me, brother, you were."

"And now?" Brother Gregory looked away, his brow furrowed. "You won't—"

"No! That is behind me." He paused and stared into the old man's eyes. "As far as I'm concerned."

Brother Gregory shook his head sadly. "How soon the poison of the world invades us once the door is opened. You need not fear, my brother. I am the only one that knows."

Brother Felix glanced toward the office. "And your files—?"

"My files are locked to all but my eyes." The old man got to his feet and stood close to Felix, looking up into his eyes. "My brother, go with my love." He placed his hand on Felix's shoulder. Felix reached inside his robe, as if struck with a sudden ache. He looked deeply into the other man's eyes.

"Did you pray for me this morning, brother?"

9

"Of course." Brother Gregory smiled and patted Felix's shoulder.

"And for yourself?"

Brother Gregory's eyes widened. "I did. But why—"

Brother Felix shot him precisely in the center of the forehead.

The file was locked, but easy. It was old and the lock mechanism weakened with rust. Brother Felix withdrew a file, glanced quickly through it, and stuffed it in his valise. Carrying the valise he returned to Brother Gregory's cell and stood for a moment, looking around the room carefully. Brother Gregory had fallen back in his dying convulsion, landing in a sitting position in the chair, and the force of his fall had carried the chair over. Now his legs rested on the edge of the chair seat, thrusting upward, the hem of his robe fallen back to reveal his puffy varicosed legs.

Brother Felix removed the silencer from the pistol and put both in the satchel. He opened the door to the cell and looked out into the deserted courtyard of the monastery. He left the cell, gently closed the door, and walked across the courtyard toward the highway.

Chapter 2

QUINTAIN couldn't work. He couldn't even think. He slammed the pencil down on the coding charts, ran his hand through his hair, neck to forehead, a habit of frustration that had been with him since childhood.

He looked at his watch. He rose, walked across his office and opened the latch-sprung door that blended into the panelling. Behind the door was a wash basin and a mirror, recessed in a cubicle. He stared at himself in the mirror. Alexander Quintain, rebel. Once again he had shown them. He smiled grimly at his image in the mirror. Screw up my life, will you? If you don't cut it out I'll mess up my hair. Take that!

He rearranged his unresisting hair in a poor facsimile of the style his hair dresser had cut it for and closed the door. He looked at his watch. She was late. It was already ten minutes past noon. She was always late. Part of the game, or something. He sighed. Whatever the game was. He put his ear against the door that connected with the adjoining office. Solid mahogany. He imagined he heard the brief resonance of a deep voice and a thrill of nervousness shot through him. Jesus Christ! What was he doing! Crazy. Certifiably crazy.

Footsteps in the hall. He held his breath until they passed. Outside in that hall flowed the life of Continental Investments, Inc. (Ltd. in London, *Cie* in France . . .), like a walnut panelled artery. People going to lunch. Men clustered at the elevator doors, talking in secret, self-important voices about real estate prices in London, oil leases in Saudi Arabia, the latest fix on the international exchange rate, pound pegged against Swiss Francs, which were pegged against the Reichsmark, which was pegged against the dollar (which, he expected to hear sometime had been pegged against the Spanish dubloon or the Roman Thalerus or some goddam thing, it would make as much sense to *him*). Out there the blood of Continental flowed, while in here? In here a madman brooded.

He rubbed the matte walnut of his desk with his fingertips. Could the walnut trees of the world survive much more success—many more executive suites? He remembered the vinyl top of his old desk beneath him on the fifth floor of the building. The grey drab metal of the furnishings in the tiny office he had, until three weeks age, shared with Burger. To calm his mind, he rehearsed the events in his life during the past weeks. *Truth defeats paranoia*, he said to himself—a slogan given to him by his old analyst years before.

Three weeks before he had been simply Alexander Quintain, Systems Analyst, although no door proclaimed as much. He and Burger shared a door that said "542." (Burger's birthdate was June, something, 1942, and Burger had once suggested they move to the office directly above so that they would at least have something relevant on the door.)

Although they were office mates, Burger, through some subtle perturbation in the organization chart understood only by the deepest thinkers in Personnel, had been his boss. Off and on, that is. Burger was a *Senior* Systems Analyst. Which meant that, for certain projects, he was eligible to be called, *ad hoc*, for the life of the project, *Project Leader*. And Burger always tried, usually successfully, to get Quintain on his projects.

Not that Quintain was the best systems analyst around. Not just that they were office mates, either, but because they were friends. "If we have to endure this shit to survive," is the way Burger explained it, "then we can at least make it tolerable by having those we love around us." Burger had been the first *real* human being Quintain had met at Continental when he had come to work there three years before. The sun-burned idiot in personnel who had screened him and given him the aptitude tests and who through it all kept bouncing on his heels, grinning emptily, and saying, "Good lad," had almost made Quintain run from the building in a suffocating panic.

He had suffered the personnel man, and, later, McCormick, the Manager of Systems, who had given him a pompous self-aggrandizing speech billed as an interview. He had suffered it all because he needed the job. He needed the victory, rather, of being employed.

When Mary had left him, he had bolted; quit his job and run clear out of the state. He had paused for breath in Los Angeles, looked around, and found that the city matched in some ineluctable way his state of mind. Tentatively, he settled in. Then the returns began coming in. From his parents. From Mary's parents. From, finally, Mary herself. Quintain was way 'round the bend. Nuts! Afflicted, eight years prematurely, with fortieth birthday male *dementia.* And not a mild case! No, indeed. Irresponsible! (his father had declared in a thirty-six word telegram), which, in his Father's vast lexicon of terms for describing Quintain's various pathologies, was reserved for only the most hopeless.

Messing up his hair hadn't seemed quite enough, so he had bought an *L.A. Times* and found the Continental ad for "Systems Analyst—Unlimited Opportunity." After the interviews he had gone back to his by-the-week studio apartment on Vermont Avenue, too ennervated by the whole ordeal to pursue anything else. Two days later the Personnel Man called to say, "Sorry, lad—," and Quintain had bought another *Times* and wearily circled the jobs for Systems Analysts. The next morning he was leaving for another interview when the Personnel Man called back. Continental's first choice for the job had changed his mind. Quintain, second choice, could have it if he wanted it. At that point Quintain would've taken a job as Systems Analyst in a Chinese laundry to avoid more interviews. He accepted. "Good lad," said Personnel.

The Monday morning he had reported for his first day's work, Quintain had had an attack of his old paranoia. In the crowded elevator he *knew* attention was riveted on him, although he couldn't catch anyone looking. But he could feel it. The cheap empty briefcase he'd bought the Saturday before seemed to grow in his hands. He tried to hide it with his body. His decidedly Midwestern clothes seemed to wilt and fade in the aura of the hip California dress of his fellow passengers. At the fifth floor he lunged from the elevator like a man escaping from prison. Two people got off behind him and for a moment he was sure they were following him just to satisfy some cruel curiosity at his eccentric appearance. By the time he located 542 he was sweating, his hair a tangled bush, his briefcase clutched against his stomach like a shield. He burst through the door, slammed it, and stood leaning against it, panting and squinting into the sterile fluorescence. Then he saw he wasn't alone. A round man with a bald head and a cherubic mouth glinted his glasses up at him over the desk he was sitting at.

"You," Burger said, "must be Unlimited Opportunity."

"Who ...?" Quintain panted.

"The new Systems Analyst." Burger removed his glasses, revealing large moist blue eyes.

"Yeah," Quintain agreed suspiciously, not moving from the door.

Burger stood and with that twisted little smile of his, bounced on his heels and said, "Good lad!"

Quintain shied like a skittish colt, stared into Burger's

14

eyes, and then laughed. From that moment they were
friends . . .

Now there was one light rap on his door. Immediately it
opened, and she slipped through, grinning wickedly, con-
spiratorially. She locked the door with a graceful, fluid movement, and stood regarding him, one hand on her upthrust
hip, a finger along her cheek. He blushed.

She was dressed in a gold sheath, lightly flowered, white
clog sandals, a delicate locket suspended by a gold chain
at her throat. She wore no makeup, and she needed none.
She knew it wasn't necessary.

"How is my owl?" she wanted to know, in a husky whisper.

As usual, he felt off balance. All the dashing, lover things
he rehearsed in his bed at night stuck and aborted in his
throat. She was two years younger than he, yet he felt like a
child in her presence.

"You're late," he croaked, trying to keep his voice down.

"Hurry," she replied, taking cushions from his two side-
chairs and flinging them on the floor. She turned, arms over
her head, eyes closed. Quintain got up, went to her, put his
arm around her, and pulled down the zipper on the back of
her dress. Then he lifted the dress off her head, trying not to
catch the thick blonde hair in the zipper. She was naked
underneath the dress. He began to undress.

"Jesus. We must be crazy . . ." He glanced at the mahogany
door.

She opened her eyes and made a face. "Scared?"

"Goddam right."

She shivered deliciously. "Me too." She kicked off her clogs
and lay down on the pillows. "Hurry . . ."

She liked to lie like that and watch him undress. Added to
everything else, it made him as nervous as hell. His hands
trembled over his shoelaces, pulling them into knots. He
didn't look at her, but he knew she loved his nervousness,
was watching it all.

15

His anxiety somehow heightened her pleasure. It didn't make sense to Quintain, and he sometimes wondered if it did to her. But, then, she was flakey. That's the way Burger had put it when, on his second week at Continental, Quintain first saw her and asked Burger about her.

Burger had given him one of his quick biographical sketches in which he was so adept and had ended it by saying, "Verna is a bit flakey."

"Verna?" Quintain had asked, feeling unaccountably jealous.

Burger waved a hand. "Everyone knows Verna. The way she looks, combined with her inquisitiveness, has made her a celebrity." Burger stared at the ceiling, his pencil and his lips touching. "I suspect, underneath all that sexiness, is an intelligent woman." Burger went back to his coding. "But warped."

To Burger, women fell into two categories: warped and warpable. And the Great Mating Dance, as he called it, eventually and inevitably brought them all from the latter category into the former. That was the way Burger talked, and normally Quintain loved it. But somehow, connected with the slim golden girl that he had briefly glimpsed, he found it, well, *cheap.*

"I don't know," Quintain said defensively. "I thought she looked rather . . . vulnerable."

Burger had given him a silent knowing look from the tops of his eyes.

There were footsteps in the hall. Quintain froze, listened. A firm authoritative step . . . he knew that step . . . coming right for the door. He made a panicked movement, but Verna caught him with her legs, drew him back.

"You think it's him?" Her voice was an excited purr. "Tell me," she demanded, as her legs clamped him deeply to her, "what do you think he would do?"

16

"My God," Quintain said. "Oh, my god." He tried to listen. The footsteps had stopped. *Where?*

She groaned. Her back was arched so that only her shoulders made contact with the cushions.

After that first time—was it only two weeks ago?—he had said, "Let's meet at my place—"

Sho shook her head.

"Only five minutes by car," he had urged, trying to make his voice light and sophisticated.

She shook her head. "Here," she said.

"But . . . you know," Quintain stammered, feeling somehow that he was revealing a terrible weakness. "The risk."

"Here, or nowhere."

He couldn't quite remember how they had begun. Certainly not through any move on his part. He'd been nearly paralyzed by her sudden appearance in his office.

She had slipped through the door—she had a way of slipping through doors, like an exotic dance movement—and stood regarding him with surprise, or speculation; even now he had a hard time reading her expressions.

"I thought this office was empty."

He stared up at her, stunned. "A week. I've been here a week."

She smiled languidly and walked around him, surveying him. "You look like an owl. Are you an owl?"

He took off his glasses with a trembling hand and tried to adopt a non-owl face. After that, shortly after that, it had happened for the first time. Somehow. He'd been terribly concerned about his performance, her astonishing beauty. She had the air of an expert. And the passion—Jesus! But it must have been good for her, because she kept coming back—every work day at around noon. No agreement, nothing said. She just showed up. He'd lost five pounds, missing lunch, worrying she wouldn't come, terrified she would.

Her climax was for him, as always, a mixture of swooning delight and acid paranoia. She groaned, growled, muttered deliriously, twisted and clawed. He was sure it could be heard five offices away or, more to the point, right next door through that solid mahogany.

He lay next to her, spent, his cheeks burrowed in a cushion, his rump elevated, while she smoked her cigarette. These were the only times he saw her smoke. It was a thin brown cigarette with a gold band and filter. She reached out and absently stroked his bare shoulder. "My owl," she said.

"I adore you," he muttered into the cushion. She laughed.

With his heat abated the paranoia began to dominate him. He wanted to fling on his clothes, urge her to dress, get her out of the office. The possibility of her scorn was a greater threat, so he endured his fear in silence.

That other time, when he'd mentioned his apartment, he'd seen the scorn in her eyes.

"Here, or nowhere," she'd said.

He'd muttered something about *him* being there, right next door. Quintain knew for a fact he was.

"He goes to lunch late," Quintain had informed her. "He's right there, *now.*"

"I know when he goes to lunch."

Of course she did. She would know that. Then he'd understood. She *liked* having him there, just a couple of inches of mahogany separating them. It added something. Maybe everything. Had she chosen Quintain *because* of the office? Would anyone do that happened to be there, right next door to *him*?

Kenneth Sanderson the Third. Quintain's boss. Boss of a lot of people. Senior Executive Vice-President of Continental Investments. And until Quintain's sudden elevation from the fifth floor to the thirtieth floor, the executive suites, a man known only to him by his legend, like a movie star. For

18

Quintain, Sanderson had that movie-star quality, even more so since he'd come up to the stratosphere to work for him. He was a living indictment of everything Quintain was not. Tall and muscular, where Quintain was tall and skinny. White and gold hair curling on his head like a victory wreath, while Quintain's dark hair hung lifelessly wherever chance put it. The air, the physical and mental posture, of being in *command.*

Of being master of every situation, instinctively.

In short, Kenneth Sanderson was everything Quintain would like to have been and had everything Quintain wanted —wealth, famous friends, power—and the most god-awful beautiful wife. Verna.

Quintain heard Verna's quick little intake of breath and knew immediately what had caused it before he raised his head to look. Strangely, he actually felt a release, a kind of resignation. He rolled on his back and looked up at Kenneth Sanderson towering over his naked, defenseless body like a tall building.

Sanderson's face was an inscrutible mask. In his right hand was a set of keys, the key-ring around his index finger, and he was flipping the keys and catching them with his palm. Quintain thought of all his care to lock the door and almost let a bitter laugh escape. Of course Sanderson would have keys to his own suite of offices!

Sanderson stood flipping the keys, still no expression on his face, his eyes studying the scene before him, and suddenly Quintain understood the calm that had come over him when he heard Verna's little gasp and knew that Sanderson had caught them. His paranoia had fled in the face of what Quintain had instantly recognized as the righteousness of Sanderson's position. The paranoia was grounded on a feeling of being wronged by others. But Quintain had wronged Sanderson. No rationalization existed that would change his

19

acceptance of that as a fact. The fear of being caught was realized. The agony of suspense was over.

Sanderson studied Quintain, the keys moving in light-refracting arcs—flip, flip, flip—while Quintain lay at his feet, hardly breathing, waiting for his fate to be decided.

Chapter 3

PRINCE put the Vauxhall in first and crawled up the Irish hill, swearing and sweating. Prince hated the countryside. He was a city man. He particularly hated the Irish country-side, with its monotonous unfolding of green hills and greener pastures, and its staring cows and staring oafish pea-sants. Give him a crowded, smoky Paris bistro, or some neon and plastic New York bar anytime. The Vauxhall and the weather didn't help matters. The Vauxhall cramped around his big body like a tin overcoat, and the weather was hot and spongy, the low-lying clouds pressing down like the lid on a lobster pot.

The Vauxhall's headlights slashed a wooden sign at the intersection of a side-road, and Prince pulled over and backed up until the lights were centered on the sign. Wrong road. He flipped his wrist and the pulsar wristwatch winked on. He had been driving due west from Dublin airport for nearly an hour. To stay to schedule he had to reach the side-road within ten minutes. He put the Vauxhall in gear and slammed it out onto the highway again, trying to gather some momen-tum for the hill he could see faintly looming ahead. He lit a Dunhill and made himself comfortable, tried to clear his mind. His big biceps bulged under the white shirt that luminesced faintly in the dash lights. His hands, the pride of his profession and legendary among his colleagues, dwarfed the Dunhill.

He arrived at the proper crossroad with three minutes to spare. According to the map he had received, memorized, and burned, the rendezvous was three miles into the gravel road. Somewhere around the intersection were, he knew, men with sniper-scope rifles, perhaps in the stand of oaks off to his right, crushing the moss and liverwort under their boots, or wedged into the crevices of the limestone outcropping ahead. There would be others at the rendezvous point, out of sight, watching. Deadly shots, all. If Prince had a suicidal bent, which he did not, all he'd have to do to gratify it would be to stop the Vauxhall and try to turn around. The snipers were all IRA Provisionals, recruited for the occasion because of their neutrality in this matter, and because they owed favors to both sides. Any funny business, any attempt to back out from either side, and they would make short work of the offender. Those were the rules.

For years the Provisionals and Prince's organization had had a reciprocity agreement. The Provisionals were very handy terrorists—the bomb jobs, the quick snipe-and-run engagements; whereas Prince's organization in England called The Group, were experts in the sticky work of espionage, blackmail, discreet assassination. A nice complement.

The Council, the American organization that was the other side in this matter, also had ties to the IRA, so the choice of the Provisionals to oversee the duel was a mutual one. Yet Prince couldn't help feeling a certain pride at the thought that the Provisionals were there in part because of him, because of the favor he had done them.

It had been Christmas in Belfast. At the request of the Provisionals The Group had sent Prince to dispose of a certain Protestant leader who had been causing the IRA fits— planting bombs around Belfast, making it look like the work of the IRA, in order to keep the British stirred up, Parliament on track against withdrawal, and to sabotage the cease-fire.

The Protestant leader had been heavily guarded and very careful, never leaving his fortress of a home without wearing the new lightweight tungsten mesh body armor. But all his precautions had been against the tactics of the Provisionals,

22

not against Prince's methods. Prince had only taken three days to spot the weakness in the Protestant's defenses. Then, with the help of a squad of IRA men, he had set up the assassination for a tobacconer's shop where the Protestant went every morning to buy a paper. Prince had waited in the back of the shop, as the IRA sniper on the roof across the street pumped three bullets through the window of the shop just as the Protestant and his bodyguard entered. The two men ran for the back, just as Prince had known they would. They had run right into his hands.

Prince had always been a little amused at the notion some members of his profession held about the effectiveness of the manual martial arts—karate, judo, more recently kung fu and haikado. Amused and secretly pleased, because there was nothing he liked better than going up against someone who fancied himself an expert in one of those disciplines. Prince, an amateur expert in anatomy, used the hand as it was intended—as a clamp, whereas the so-called experts chopped and hacked and poked with it, trying to make it something it was not. While the karate expert, for example, was raising his hand to strike, Prince was simply thrusting his out and grasping, gaining that split second advantage that made the difference. Of course he was also naturally gifted, endowed with huge, quick hands that he kept trained to a constant peak. He was seldom without a hard rubber ball, flexing it in one hand or the other. And he didn't stop with the hands. They were only as effective, he knew, as the vehicle that delivered them to the target. He worked his body with all the devotion of a professional athlete. He lifted weights and ran whenever he could spare the time. His body had the sleek gloss of toned muscle, but he was careful not to overdevelop it. His chest was a particular worry—he had inherited round, cable-shaped pectorals, and he worried that age would eventually shorten them and make him the half-beat too slow that would mean the end of his career, if not his life. But that was the future, and Prince had learned not to let his thoughts linger over the future. In the present he was at the peak of his physical capabilities.

Which is why the target in Belfast hadn't had a chance. Prince knew that when the firing started, the target and his bodyguard would make for the alley, away from the firing, leaving their men on the street to deal with the sniper. He knew the guard would come through the door first, clearing the way, with his gun out. Prince's right hand darted out, gripped the guard's gun arm at the wrist, and crushed the man's ulna, which made him drop the gun. At the same time his left hand, the slightly better one, had clamped on the target's throat. As he positioned that hand, he slipped the right down to the guard's carpal area and began to crush those bones—not too quickly—because he wanted to paralyze the guard with pain, and he knew if he went too fast there was a danger that shock would protect the gunman from the pain and make him a problem.

He wanted to go quickly with the left, and he did. A split second to feel the correct position on the throat, and then he clamped down with full effort. He felt his thumb splintering through the thyroid cartilage, collapse the trachea, and finally plunge through the larynx to grind against the spinal medulla itself. Then, with a sudden twist, he snapped the neck, and dropped the body of the target and turned to deal with the gunman, who was frozen in agony. It was all over, he estimated, with professional pride, within five seconds ...

Prince braked the Vauxhall to a crawl. He was less than a mile from the rendezvous, several minutes ahead of schedule, and as he used up that time, he searched the terrain, storing quick snapshot impressions for later use. Off to his left was a heath, shimmering in the light of a moon that had broken free of the clouds for a few minutes. The heath was silvered over with bog cotton and some other sedge he couldn't identify. But it was too far away to be a factor. Ahead, rising

24

gently on the horizon, was the pasture that was the rendez-vous. It was rough and bristly, dottled with crowberry and dwarf juniper, and crested at a rise with a stand of mossy old oaks. Beyond, in the far distance, the roof of a building rose above another gentle hill—a barn, or a farmhouse, he couldn't tell which. To his right, the limestone outcropping continued, dwindling away on the horizon to a low hard spine splitting the ground. He guessed that the IRA snipers were in the heath and the limestone, giving them a good triangulation of the pasture. The observers would be there, too—separated, of course. Probably one in the heath, one in the limestone. The terrain offered little in the way of a weapon—an oak limb for a club, perhaps a limestone rock for bashing. Which was fine with him. He had all the weapons he required attached to his wrists.

But he was on guard against over-confidence, the worst enemy he had in his profession. Even though it looked like all the advantages would be his, he didn't dwell on that. Instead, he once again went carefully over all he knew about the man he was to go against in less than twenty minutes.

Felix. That was the name Prince knew him by, the only name he had ever known him by, just as Prince had been his only name for nearly twenty years, since it had been assigned to him when he first entered the profession. Even then Felix had been a whispered legend among those in the profession. At one time, early-on in Prince's career, Felix had been something of a hero to him. Prince had coveted for himself a reputation as legendary as Felix's—the muted awe when his name was mentioned, the bits and pieces of his exploits that circulated in the profession. As Prince had gained a reputation of his own, he tried to tell himself that he was as much of a folk-hero in the business as Felix was.

The difference in their styles couldn't be sharper. Prince was a specialist. His hands were everything. While Felix was an eclectic, using whatever technique and weapon fitted the occasion, he wasn't a dilletante. Dilletantes didn't survive in the profession. Felix had been tough, agile, quick-witted ... *had* been? Prince caught himself. *Was still.* Prince had grown accustomed in the past month to thinking of Felix as dead.

Felix must have gone to very deep cover during that month. Not a word, not a breath to contradict the assumption that his body lay rotting in an Arab-dug grave in that American desert where the operation had exploded in Felix's face.

Then he had surfaced, resurrected. And the first thing he had done was call Prince out. Prince's immediate reaction had been pride. Then excitement at the opportunity the challenge offered to become recognized finally as the best in the world.

Yes, he was proud to be called out by Felix. The custom had been introduced by Felix and some of his contemporaries more than twenty years before. Since then there had been perhaps seven or eight challenges issued, seven or eight confrontations on the field of honor enacted, each one becoming a part of a legend that, inside the profession, carried all the mystique and folk-lore that a few of the great heavyweight championship fights did in the outside world.

Of those challenges, Felix had fought and won two. Every confrontation had been between the greats of the profession. To be called out by Felix was indeed an honor. It elevated Prince to a place that he himself hadn't believed in his heart he occupied. He considered it great good fortune that The Group had sent him on the mission to assist the Arabs in Arizona. Because he had been there, Felix was even now waiting to meet him on the field of honor.

Prince had no doubt about the outcome. He would burn Felix, and then would occupy for all time his rightful place as one of the Greats of the profession. It was indeed sweet compensation for the ever-increasing number of seedy, squalid assignments that he was getting—that every member of the profession was getting. With the advent of more sophisticated electronic techniques, high-altitude spy planes, and public scrutiny of intelligence activities, the profession had gone steadily down hill, degenerating into a back-water of the intelligence community, looked down upon by the public and the bureaucrats alike.

Prince reached the rendezvous point exactly on time. He parked where he had been instructed, on a rutted trail, and stepped out of the car. Although he had never witnessed one of these duels, he knew the procedure by heart. He quickly stripped to bare skin. The rules of the challenge dictated that he and Felix go against each other with nothing more than their native skills and whatever the terrain afforded in the way of weapons. Each man was permitted a wristwatch to time his arrival at the rendezvous point, and then even that was to be flung away. Too many clever things could be done with watches, turning them into weapons as lethal as guns.

Prince walked gingerly to the center of the field, took off the watch and held it above his head for the IRA men to see, and threw it as far as he could. He had deliberately arrived at the center of the field early as a show of confidence, a psychological edge. While Felix scrabbled around in the bushes for weapons, he would be aware that Prince stood calmly waiting for him with no need for anything but his hands. Prince mentally counted the seconds using the old sentry method, and did a strategic examination of the terrain, noting escape routes, hiding places, holes and hummocks that might cause fatal stumbles.

Prince thought he knew the kind of make-shift weapons Felix would come up with. He had put his own mind to the task for several hours, fitting himself into Felix's place. Felix would need weapons that would maintain distance, and neutralize Prince's hands. If Prince ever got a hand on him, it would be over in seconds. Two things afforded distance. A pole or club, and some kind of projectiles, like rocks. Prince was sure Felix would go for the pole. Perhaps a tree-limb, or a fence post. He wouldn't go for both pole and rocks, since the weight would make him clumsy.

The second problem Felix had was finding something to kill with. Felix was a karate expert, but he would never be so foolish as to match his hands against Prince's. Prince had thought about this for two hours, finding and discarding solutions. Finally it had come to him. Felix *would* use karate. He had no other choice. So he would try to neutralize the threat from Prince's hands, and then move in for a killing blow. Prince almost felt sorry for him.

Prince kept counting, hesitated, and checked his count. If he hadn't missed a beat, and he was sure he hadn't, Felix couldn't make it. To be at the center of the field at the appointed time, he would have to make a head-long dash. And no barefoot man was going to make that kind of dash over that rough ground. Prince felt a throb of disappointment. If Felix appeared too late he would be cut down by the IRA men. Prince decided he wouldn't show. Felix was no more suicidal than Prince.

Then Felix showed.

Except he wasn't running. The horse under him was.

Prince almost laughed, the sight was so ludicrous. There was Felix's scrawny old body a-straddle a farm horse, bare heels beating its flanks, a make-shift halter in his left hand— the same hand that held a long oak limb—making straight for the center of the field and Prince. Then Prince was outraged. He almost yelled out that this was a cheat. Technically, of course, it wasn't. Farm animals certainly qualified as resources under the code.

With a curse for allowing himself to be distracted by the sight of Felix and the horse, Prince snapped his mind back in focus. He quickly scanned the approaching apparition, his mind deadly serious. Felix was bent over, the pole in his left

28

hand along the horse's neck. His right arm was hidden by the neck of the horse, clinging to the mane.

Something flickered and died in Prince's mind, something out of place, but he didn't have time to search for it because by that time Felix and the horse were on him. Prince bent his knees slightly, readying himself for his move. Once he got that pole in his hand, the rest would be easy.

Prince made a feint as if to retreat, and then lunged at the pole. His hands were too quick for Felix and he felt his left close around wood, and for a moment he and Felix were joined by the pole.

Suddenly Prince knew what was wrong, but it was too late. Felix had let go of the pole, sending Prince reeling off balance at the sudden release, and had his right arm up, revealing the pitchfork and driving it straight for Prince's chest. Prince, off balance, the pole still clutched in his hand, could do nothing but watch it come. It seemed forever. The tines caught the moonlight, and flashed. As he felt them enter his chest, felt the skin tear and the cartilage and bone begin to rip apart, he knew he had gotten himself in this situation by his own carelessness. When he saw Felix charging with that pole in his left hand he should've known. Felix was right-handed. The danger would come from the right hand.

Prince's mind was fogging with pain. Felix was driving the horse at him, trying to implant the pitchfork deeper. Prince was weak with the pain and shock. Then anger saved him. He planted his feet. He was Prince! No one was going to burn him this way! He twisted his upper torso out and away from Felix's charge, and all the years of conditioning paid off. The tines of the pitchfork were deeply imbedded in those cabled pectoral muscles of Prince. Felix made one desperate, lunging effort to pull the pitchfork free, and then the horse carried him past.

Prince staggered and fell to his knees. He got a hand up

B

to hold the pitchfork, but he couldn't free it in the time he had. Felix was off the horse and coming at him. Prince lurched to his feet holding the pitchfork handle in his right hand, keeping it at right angles with his body, as he brought his left up. Felix simply leaped quickly to Prince's right, and his hand flashed toward Prince's exposed neck. Prince managed to spin with the blow, as he had been trained, but the pitchfork slowed him. The blow caught him high on the neck, and dropped him to his knees again. Prince bent forward and let the ground support the pitchfork handle, freeing both hands to meet the next attack. But it never came. Felix ducked, and when he came up he had the pitchfork handle in his hands. Prince stared at him across the feet separating them, his mind fogging again. He shook off the fog, and tried to stand. But Felix planted his body solidly in the turf, and leaned into the handle. Slowly, agonizingly, Prince yielded, going back first to sit on his heels, and then toppling backward onto the ground. Felix went with him, coming up over Prince and hanging his weight from the handle until his feet literally left the ground. Prince's chest was gushing. He got his hands on the handle, but they were as weak as a baby's.

His eyes locked with Felix's, and as the pitchfork gave suddenly and horribly to meet the ground under him, anger took him for a moment to a lucid plateau.

"I'm *Prince!*" he shouted . . .

And died.

Chapter 4

WHEN DIAMOND was certain Prince was dead, he lowered the binoculars and said to the IRA sniper on his left, "That's it."

The sniper slung his rifle and waved his arm in a high slow arc. Another sniper rose from the limestone formation where Diamond stood and, across the meadow, two figures stepped from the trees. They all advanced toward the center of the field.

The horse grazed peacefully at the edge of the field. Felix was disappearing into the trees. Prince lay where he had fallen, pinned to the ground with the pitchfork. As he passed by, the horse raised its head and looked at Diamond indifferently.

Diamond went over what he had seen, impressing the event indelibly in his mind. He knew that when he got back to the States The Council would want to hear every detail. Excitement still welled in Diamond. He had never witnessed anything like the duel.

When The Council had been contacted by Felix, when they had recovered from the shock of finding a man they had thought dead was very much alive, and got down to discussing the duel Felix had asked them to arrange, Diamond had been adamant. He was the Chairman of The Council, and he would arrange the duel and be the observer. Each member of The Council had had a passionate reason why *they* should observe, but Diamond had dug in stubbornly and finally they had given in on the condition that a special meeting be convened when he returned so they could share his experience at least vicariously. Diamond didn't blame them for envying his position. In all his years in the profession this had been the first opportunity he'd had to witness such an event.

As the men gathered around Prince's body, one of the IRA men put his foot on the corpse's chest and heaved the pitchfork free. Two others, their rifles slung, picked up the body and staggered off with it in the direction of Prince's car.

"Need any help?" Diamond asked the Irish leader.

"Well in hand. We'll cover you out of here. When you reach the highway, you're on your own."

"The Group's observer?"

"On his way. His man lost, so no reason for him to hang about."

Diamond found Felix beyond the oaks, dressed and standing quietly beside a pale green Audi.

"Well, Felix," Diamond said nervously. "No good to ask where you've been, I suppose. The Council is a bit curious."

Felix stared at him for a long moment. "I am a member of The Council."

"Still, it would seem that you could've gotten some word to us."

"Who could I trust?"

"Of course. But why did you come out of cover now?"

"I got word that The Group, Prince in particular, had a hand in trying to burn me in Arizona. All I was waiting for was to find out who it was."

"Word? From ... ?"

"Never mind. I have my contacts. Tell me what you know. Who on The Council betrayed me?"

Diamond resisted the impulse to avert his eyes from Felix's steady gaze. "Stone and Cutter."

Felix paused, thinking. Then he mentioned Stone's and Cutter's real names. Diamond nodded. "They stole money from the legitimate side of the company. The Council had to

32

replace it when we found out. We can't afford a government audit right now . . ."

"Never mind that," Felix waved aside talk of business. "Why did they betray me? Who was Prince working with in Arizona? He had a squad of professionals, and they weren't from The Group."

Diamond shrugged. "You and I can both guess who was with Prince . . ."

"The Arabs," Felix said flatly. "That group of fanatics led by the one they call the Colonel."

Diamond nodded. "Stone and Cutter needed money—needed it fast. They thought if they betrayed you, and you were burned, the flap it would cause on The Council would cover their escape."

Felix smiled grimly. "And also remove their greatest danger."

Diamond sighed wearily. It had been a long day. "Yes. You need not remind me, Felix, that you are the best professional in the world. You proved it again today. Of course Stone and Cutter breathed easier when they thought you were dead."

"And now?" Felix stared into Diamond's eyes. Diamond fought down an urge to shudder.

"Stone and Cutter had an accomplice, a computer expert. They believe they've arranged it so it appears he was in it alone, that he took the money by himself."

"And The Council?"

"We've let Cutter and Stone believe they're safe, that only the computer man is implicated. Naturally, when we discovered you were alive, we knew you would want to deal with them yourself."

"You were right. But what's to prevent this computer man from taking to his heels?"

"He works for the company, of course. But he's an outsider to The Council. He doesn't even know you exist. Don't you see, Felix—it's perfect. Stone and Cutter will make sure he stays around, because they want him to take the fall for the embezzlement. They'll stay around themselves, because they believe they're safe." Diamond cut himself off. He knew he was over-selling to Felix, and he damned himself for it.

"I intend to get the truth out of them before I kill them," Felix said. His eyes pinned Diamond, searching his face almost hungrily.

Diamond knew Felix was searching for his reaction. Felix had never trusted him. To divert Felix's attention, Diamond looked at his watch, and said, "I've got us booked out of Dublin Airport in two hours."

"I'm flying from Heathrow," Felix announced. "I've some business in London first. Did you bring documents for me? I'll need to carry a gun on . . ."

Diamond produced a plastic sheathed card from his wallet and handed it to Felix. Felix stared down at it. "What is this . . . ?"

"They've put out new ID since you've been . . . away. That's a CIA pass. Gives you total diplomatic immunity. It's registered against your fingerprints in every major capital . . ."

"All right." Once again Felix waved away talk of procedures. "Do nothing until I arrive."

Diamond drew himself up. "I am Chairman of The Council. Don't give me orders."

"Do nothing until I get there—please." Felix's smile was a grim scar in the moonlight.

Diamond stared silently at Felix for a long moment. Finally, he nodded.

"This outsider—" Felix said. "This computer expert that was behind Cutter and Stone—what is his name?"

"Quintain," Diamond replied. "Alexander Quintain."

At Dublin Airport Diamond checked in at the airline desk and then walked to a bank of public telephones. He popped

34

the clasp of his watch band open and a small piece of paper fell from it into his hand. He dialed the Dublin phone number written on the paper, and then burned the paper with his lighter.

"Yes."

"Heathrow Airport," Diamond said. "I don't know when. The next day or so, I'd guess."

"We'll take care of it."

The line went dead. Diamond walked to a bench, sat, and waited for his plane to be called.

Chapter 5

QUINTAIN'S calm lasted but a moment. Two thoughts swept it aside, leaving a void for the fear to fill. The first was, *Damn Burger, for getting me into this.* Which he instantly recognized as unfair, and typical—blaming others for his own mistakes. With that self-criticism, instead of damning Burger, he began to wish he was there, to help him by saying something clever to Sanderson. Burger was good at that. The clever quip that turneth away wrath. Quintain was not.

Fear pierced his shock, and Quintain became aware of Verna sitting naked beside him, gazing up at her husband, and he wondered at her calm. Didn't she know the danger she was in—they were both in? Didn't she realize that their lives were on the line . . . ?

Quintain had never doubted from the start that if Sanderson caught them the consequences would be brutal. Sanderson was one of the heroes of the world, and you didn't mess with a hero's woman if you cared for having your head attached to your body. That was Quintain's closely held belief about heroes. And if you were a hero's wife, you might be a *little* safer (in that the hero would go for you last, perhaps), but not much. That's what Quintain wanted to shout at Verna in that split second eternity they sat staring up at Sanderson towering over them. He wanted to jar the calm and complacency that seemed to come so easily to her.

Yes. He'd gotten himself into it. No one forced him to take the job. In fact, Burger had put it just that way.

"No one's forcing you, Slick." (Burger had taken to calling him Slick after an encounter they had had with a pair of stewardesses in a bar. Quintain knew it was Burger's way of satirizing his ineptitude with women, but, nevertheless, Quintain rather liked it.)

When Quintain had told Burger about the job offer it had been at the end of an exciting and confusing day.

"Burg, if I tell you something, can I rely on your discretion?"

Burger brought his round body to a posture of military attention. "I swear t' ya, Billy Boden, they's not a bloody limey h'alive kin wrench it from me."

Quintain frowned, trying to place it. "I give . . ."

"Victor McLaglen, in *The Informer*," Burger said proudly.

Quintain laughed. "That was a *cockney* accent!" Burger was famous for his atrocious imitations. "Not even a *good* cockney accent."

"Cockney, h'irish, alls th' same to me, Guv. Now wots this bloody awful secret?"

"I'm scared shitless of Sanderson."

Burger laughed heartily. "Jesus, Slick—so's everybody in this building."

Later, in the bar of the restaurant where they went to have dinner, Quintain hoisted his first Gibson, and said, "Everybody in the building doesn't have to work for Sanderson."

"So?"

"So he makes me so goddam nervous I can hardly croak out a word in his presence."

"If you ask me," Burger replied solemnly, "that works to your advantage. Your most effective conversational asset is silence."

"Jesus, Burg! What would I do without you around to pump up my ego?"

"You'd go—" And Burger made a noise with his lips like a deflating balloon. A woman down the bar turned to stare at him, and Burger shrugged at her and gave her an angelic smile.

Quintain had two quick Gibsons at the bar, and ordered a third when they were shown to their table. He began to feel brave. "I guess I'll just take that job."

"There you go, Slick. Grab that bear by the tail."

"Assistant to The Senior Executive Vice-President," said Quintain, rolling the words on his tongue.

Burger laughed over a forkfull of prime rib. "There's not a portal in the building wide enough to hold that title. You'll have to install a garage door."

Quintain didn't join Burger's laughter. His bravado had gone as fast as it had come. "Why me?" he asked, frowning.

"Now there's an original question. Have you ever thought of giving up computers for philosophy?"

"No, goddamit, Burg. I mean it. Why pick me? Sanderson doesn't even know me."

"Because, laddie, he needs a systems man. And, even though I've seen your work, I have to admit you pass for one."

"Christ—there're a hundred systems men at Continental."

Burger sighed. "Okay, Slick. I'll give you the chronology —although I can't imagine anyone being interested in anything so boring." Burger took a dark thin cigar from his coat pocket and lit it. With his round bald head, his baby's cheeks, his glasses glinting in the low light, and the cigar in his mouth, he looked to Quintain like some puckish elf who had just stepped out of the Black Forest.

"Sanderson needs a systems man," Burger continued after he'd gotten his cigar going. "He has some wild-ass idea that he wants to personally implement. Don't ask me what it is. The workings of Senior Executive Vice-Presidents' minds and the Orphic mysteries are all one to me. Besides, he didn't tell McCormick; and, therefore, McCormick didn't tell me . . ."

"He didn't tell me, either," Quintain replied with a worried frown. "Just said it was something he knew I could handle."

38

"Which means nothing—" Quintain raised an eyebrow. "Look—one of the rules of membership on the thirtieth floor is that you have to speak inspiringly to the lessers on the other floors. Anyway, you want to hear this goddam story, or not—?"

Quintain shut up.

"Okay," Burger said, eyeing the end of his cigar suspiciously. "So Sanderson has some pet project. It requires the use of a computer. Ergo, he goes looking for a computer man. And who's got the computer men? Why, our beloved chief, McCormick, of course. So Sanderson summons Mac, and gives him the honor of sharing his personnel problem. Now, you may not have noticed, because he disguises it so well, but Mac does have an ounce or two of shrewdness. Particularly when it comes to protecting his own ass. He's in a bit of a bind, with this request of Sanderson's. Like any good computer executive, Mac abhors losing even the tiniest little crumb of his empire. And Sanderson has made it plain that the man that goes upstairs will still have his salary charged against Mac's budget—"

"Aha!"

"Indeed, aha, and in fact, ha ha. The only thing Mac will get out of this whole thing is a little appreciation from Sanderson which, believe me, on the present market, won't buy you a hot cup of coffee. *And* he stands to lose a warm body. So Mac does the only decent thing—he starts looking around for the systems analyst whose absence will hurt him the least."

"Thanks a whole fucking lot!"

"Now, now, Slick," Burger held up the palm of the hand with the cigar in it. "Hear me out. You ain't been gored near as bad as you think."

Once again, Quintain shut up.

"So Mac ropes me in on the deal. Hell, I say, I'll take the job, and start giving him a whole routine about what a lazy

39

shit I am. But he's not buying. Wants to keep me around, I suppose, because I have such a good ass for kicking. So—when I see I can't have the plum, I make up my mind somebody I love will. And who do I love most—?" Burger grinned around his cigar, his glasses glinting at Quintain.

"You mean—?"

Burger nodded smugly. "I convinced Mac that you are the most useless turd in the whole department. Which, considering our department, is some kind of worldwide honor."

Quintain grinned, feeling a whole gin-cloud of love for Burger. Then it hit him. "But, Jesus—what if I turn it down?"

Burger shrugged and made a petulant moue. "Christ, Slick! I never thought you'd think twice. I thought you'd be like me—jumping at the goddam thing." Burger stared morosely at the cigar butt. "If you turn it down, I'll make it right with McCormick—some way."

Quintain waved off the suggestion with a drunken slash of his steak knife that nearly decapitated one of the plastic flowers in the center of the table. "I'll take it!" He had cried. "I'll take it!"

What else could he do? Stay where he was and have McCormick thinking of him as the most useless turd in the whole department? With all the best, loving intentions in the world, Burger had put him in this situation.

Damn Burger for getting me into this!

Kenneth Sanderson the Third actually smiled! A half-twist of his lips that, from Quintain's perspective, looked sadistic and malevolent. He's going to enjoy killing me! Quintain thought, his mouth agape.

"Close your mouth and put on some clothes," Kenneth Sanderson the Third said. "You're ludicrous."

Quintain closed his mouth, leaped up, and began trying to pull his pants over a trembling leg with trembling hands. Sanderson could've told him anything, to jump out the window, and he would've done it, instantly.

While he struggled with his clothes, Quintain listened to Sanderson and Verna talking with an aural acuteness that was almost painful.

"I know what you're doing," Sanderson said.

"Do you?" Verna smiled lazily up at him.

"There are limits, Verna."

"Are there? Are there limits, Kenneth?"

"Goddam it!" (Here it comes, Quintain thought. She's done it now. She's gotten him mad. Quintain wondered how he was going to make a run for it with one leg in his pants.)

Sanderson visibly controlled himself. "Get dressed."

Verna rose to her feet in one fluid movement and picked up her dress. "I didn't know there were limits, Kenneth. You should've told me. I thought just the opposite—"

"Shut up!" (Quintain jumped a foot. Verna took it calmly, snaking into her dress. Quintain cautiously reached out a toe, snagged his shirt which was lying between him and Sanderson, and inched it toward himself.)

"Are you setting out deliberately to ruin things for us?" Sanderson asked his wife. "Weren't you aware of the risks?"

"Of course." She smiled in the way that (formerly) drove Quintain mad with lust. "That's the point. You have said yourself, on many occasions—"

"All right," Sanderson said wearily. "You insist on baiting me. But get this. You are going to behave yourself, until—" His eyes swung around to Quintain, who was trying frantically to undo the knots in his shoelaces.

"Get out of here!"

Quintain jumped up, one shoe on, the other in his hand. "Yessir!" He limped for the door.

"Ah—Quintain—"

"Yessir?"

"Take the rest of the day off. Be in my office at nine in the morning."

"Yessir!" Quintain bolted out the door, down the hall to

41

the elevator, and flung himself on it when it arrived. A grey-haired woman on the elevator stared and cringed against the wall. A man in a suit carrying a briefcase gave Quintain one surprised look and then pretended he didn't exist. Quintain was too busy with his own problems to notice. He knew exactly where he was going.

He leaped out at the fifth floor, was peripherally conscious of his shoulder grazing a young man carrying a stack of boxes, but didn't hear the thump of the boxes falling to the floor, or the stifled curse that followed, because by that time he was already at Burger's office door.

Burger looked up with that slightly bored, noncommittal half-smile he affected until he identified intruders, and then his mouth fell open, and then his eyes widened, and then he snatched off his glasses and looked accusingly at them as if they had betrayed him.

"Jesus, Slick—what's the matter?"

"I've got ..." Quintain panted, "to ... talk to you."

"Hey—the building's not on fire, or anything—?"

"No. I've got ... talk to you."

"Okay. Sure."

"Not here!"

"What? All right. Sure. Let's see—first let's get that other shoe on. There's a good lad. And tuck in that shirt—and the zipper. Where's your coat and tie? Never mind. Tell me later. After we administer a little emergency treatment. If I ever saw a man who needed a drink ..."

Burger, as Quintain knew he would, took him in hand. Got his clothes straightened out, put an arm around his shoulder, and led him carefully, as if he were a fragile old man (which, in a way he had become in the past few minutes) down the elevator, out onto the street, and into Tony's bar in the next block.

They sat in a booth at the back. Half-way through his first Bloody Mary, Quintain's trembling abated enough that he didn't have to use both hands to pick up the glass. Burger waited patiently, making it plain through his relaxed posture and his little half-smile that Quintain should take his time, that he, Burger, had all day and all night if necessary. Quintain was very grateful to have a friend like Burger.

As Quintain told Burger the story, the horror of his situation came flooding back and by the time he finished he was staring morosely at the celery stalk in his third Bloody Mary.

"Jee-sus!" Burger whispered reverently. "Verna!" And then looked at Quintain in a way that communicated a lot.

For all his round physique and babyish, petulant mein, Burger was a killer with women. Quintain had tried to analyze, in the hope he could emulate it, what about Burger attracted women to him like iron filings to a magnet. But he hadn't been able to. He supposed it was the devilishly innocent look he could get in his eyes, or maybe the quick quips that made them laugh, or maybe even that old bromide about the virility of bald men—or maybe all that and more. Whatever, analyzing it hadn't helped Quintain in the least. Now, here was the student telling the maestro that he had just played at Carnegie Hall to a packed house.

"Verna!" Burger repeated in awe.

Even with all the anxiety besetting him, Quintain couldn't help feeling a little proud.

"I know for a fact," Burger said solemnly, "that Verna has never put out for anyone else at International."

"For a fact ... ?"

Burger lowered his head modestly. "I gave her my best shot."

Quintain couldn't help laughing. "And if Burger can't score ..."

"Exactly." Burger smiled broadly. "Until ol' Slick came along."

Quintain's laugh died in a groan. "Burg, I am in trouble. Big fucking trouble."

"That's the kind you're in, all right," Burger replied, his eyes glinting. Then, suddenly serious, "But maybe not. Let's analyze—"

"Analyze, hell. It's simple. If Sanderson doesn't decide to kill me, after all, he'll fire me."

"Wait. You're not using your head. I can see Sanderson getting physical in the, ah, heat of the moment. But that moment's past. He's too cool to rough you up after the fact."

"I hope you're right. But the job's down the drain."

"I don't know. Why didn't he can you right off? Why make an appointment to do it?"

Quintain shook his head slowly. "I don't know. It doesn't matter. I'll have to quit, anyway."

"Whoa! Why do you say that?"

Quintain looked up in astonishment. "You think—you *actually* think I can go back and work with him like nothing happened—?"

Burger tapped his lower lip with his celery stick. "Sure. That's it! Sanderson is the man of the world. Jet-setters, he and Verna. Even though he's probably raging inside, his code says, take it like a sophisticate—*savoir faire*, and all that. 'Had a go at the little woman, did you old chap? Heh, heh. Bloody good joke on me.' ..."

"You know what you are?" Quintain asked. "You are nuts."

Burger shrugged and smiled his angelic smile. "Well—it's as good a theory as any, right now."

"I'm never going back," Quintain muttered.

"Suit yourself, Slick. But I don't see what the harm is in at least going in tomorrow and seeing what he has to say. Hell—" he added gruffly, "I'd hate to see you go. You're about the only one left at Continental that makes sense."

After the Bloody Marys they switched to scotch. Quintain told Burger how the affair with Verna had started. With the scotch melting his fear, it now all seemed to Quintain somehow ludicrous. He couldn't stop laughing, and soon Burger

44

joined in, and they leaned across the table gasping and pounding each other on the arms.

At five o'clock the Continental crowd began to drift in. Pendelton, the Vice-President of Personnel, walked by their booth shepherding Miss Palmer, a little grandmother of a lady who worked in accounting. Pendelton's eyes flickered over Burger and Quintain and he gave them a curt nod. He was a dandy little man, dressed in his customary suit and vest with a half an inch of starched shirtsleeve showing the gold cufflinks at his wrists.

Miss Palmer paused and stared into the booth near-sightedly through her steel-rimmed thick glasses. Pendelton continued on to the bar.

"Mr. Burger and Mr. Quintain," she said. "What are you boys up to?"

Burger held his glass up to her. "Getting gloriously drunk, Miss Palmer."

"My, my," she said with a devilish smile. "I can see that the young ladies will need police escorts tonight.'"

Burger leered at her. "Especially you, Miss Palmer." Miss Palmer chuckled throatily. "Buy you a drink?"

Miss Palmer looked over her shoulder to the bar where Pendelton was sitting, looking impatient. "Better not," she whispered, with her finger to her lips. "Mr. Pendelton has first rights on me tonight."

Burger watched her walk primly to the bar and climb up on a stool by Pendelton. "Thirty years ago I'll bet she was something."

Burger turned his attention to Quintain. "Pendelton didn't seem overjoyed to see you, Slick. You think he holds a grudge?"

Quintain colored slightly and shrugged. The incident Burger was referring to had occurred nearly two years before. Quintain had blocked it out of his memory, as he might an old illness. In a way it had been—the paranoia had had a

45

grip on him every bit as tenacious as any physical illness.

At ten o'clock of a grey February morning, Burger had been tied up and Quintain went ahead to the canteen on the second floor of the Continental building to wait for Burger to join him for their morning coffee break.

The canteen was crowded, but Quintain managed to get a small table near the door. Pendelton was at a table across from him, drinking coffee with a group from personnel. Quintain put his coat on the back of a chair to indicate the table was reserved and went to the coffee machine. He was sweating by the time he reached it. He was sure every eye in the room was riveted on him. Crowds did that to him. As he put his coins in the machine his back crawled with the impact of those eyes. He had worked at Continental for a year, and yet he hardly knew anyone in the room. It was a room full of hostile strangers with but one mind, and that mind was focused maliciously on him he was sure, waiting for him to make a fool of himself. He quickly obliged.

As he turned with the coffee in his hands, they began to tremble, and the coffee sloshed over the rim of the cup and stained his pants. He kept walking, in a half crouch, the coffee cup clamped in both his trembling hands. There was nothing else he could think to do. The trembling became worse. He kept his eyes on the floor as he inched painfully toward the safety of his table that now seemed a mile away. The coffee spilled again, this time splashing his shoe. Over the buzz of voices in the room someone laughed. He was sure that that laugh was directed at him. Anger rose in him like a hot knife. Then, suddenly, Pendelton was at his side, taking the coffee cup from him.

"Here, let me have that. Are you all right—?"

Quintain spun in one blinding moment of raw instinct, and with his forearm slammed Pendelton up against the wall of the room. The rest of the coffee spilled down Pendelton's immaculate vest. A hushed silence descended on the room

46

like a curtain. Pendelton stared into Quintain's face with stark terror.

"Now, now ..." A hand gripped Quintain's shoulder and turned him away from Pendelton. Quintain spun with his fist ready, and stared without recognition into Burger's round, benign face.

"Hold on, there, Quint," Burger said with a small grin and wary eyes cutting at Quintain's raised fist. Quintain lowered his fist, stared wildly around at the shocked faces, and then ran from the canteen. Burger assured him later that he had squared things with Pendelton by telling him Quintain had just been through a tragic personal experience. Not exactly a lie, except that that tragedy of his divorce was nearly a year old at the time.

As he sat in the bar with Burger, the horror of that moment came flooding back to him. The memory of the sudden release of his hostility in the canteen that day was a painful scar on his soul. He got up from the booth and stood for a moment until the floor stopped swaying under his feet. Burger looked up at him questioningly. Quintain carefully made his way to where Pendelton and Miss Palmer sat. He extended his hand to Pendelton.

"Never apologized," Quintain slurred. "Sorry. Didn't mean it."

Pendelton, looking embarrassed, took Quintain's hand and made some vague sound of acknowledgement. Miss Palmer put her hand on Quintain's shoulder, and laughed.

"Dear boy," she said gaily, "you are getting sloshed."

Burger and Quintain left the bar shortly after that. They took a cab to a Mexican restaurant on Western Avenue. On the way Quintain was lost in his reveries. Through the fog of alcohol clouding his mind, he relived again his violent reactions to his paranoia, and wondered as he had done often in the past at the sudden rages it could induce. The psychiatrist he had gone to had tried to explain it, but Quintain never

47

fully understood it except on an intellectual level. It was as if all the imagined and real plots against him were a catalyst that built up the violence until it had to erupt. That was one of the reasons Mary had left him. He had never harmed her physically, but he had frightened her greatly whenever he had flown into one of his rages in her presence, shouting incoherently, breaking dishes, furniture, whatever came to hand.

The heavy Mexican food sobered them a little—just enough to let them launch into the drinking again at Burger's apartment. Burger urged Quintain to see Sanderson the following morning. Quintain, with the aid of all the alcohol he had consumed, began to think the whole Sanderson business wasn't as serious as he had imagined. By the time he staggered out of Burger's apartment at one in the morning, he had assumed a rather arrogant attitude about his ability to handle Sanderson.

What the hell, he told himself. Might as well go in in the morning and see what the man has to say.

Chapter 6

FELIX took a seat on a bench in the Pan American waiting room at Heathrow Airport outside of London, opened the London *Times*, and lit a cigarette. Felix didn't smoke. He hated the taste of cigarettes, but he always carried a pack, along with the polished chrome Ronson in a little velvet case. He carried them for times like this. When he wanted to look behind him. And the Ronson was a good mirror.

The man was there. Across the lobby, at the ticket counter with his back to Felix. It was a professional surveillance, he knew that. He'd first spotted it after he'd gotten in the cab at the rental agency in London where he'd turned in the Audi and picked up a cab. It had been a relay tail. First a green Jaguar XJ–6 following several cars back. When Felix had picked up the Jag, it had been one of three candidates. Then a blue Rover had made a right off a side street to pull in ahead of the cab, and the Jag dropped off. Then he had known for sure that he was being tailed. The Rover sped ahead when a black Renault picked him up from behind. The Renault stayed on until they were clear of London, and then the Rover reappeared ahead, the Renault dropped off, and the Rover led the cab all the way to Heathrow.

Felix dropped his satchel on the floor of the cab, got out without it, paid the driver, and walked almost to the entrance before he spun around and ran back yelling at the cabbie who was just pulling out into traffic. Up the way, in the passenger pick-up lane, a man in a plaid jacket was getting out of the passenger side of the Rover. Felix retrieved his satchel, and went into the terminal. He was certain no one else had gotten out of the Rover. Which didn't prove any-thing. The other cars could be arriving outside at that moment.

Felix stubbed out the foul-tasting cigarette, and, pretend-ing to read *The Times*, thought his situation through very carefully.

It could be simply a surveillance. If that was the case, it was probably those idiots in the Council, wanting to keep track of him, suspicious and distrustful about his month's absence.

He speculated for a moment that the surveillance was somehow a result of his killing Brother-Abbott Gregory at the monastery. But the man watching him didn't have the look of a policeman. The situation just didn't smell like a police surveillance. Besides, he had covered his tracks well. The file he had taken from the Abbott's cell was the only link between Brother Felix and his real identity, other than the Abbott himself.

Even while speculating that the people following him might be there because of his murder of the Abbott, Felix did not question the wisdom of that murder. The Abbott and his files had been loose ends, and Felix never left loose ends. He had learned long ago that inattention to such details could cause, in the most unexpected ways, fatal consequences for someone in his profession.

Felix took a small tin from his vest pocket and popped a breath lozenge in his mouth, to remove the taste of the cigarette. He was dressed in a beautifully tailored worsted suit, a dark blue silk shirt, and a light grey tie. His tonsured pate was covered with a toupee that had been especially made and fitted for him. He looked like an elegant, slender, though rather severe, English businessman, although when he spoke the faint edge of a Slavic accent showed. When he put the lozenge tin back, he let his hand briefly feel the large comb clipped to his inside coat pocket.

He got up, folded the paper under his arm, and walked to the ticket counter. The man in the plaid jacket was in a phone stall, pretending to have a heated conversation with someone. Felix pulled out his ticket, and showed it to the girl behind the counter.

"Pardon me. Is this flight on time?"

"Yes sir," She gave him a plastic smile. "Flight Forty-nine, to New York, boarding eleven-thirty at gate B ..."

While she was going through her routine, Felix was reading the flight board on the wall behind her. There was a flight to Paris boarding now. Too soon. There was another in thirty minutes. A bit late, but it would have to do. He would have to gamble that they hadn't set up an assassination in the middle of the Pan Am waiting room.

He went back to the bench and pretended to read his paper for fifteen minutes, and thought through his situation. He had to assume it was an assassination. Three times during the fifteen minutes he lit a cigarette to keep track of the man in the plaid coat. The man was staying well back, which either meant he was acting as back-up to the actual assassins or the strike was to be somewhere other than the waiting room. Felix had given himself a margin by putting distance between himself and others in the waiting room. He chose a place on the end of the bench, and spread parts of the paper beside him for several feet to discourage others from sitting by him. If they were professionals they must know he wasn't going to let himself be trapped in a restroom or an empty corridor. The announcement for his flight came over the PA system. He stood, picked up the valise, and leaving *The Times* on the bench started for the boarding gate. If there were no other moves, no other indications, he would simply get on the plane, carefully checking who followed him on. They might try it in flight, but he doubted it. No professional would put himself in that kind of position, trapped in an

51

aluminum prison thirty thousand feet in the air, with a corpse on his hands.

Felix found the airport security office and waited patiently while two uniformed men studied his CIA pass, took his fingerprints, and transmitted them to London for verification. Then he was led through an interior corridor by a young woman and out into a main corridor where the woman passed him through the security checkpoint at his boarding corridor, with his gun still in his valise. That was little comfort to him. He knew that the men watching him would have the same privileges.

As he walked down the boarding corridor he followed a slender woman in a tweed traveling suit carrying an expensive-looking leather flight bag. Gate B, where he was to board, looked normal. A bored passenger agent checked the ticket of the woman in the tweed suit against the passenger list while Felix stood waiting with a look of weary patience on his face to disguise the careful surveillance he made of the waiting area. A stewardess in a crisp blue Pan Am uniform hurried into the boarding tunnel, her heels clacking efficiently. A maintenance man in grey coveralls with a Pan Am logo on the pocket stood on a ladder by the gate sign, changing a fluorescent light fixture in the ceiling. The waiting area was empty. Those who had been waiting were by now on board, an unwatched TV set flickering in the corner of the lounge. Through the windows Felix could see the silver nose and a section of the fuselage forward of the wings of the Pan Am jet, the empty first class windows staring back vacantly at him.

The passenger agent finished with the woman, waved her through, and checked Felix through. The woman was halfway down the tunnel when Felix entered. Behind him the agent was in an argument with a passenger about some mistake on his ticket and the agent was directing him elsewhere for correction, and the man was arguing loudly and belligerently. Felix was well into the tunnel, the woman in tweed and the stewardess ahead at the door of the plane, when it hit him. The empty windows! Possible explanations flashed through his mind: a small first-class passenger list, but the agent had checked Felix's ticket against a manifest that had looked quite full; or, for some unaccountable reason those passengers already aboard were sitting everywhere but in the forward port window seats—unlikely, improbable ... these thoughts strobing across his mind unassisted in the time it took him to pop open the valise, shove his hand in, grip the automatic, no time for the silencer, and send a shot through the soft vinyl of the valise into the chest of the stewardess, her body spinning and falling away into the interior of the plane.

The woman in tweed had her back to him, which gave him time to pull the gun free, letting the satchel fall, and he fired as she turned, her right arm raised so that the heavy caliber gun in her hand was in that very military, very professional ready position, and he caught her in the side of the chest under the raised arm, having learned so long ago that the memory of learning was gone, that you fired for the big areas of the body first, putting your opponent down before trying any fancy marksmanship to the very few instant-killing spots on the human body.

As he saw the woman in tweed fold herself into the floor with a grunt and a whispering, sad sigh, he was aware of a sudden dimness, a damping of the light in the tunnel to just the weak glow of the light tubes along the side of the roof, and he was turning and crouching in the same swift movement, the gun hand forward, sweeping ahead of his turn, when a violent, knifing blow numbed his right arm and sent the gun spinning away up the tunnel toward the still form of the woman. Felix instinctively let his body collapse so that he was squatted on his heels, his chin crammed firmly against his chest protecting the vulnerable throat, knees pressed together to protect the crotch, his good arm across his stomach.

The next blow hit him high on the forehead at a spot in space where his throat had been a microsecond before. Though it was off-target, and glancing, the blow rocked him back and set up a roar in his ears; and as he rolled to his left, away from his opponent, he realized he was up against a very talented professional indeed, one of perhaps a dozen people in the world who were that capable in the ancient art of karate. As his left shoulder hit the floor of the tunnel, he let his legs unwind with a snap toward the direction the blows had originated, and felt one foot hit something, and heard a thump on the floor. He came up in a crouch across the tunnel from where he landed, the large comb from his inside pocket clasped in both hands. The passenger agent was just rising from his knees where Felix's kick had put him, his right hand groping inside his coat at his waist. Felix wasted no time in deluding himself that he could take the man at karate. He took one step, arms out like a football player, and drop-kicked the man in the lower stomach. The man lunged, arms out, trying to encircle Felix's legs. Felix's next kick was off-balance as he evaded the man's arms, and landed on the cheek instead of the bridge of the nose where he had aimed it. But it was enough to rock the man up against the wall of the tunnel, enough to give Felix time to strip the dummy comb from the thin tungsten steel knife, and throw himself, shoulder first, into the man's chest, pinning him, driving the blade into his throat.

Felix untangled himself from the man's body, retrieved his valise and his gun, and screwed the silencer onto the barrel of the gun. A vinyl accordian door had been drawn across the end of the tunnel that led into the waiting room. As he stripped off his coat and peeled the toupee off of his head he assessed his situation. The man in the plaid jacket was still out there, probably in the waiting room. Then he saw how they had done it. The man on the ladder had changed the gate sign! Felix silently cursed himself for not noticing that he had arrived at Gate B before passing Gate A, which this obviously was; the plane attached to the tunnel probably waiting to be cleaned and serviced. He took his black cassock from the valise, and stuffed his jacket and toupee in. How many others were out there, he didn't know. He needed to do two things. Find out who they were, and get out of the airport. He slipped the cassock on over his clothes, and shoved the gun into the waistband of his pants, leaving a gap in the front of the cassock, so he could get to it quickly.

A jet was warming up nearby, the whine of its engines washing away other sounds. He doubted that the shots were heard beyond the waiting room. If the man on the ladder had heard them, he wasn't going to be sticking his nose through that folding door to find out who had won until he had back-up. And from what direction would that come? Suddenly Felix knew.

He ran to the door of the plane. The stewardess was sprawled on her back in the vestibule, her coat open, exposing the small caliber pistol still in its holster at her waist. Felix ducked into the vestibule and flattened against the partition. He could see the pilot's compartment through the open door in front of him. Empty.

The woman in tweed groaned softly. He turned, bent, got his arms under her, and stood her on her feet against the partition. Her eyes were open but glazed with shock. Her legs wouldn't hold her. Felix slapped her sharply. The eyes blinked, focused, her legs straightened, and Felix pushed her into the open doorway to the first-class compartment. She stood swaying like a drunk, her shoulder bouncing off the edge of the partition. A man's voice came from the cabin. An indistinguishable question. Felix stepped out behind the woman, pushed her down, and fired. The bullet caught the man in the plaid coat in the shoulder, spun him staggering back down the aisle. The second bullet hit him in the base of the spine and slammed him face down in the aisle. Felix ran down the aisle, put his hands on the seat backs to leap the man's body, and continued to the cabin door in the tourist section. It was closed but unlatched. He peered through a window beside the door for an instant, then shoved the door open with his shoulder, dropped the valise out, turned, and dropped softly to the concrete apron. He tucked the gun back in his waistband, straightened the cassock, picked up his valise, and walked briskly toward a service entrance to the building. He held the valise pressed against his thigh to conceal the bullet hole.

Inside the service entrance a man in a white uniform with noise suppressors around his neck stopped him.

"You can't come through here," the man said. "Employees only—"

Felix turned, all meek confusion. "I'm sorry. I've lost my way, and my plane is leaving—"

The man glanced at the ticket Felix held out, and looked for a moment at the cassock and tonsured hair. "Okay, Father. You can still make it. Through that hall and up the stairs at the end, turn left at the top to Gate B . . ."

Felix turned right at he top. The ladder was still there, but the gate sign now displayed an "A." He stopped by the wall next to the opening to the waiting room, pretending to study his ticket. When the main hall was clear, he ducked around the corner, his hand inside his cassock on the gun butt.

The man in the maintenance uniform stood at the window, his back to Felix, trying to peer into the first-class cabin of the plane. Felix dropped him easily with a chop at the base of the neck. He opened the folding door far enough to drag him through, and closed it. He revived him quickly, and using the knife very sparingly, began to interrogate him. The man wanted to talk. Was eager to talk. And did talk in a breath-

56

less spate of Arabic. When Felix was satisfied the man knew no language he knew, he disposed of him quickly, carefully closed the folding door on the bodies in the boarding tunnel, and made his way to the ticket counter. He bought a ticket for Paris and boarded the plane moments before the door closed. Within five minutes they were in the air, gaining altitude for the turn toward the channel and Paris.

Felix folded his weary body into the seat, and relaxed. He was out of danger for the moment. He knew now who had tried to burn him in the airport; the same fanatical Arabs who had tried in Arizona. And someone had told them where to find him. Someone on The Council, because by now they would've all known he was planning on leaving Europe from Heathrow. Diamond had returned to the United States, and The Council would've demanded all the information he had about Felix. But who on The Council? Who was the betrayer. Cutter, Stone and this Quintain, as Diamond had told him? Possible. But too pat. Too neat. Felix sighed, and let his head roll back on the seat cushion. Before he fell into a fitful sleep, he promised himself that Cutter, Stone and Quintain would gladly tell him everything before he killed them all.

Chapter 7

WHEN QUINTAIN quit psychotherapy he gave himself and Mary a lot of sensible, vacuous reasons. It was too expensive. He was cured. The psychiatrist was sicker than he was. (Which was true, but probably made him no less effective in his work.) Mary didn't buy any of the reasons. She left. Quintain didn't buy any of the reasons either. But that didn't prevent him from selling the hell out of them to Mary. She left anyway.

He never told her the real reason he quit. Of course, he didn't know the real reason at the time. Had he known, he wouldn't have told her anyway. The real reason came to him six months later in Los Angeles, on a bus, rumbling along Wilshire Boulevard. It came to him borne on a wave of numbing anger. The bus was almost empty. He was returning from a movie, his only form of diversion during his first year in L.A. In the movie, the hero had overcome his enemies with righteous violence applied indiscriminately. (Quintain no longer remembered much about the movie—just the jumble of karate chops, machine-gunnings, and knifings.) Quintain suddenly was afflicted with a blinding desire to confront *his* enemies, to deal with them violently, to create the peace for himself that only being surrounded by the carnage of his attackers would bring. He stared suspiciously around the bus. Wouldn't you know? Empty. Except, of course, for the driver, who was protected by a brass sign warning it was a misdemeanor to engage him in conversation.

As his anger ebbed, Quintain saw why he had quit therapy. He was afraid to face his own anger. Just as it had frightened

Mary, and had eventually made her run, it frightened Quintain and made him run from confronting it. Because he saw that if he did, he would be forced to search for reasons for it, and there were none. He knew that in his rational times. There was no reason for his anger. His enemies were vapors. To attack them would be like attacking smoke.

The incident with Pendelton in the company canteen had represented a setback. It had frightened him. The old paranoid in his head had emerged and whispered dire things. Quintain had fought it down. Burger had helped, largely unknowingly, by giving Quintain the benefit of his sane, satirical perspective on life. Then, strangely, Quintain had overcompensated. He had lost his ego discernment. He became convinced that everything he saw as inimical to his well-being was a product of his imagination. The pendulum swung too far. Before it could swing back, he was promoted to become Sanderson's assistant.

The job was a strange one. Quintain placed constants in a computer program, and had the program run in the data center. That was it. Sanderson gave him the constants. The program came from the program library, not even written by Quintain. Each afternoon at two o'clock, Quintain would go into Sanderson's office with a pad of paper, write down the constants Sanderson dictated, take them to a keypunch operator on the third floor and have the constants punched into cards, and turn the cards and program over to the input clerk at the data center. The following morning at nine o'clock, Quintain would pick up the program from the data center, along with a listing of the constants that he could check against his pad of paper to make sure the right constants had gone into the computer, and not until two o'clock would the whole cycle start over.

After a week of this, boredom and curiosity aroused a determination in Quintain to find out *what* that program did that he fed to the computer so mechanically every day.

He called the data center and entered a request for computer time. He knew he could read the listing of the program's instructions that he had in his desk drawer to find out what the program did, but it was faster to set up a test case on the computer and let the computer tell him.

Five minutes after he had made the request for computer time, McCormick, the Manager of Systems called and said he wanted to see him immediately. Quintain went down to his old boss' office, and was ushered directly into McCormick's presence.

"Did you request computer time?" McCormick wanted to know in his typically blunt way.

Quintain said he had.

"What for?"

"Uh ... I wanted to analyze the program I run for Mr. Sanderson."

"What for?"

Quintain was beginning to get a little irritated. "To find out what it does. I don't work for you any more ..."

"Forget it."

"What?"

"I said forget analyzing the program." McCormick leaned his beefy, bare arms on his desk, and pointed his pipe at Quintain. "Look, here, Quintain. We can't burn up valuable computer time to satisfy idle curiosity."

"Idle curiosity!" Quintain was indignant. "It's my job to know what I'm doing."

"No it's not." McCormick lit his pipe in an off-hand way that made Quintain furious.

"The hell it's not!" Quintain stood, his face flaming. "We'll see if it's my job or not ..." he turned to leave.

"I already spoke to Sanderson."

Quintain spun around.

"He agrees with me."

60

Quintain felt as if his legs had been knocked from under him. "Uh . . . oh."

"In fact, he called me," McCormick went on.

"Well," Quintain said weakly, "if that's what Mr. Sanderson wants . . ."

Quintain went back to his office, hollowed out with defeat. He sat at his desk brooding. It was obvious Sanderson didn't want a System's Analyst on this job—he wanted a mindless drone, a robot. But to not know the logic of the program you were responsible for? Quintain couldn't understand it. It made no sense, and it went against all of his training and experience. Idly, without thinking what he was doing, he took the program listing from its drawer and put it on the desk. It's a good job, he told himself as he absently riffled the pages of the listing. Nice office. Good pay. Verna. Jesus! The thought of Verna brought him leaping up out of his reverie. He jerked his hand from the listing as if burned. He picked up the listing, threw it in the drawer, and kicked it shut. That's all he needed. To have Sanderson find him going over the program listing when he so obviously wanted Quintain to keep his nose out of it. He made a vow never to look at the listing again. If Sanderson wanted a robot, he would get a robot . . .

He awoke in his bed fully clothed, feeling like he had been painfully bound and cast into a blizzard to die, his first thought that, at least he had never disobeyed Sanderson about the listing. He can't have *that* against me. He laughed —a short, dry croak. He'd been caught with Sanderson's wife and he was worried about some stupid program!

He wondered for a confused moment what was causing the roar of cold air in the bedroom, and then he remembered. When he had staggered home from his evening with Burger he had turned on the air conditioner to air the bedroom, had

c

flopped on the bed to wait, and of course had promptly gone to sleep.

He hopped on numb feet and aching ankles to the air conditioner and turned it off. His alarm clock on the floor by the bed told him it was a quarter past eight. He stripped off his clothes, letting them fall where they might, turned on the hot faucet in his shower to maximum, and stepped into the steam.

His head felt like it was disassociated with his body, floating somewhere in a murky space of its own. When the feeling returned to his limbs he mixed in a little cold water and thrust his head under the spray for several gulping, sick minutes. Then he held his breath, shut off the hot, and cranked the cold on full. Just at that point where he felt like he would scream with pain, he stepped out and wrapped himself in a towel.

While he shaved and brushed his teeth, his awakened thoughts began to glow greenly around their edges with the old paranoia. In less than an hour he was due in Kenneth Sanderson the Third's opulent office. The night before, in the ambience of comraderie and booze, it had seemed a jolly brave thing to do to show up in Sanderson's office to match sophisticated drolleries. In the yellow smog-light of day Quintain knew he wasn't sophisticated enough, or droll enough, or, most of all, brave enough to match anything with Sanderson.

Aside from that, and more to the roots of his anxiety, there was The Grand Scheme of things. Behind that always, Grand Schemers—or, now, The Grand Schemer, Sanderson. Grand Schemes made themselves known to Quintain through unanswered questions. In this case, why did Sanderson want him in his office at nine? Why did he dismiss him from the scene the day before so offhandedly? What was he planning to do to Quintain at nine o'clock on an ordinary, work-a-day Friday? (Ordinary days, prosaic familiar settings, were, somehow, to Quintain more ominous than days that were special, like holidays, or settings that were unusual, like Disneyland. Who ever heard of an evil conspiracy coming to fruition on the Fourth of July at Disneyland?)

The Grand Scheme provided the answers. Sanderson wanted him there at nine because he had known when he dismissed Quintain he would need a night to devise a punishment horrible enough to match Quintain's crime. He had dismissed him so casually because he didn't want Quintain to panic and run or to show up with a phalanx of tough L.A. cops armed to the teeth with riot guns and tear gas.

Quintain heard the word "paranoia" bouncing around in his skull, echoes of other voices—Mary's, his psychiatrist's, his father's—and he could label what he was feeling with that word. Three thousand dollars and a year of therapy had given him that. But he couldn't really feel it, attach it deep in his gut to what was happening to him. The old sick rationalization kept haunting him—what if, this time, it wasn't really a delusion? What if Sanderson was really going to do something . . . hideous? Quintain shuddered and nicked his chin with the razor. Explain that away, Mr. fat-little-psychiatrist with the sleepy eyes and sneaky grin and forty-dollars-an-hour fee.

Now, Mr. Quintain, what evidence, what hard facts, do we have here?

Jesus Christ, doc, I've been banging his wife! (Ironic, disgusted chuckle.)

Still—what do you know about their marriage? What do you know about the arrangements, the understandings, between two people you describe as sophisticated beyond your understanding? And didn't you say she said something about an understanding—implied an arrangement? And didn't she seem calm, even—?

Enough, already, Doc! It's guys like you that get guys

like me to let their guards down, so guys like Sanderson can—.

Can what?

What? There it was. The unknown factor. The crippling inability to see inside heads and read motives. To know what people were *up to*. So you were left with no choice but to sniff out clues, put events together, and penetrate the designs of the Grand Schemes. Always assume the worst, and you'd be on guard. Mary had pointed out that that didn't leave much time for living, for enjoyment. Just the kind of talk that got you to lower your guard for that split second when—*zap!*—they'd get you. Okay, she'd said, in that small, flat voice that meant she was talking business, laying out her decision with no chance of appeal, get some help, or I'm leaving. She'd left anyway a year later. Three thousand dollars down a rat-hole called *help*.

Now Mary was remarried. A building inspector for the city they had lived in. Although Quintain had never seen the man, he had an image of him—big, raw-boned outdoor type, given to wearing Pendelton shirts, and elk-hide construction boots, striding around town condemning buildings right and left, as unparanoid as a man could get. Who needed paranoia, when you were big and capable, IQ around the median (Quintain took a great deal of solace from an article he'd read that said paranoia and intelligence had a high positive correlation)? Too dumb, for Christ's sake, to even *realize* there were all those plots hatching away in the darkness of *their* minds?

Quintain braced himself on the sink, let his head hang between his shoulders, and took several deep breaths, holding them long in his lungs, and letting them out slowly. It was one of the other things he'd gotten for his three thousand, and it did help, he had to admit. He raised his eyes to his image in the mirror. Long, angular face, eyes the color of denim that had been too long washed, lank brown hair, the skin pocked on the cheekbones with the moon craters of adolescent acne, tanned to the orangish Southern California badge, the Midwestern pallor buried there somewhere, ready to pop out with a month or so away from the smog-strained sun.

The phone rang.

Quintain padded bare-chested, dressed only in pants, through the bedroom, across the small living room, and plucked up the receiver from the phone that rested on the short bar that divided living room and kitchen.

"Hey, Slick—what the hell brand of kerosene were we drinking last night?"

"Burg—where are you?"

"Why, I'm down here in my office at jolly old Continental Investments, Inc, smiling and nodding in my usual ingratiating way, and trying to pretend that I haven't got my head wired to my neck with a bunch of paper clips."

"Hangover?"

"You just won the first national competition for superfluous questions. Why aren't you down here sharing your suffering with your peers?"

Quintain paused, swallowed painfully—

"Hey, now, Slick—you aren't going chicken, are you? By God, when we parted last night—I should say this morning—you sounded like John Wayne with a gun in each hand—"

"God, Burg, I don't know. Maybe I should just chuck the job."

"No moaning, Quint, for God's sake. Have some pity on my poor old hung-over ears."

"Okay. It's like this. I've thought it all out—"

"Screw that."

"What!"

"I said, screw that. I know how you think—how that mind of yours, left unfettered, scampers around sniffing for disaster. Now just get a good grip on something, and listen to me. I've been doing a little sniffing around on my own. Our friend was in early this morning for some meeting up in Valhalla. I checked with two secretaries up there, and you know that *nobody* knows more about the emotional climate around here than secretaries. And they tell me that The Third is his old, bouncy, self-confident self, shaking hands and slapping fannies with his usual elan."

"You—you really checked?"

"Hell yes. I thought you'd be in by now, and would want to know. All the scam seems to indicate that decapitation and mutilation are the last things on Sanderson's mind."

"I wish you wouldn't put it quite that way."

"That's the spirit, Slick! If you can laugh after what you drank last night, you've got size ten balls."

"So has Sanderson."

"Eight and three-quarters. Checked it with his tailor."

"Listen. I really appreciate this."

"Then show it. Get your ass in here. Set that square jaw and look the man in the eyeballs. If you go, who will help me dissipate this athlete's body?"

Quintain dressed quickly, left the apartment, ran to the bus stop, and got on a bus before the glow of confidence his talk with Burger had given him could begin to fade.

But it faded rapidly in the elevator going up to Sanderson's office. His knees buckled, and his throat and mouth felt like they had been swabbed with rubbing alcohol. Only the fact that he was in the building, actually on his way up in an elevator that couldn't be reversed, kept him going. He felt carried by The Fates. If They wanted him maimed or killed, so be it. He went into Sanderson's outer office, spoke to the secretary, and allowed her to admit him to The Presence in a dull hypnotic haze. Only when he was standing in front of his desk looking into the big handsome face of Kenneth Sanderson the Third did Quintain allow himself to realize where he was.

"Quintain," Sanderson said, nodding. After a more careful look, he added, "Why don't you sit down. Would you like coffee? You look a little pale."

Quintain sat mechanically in a chair, and took the coffee cup from Sanderson with nerveless hands. "Hard night," he mumbled. "Probably coming down with something." And then added inanely, "It's going around."

Sanderson leaned a hip elegantly clad in English worsted against the edge of his desk and said, "We might as well get right at it."

Quintain spilled a dribble of coffee on his pants without noticing it.

Sanderson took a cigarette from the teak box on his desk, lit it, and blew smoke at the ceiling, studying it with a frown, as if trying to decide if the tiles had been correctly installed. "Quintain, I'm going to tell you something that I trust won't leave this office."

Quintain nodded several times, realized what he was doing, and stopped himself with an effort. He had a sudden image of himself sitting there nodding like a robot, unable to stop even when Sanderson called in two strong men to carry him out, still nodding all the way.

"My wife—" Sanderson began. "Ah, Verna and I, have never subscribed to what might be described as conventional conduct. We've always felt that people should make their own rules on questions of personal morality." Sanderson paused and studied the end of his cigarette. "It's been a good marriage, Quintain. Exciting. Unbound by all the silly little games and rules that warp so many. Do you follow me?"

This time Quintain managed to limit himself to two nods.

"So—what happened between you and Verna is not something that causes me the concern you might expect. I'm not all caught up in proving my manhood through possessing another human being. People who are, it seems to me, are proving just the opposite. And it's happened before, with both of us."

The fact that Sanderson hadn't met his eyes since he began to speak gave Quintain a little courage. He tried to relax his stiff posture, and actually to taste the coffee.

"So," Sanderson went on, smiling sardonically, "you might well ask why I was a little upset yesterday—"

"Oh, no—" Quintain croaked.

"It was because of the *location* she—you and she chose. I mean, right next door to my office. I have a certain professional standing here that I have to maintain, Quintain. Surely you can see that."

"Yes sir. I tried—" Quintain blurted, and then caught himself.

Sanderson nodded. "I know. I'm sure the office was all Verna's idea. And, with one part of me, I appreciate it. Admire, even, the daring of it." The smile faded, and for the first time Sanderson looked into Quintain's eyes. Quintain suppressed a shudder. "But it's over," Sanderson said. "It will never happen again in a way that could cause me professional embarrassment. Verna understands that now. I hope you do."

"Oh, yes sir. I wouldn't—"

"Let me spell it out. As far as you and Verna are concerned, it's over, period. Here or any place else. And that's not just my feeling—Verna feels the same way. Clear?"

"Oh, no. I mean yes! I wouldn't—*couldn't* even think—"

Sanderson somehow had Quintain on his feet, walking him to the door with a large hand on his arm. He stopped him in front of the closed door.

"I was sure you'd get it without a lot of explanations, Quintain. You're a bright fellow. I've been very pleased with your work, and I predict you're going to move along very nicely in the company. After all," Sanderson chuckled confidentially, "having me in your corner won't hurt."

"I—I enjoy the work—"

Sanderson patted his arm. "Good. One other thing—since you're working up here with me, there are certain social considerations that go with the job. Do you own a dinner jacket? Never mind. My secretary will give you the name of a place where you can rent one. We're having a little gathering tomorrow night at our beach place—Jenny will give you directions. Around eight. There are some people that are going to be there you should meet." Sanderson opened the door. "Be there, won't you. Sort of a command performance, you know."

And Quintain found himself, still clutching the coffee cup, on the other side of the closed door.

Burger couldn't seem to stop chuckling and hammering Quintain on the shoulder with his fist, while Quintain grinned foolishly.

"Jesus, Slick," Burger said admiringly. "You go up there like the condemned man to the gallows and come back with the crown jewels. I have to plot and scheme to get into that party, and you trip up there and come back with an invitation from the golden boy himself."

"You—!"

"I'll be right there with you, Quint, rubbing the slightly frayed elbow of my dinner jacket against yours."

Quintain sat in his old chair and stared up at Burger. "How the hell—?"

Burger grinned. "I didn't wangle an invitation in quite the imaginative way you did. You know Chris Bell—?"

Quintain nodded. Christine Bell, the Director of Public Relations for Continental, was known to everyone in the building.

"She's invited, she gets to bring an escort, and I courageously volunteered to play that role."

"I thought she was married."

"Was. She's in the throes of a divorce, and needed an

understanding, tender companion for the big bash. I managed to get my application in ahead of the crowd."

Quintain stared at his round friend who was pretending modesty, smiling owlishly and rubbing a thick cheek. After knowing Burger for so many years, he knew he shouldn't be surprised at anything he did. But Christine Bell! Escorting her to the kind of party that Quintain had only read about in gossip columns.

Quintain actually had little personal acquaintance with Chris Bell. Being in charge of Public Relations for a company like Continental, which was sensitive to the point of obsession about its public image, naturally thrust her into a prominent position in company affairs. Anything that smelled even remotely of newsworthiness had to go through her office, and as a consequence she became involved in a lot more of the day-to-day operations of the business than she would have in a similar position for a company that handled public relations in a more routine manner. That involvement had given Quintain his one and only contact with her.

About a year before he had been assigned to design a computer system to convert Continental's payroll from manual to automated. A data processing periodical had heard about it, and wanted to do a feature on it. The conversion was nothing out of the ordinary, in fact quite standard, but the magazine had thought it newsworthy that a company as large as Continental had waited so late in the computer age to convert an accounting application that most companies had automated years before.

Chris Bell had, through her secretary, invited Quintain up to her office to discuss how he should handle the interview with the magazine. She was small and vulnerable looking, with the face and figure of an adolescent—large, dark eyes, a small, full mouth—but when she spoke she quickly erased the little-girl impression. She was sharp, decisive, no-nonsense, and she had made Quintain feel vaguely inadequate, as if he had been confronted with a friend's precocious child who turned out to know more about everything than he did.

After that meeting he had asked Burger about her. He'd had an uncharacteristic urge to know more about her, to find out what the circumstances of her private life were. Burger, who seemed to know everything about everyone, told him she was married to a lawyer, a young maverick in the public defender's office who was said to have a bright political future if he could learn a few more manners when dealing with the establishment. Burger had said she was an honors graduate from Vassar who had started out with pretensions of being a novelist, but who had quickly found her talents were better rewarded by the business world. Those talents, coupled with a distant blood relationship to old General Frawley who had founded Continental, had quickly vaulted her over the heads of other members of the PR department, into the position of Director. The news about her husband hadn't mattered to Quintain—he had already marked her as one of the girls that were out of his league. In fact, almost any girl he found interesting was so marked. They were, like Chris Bell, always too bright, too aware of themselves and confident about what they wanted from life, for him to imagine they could ever be interested in a nervous, paranoic computer man named Alexander Quintain. For a week or two his meeting with Chris Bell had left Quintain with a vague residue of remorse that he would never know the vulnerable little girl behind that hard, bright exterior, even if, indeed, such a creature existed outside of his own wistful imagination.

Quintain went thoughtfully back to his office, sat at his desk, and stared at the pool of lamplight on the coding sheet in front of him. He thought about Verna Sanderson. He thought about her quick, nervous energy—the thrusting, compulsive way she had used him sexually. And he knew, with a piercing insight that surprised him with its sharp, quick pain, that he was nothing to her—that he had been nothing but a device. A tool to gratify some twisted need for the heightening effect that danger brought to the sexual act. He mourned for a brief moment the might-have-been, the still-born opportunity to be lovingly in touch with another human being that their affair might have presented. Then he sighed, and let the mourning pass.

Verna would be at the party, and he knew how it would be. If she noticed him at all, it would be with that cool detachment of the hostess regarding the stranger-guest. He knew that he would obey the unspoken code from Sanderson that he react in the same impersonal way. Don't rock the boat, boy, or they'll haul you very quickly outside the circle of the tribal campfire and drop you on your ass in the cold night, without job, without friends.

He had been caught by Sanderson up to his armpits in a cesspool, and somehow he had been miraculously hauled out, cleaned off, and sprayed with a heady essence-of-success perfume. On the following evening he would be sharing drink and food with the powerful. Burger had given him a quick, dizzying resume of the guest list. Besides all the movie stars, international financiers, and jewels from the jet-set firmament, it was rumored that General Frawley himself would make one of his rare public appearances.

Brigadier-General Lucius Darwin Frawley, founder of Continental Investments, Inc., was a very private person. Most of the people Quintain worked with at Continental's corporate headquarters had never laid eyes on the man. Around the hallways and coffee bars of Continental he had assumed the proportions of some mythical god-head from whom, unseen and mysteriously, all policies, beneficences and major decisions flowed. It was speculated that his reclusiveness was the product of his army background re-enforced by the strange corporate nature of Continental itself.

Frawley had been one of Wild Bill Donovan's aides in the

OSS during World War II, in charge of liaison with European underground movements. Then in 1947 he had been one of the small group of men who had organized the CIA. He had stayed on for three years, then retired to seek his fortunes in the business world. The search had been short and fruitful. Through contacts he had made in the intelligence community throughout the world, Frawley invited exactly twelve men to join him in an unlimited partnership, its objective the amassing of wealth for the benefit of the thirteen wherever opportunities arose.

The original founders of the partnership had been among the wealthiest, most influential men in the world. What drew them into an organization with a man who had scant credentials in the world of finance, was the method of operation that Frawley proposed for their endeavors. Each of the other twelve partners had a unique area of specialization. One was an expert in petroleum exploration and marketing, another in international currencies, another precious metals, and so on, the composite group covering every area of natural resources and markets known at that time. Frawley's idea was that the partnership would form a pool of knowledge unavailable anywhere else, and through sharing that knowledge, Continental would be in a unique competitive position. What sealed the deal was Frawley's own area of contribution—intelligence. By applying the techniques of intelligence to the acquisition of advance inside information about everything from proposed mergers to the spot price of silver, Frawley had placed his partnership in a position of tremendous advantage.

Frawley had been careful to work within the laws of the countries in which the information was gathered. That is, he had managed to go to the outer limits of those laws, but never beyond. He had been so successful that several countries had rewritten major sections of their civil codes in response to the ways Frawley had operated. When that happened his organization would simply regroup, study the new laws, and launch another beach-head on their outskirts.

From the start the company had been owned on an equal-shares basis by the thirteen, and it still was. Over the years partners had died, or had retired, and been replaced with no difficulty. The routine operations of the partnership had grown until it had become advantageous from an organizational and tax standpoint to form a separate corporation, duly incorporated in the state of California, to handle them. An accounting department, a legal department, a computer operation—all the standard organizations for servicing a business—had been brought together under the legal name of Continental Investments, Inc.

The company was wholly owned by the partnership through a complex preferred stock arrangement, and the activities of the two organizations, the partnership, and the service company, were coordinated by an interlocking group of executives known as The Council. Since the company was privately owned, it didn't publish annual reports. The people at Quintain's level, and higher, knew only enough about the company operations to do their jobs. Quintain didn't even know who was on The Council, and no one he worked with, including the usually all-informed Burger, knew. Even less was known by the general public. Christine Bell and her efficient Public Relations staff saw to that.

Continental was heavily populated with ex employees of intelligence agencies—ex-CIA, ex-FBI, and even some now-elderly ex-OSS men. Even Burger had come from the CIA where he had been a computer programmer at its installation in Virginia. This, coupled with Continental's aversion to publicity, gave the company a flavor of surreptitiousness that Quintain did not mind. He was a private person himself, and he preferred working for a company that didn't prod and poke its employees with all the sophisticated psychological gimmicks designed to discover what "motivated" them.

74

The disadvantage was that Quintain knew very little about what the company did, or how it was organized to do it. He had his job—before moving up to the executive suite, designing payroll systems, and now, putting various esoteric constants into some kind of an investment analysis program at Sanderson's direction—but beyond the details necessary to accomplish those tasks he knew very little. And Quintain had an active curiosity coupled with a mind that, when it wasn't crippling itself with paranoic delusions, was very good.

So the party at the Sandersons was an opportunity to perhaps scratch his itching curiosity a little. To pick up a few more pieces of the puzzle called Continental Investments, and turn them and fit them into the other few he had. It was a game, much as computer programming was. Both harmless. So he thought.

But, then, he didn't know what they were planning for him.

Chapter 8

AS QUINTAIN drove up the old coast highway toward Malibu, he downshifted on the curves and used the added compression to accelerate the MG through them, taking pleasure from the way the old car hugged into the highway. On one broad curve he looked to his left at the breakers riding high onto the sand in the moonlight, and decided he felt good.

The MG was the only luxury he had allowed himself since his break up with Mary. Self-denial somehow seemed to quicken the healing of the wounds. He had found the MG through his odd reading habits. The classified section was his favorite part of the paper. He enjoyed reading the disguised, plaintive little cries for help in the Personals, the strange get-rich-quick schemes and cryptic messages in the Announcements. One Sunday, almost a year before, a small ad had seemed to leap out at him from the Antique Car section. Someone was offering an MG TD in running condition for fifteen hundred dollars. The ad stated the opinion that the car was restorable. Quintain impulsively called the number listed, made an appointment, and took a bus out to Alhambra where he had found car and owner. On the bus ride out he had known he was going to buy the car. With that realization came the hope that his suffering over the divorce was finally over.

The car was in miserable shape: upholstering worn to shreds, dented fenders, the body more covered with rust than paint. But the engine started on the first turn and idled smoothly. He offered the young student selling the car a thousand and immediately agreed to his counter of twelve-fifty.

Quintain had been slowly restoring the car, doing what work he could himself, shopping around for the best prices on the work he couldn't do. The car had new upholstery, the dents had been fixed, and they and the worst rust spots sanded down and primed so that the car was a pie-ball color of grey and original faded green.

The rented evening clothes made Quintain feel a little decadent, giving him a comfortable aura of luxury. In some way he couldn't verbalize, the clothes seemed to go with the car, as if they were in tune at some spiritual level. The MG had a right-hand drive, which added to Quintain's sense of risk, of being slightly out of control of the car as it hummed steadily along the coast at sixty miles an hour. And the unfamiliar elegance of the evening suit had that feeling, as if he had assumed an outer shell that would thrust him in the way of adventure. The purpose he had adopted for the party, to ferret out information about Continental Investments, combined with the images cast by the car and clothes, made him feel rather dashing.

The Sanderson's beach house at Malibu was a huge structure of glass and wood, clinging to the ridge of a low cliff and spreading in a zig-zag along the ocean front. Down the northern slope of the cliff three terraces had been cut. Patios and outdoor cooking facilities on the first, a rectangular swimming pool of pale blue tiles on the second, and beach cabanas and white sand on the third. The terraces were ablaze with Japanese lanterns. A bar was set up on the first terrace, and a large barbecue was blazing with manzanitas wood, attended by two men in white uniforms, in preparation for the steaks that were piled on platters on a table at their side.

Quintain parked the MG among the Mercedes, Jaguars, Cadillacs and one frost-silver Rolls Royce gathered in the wide circular drive, and was shown through the house and out toward the first terrace by an elderly maid dressed in white-frilled black uniform. He stood for a moment at the top of the railroad-tie steps that led down to the terrace, surveying the scene. Perhaps fifty people were on the terrace, pulled into little clumps of two, three, four, by some social gravity, sipping drinks. Quintain was struck by the absence of loud laughter, voices raised in revelry or drunken argument. There was only a discreet murmur under the music that was piped through the big speakers at either end of the terrace. Quintain, as he began his descent, questioned his strategy of arriving an hour late. He had hoped to slip into the party unnoticed in the throng, but it now seemed that the logistics of getting down to the terrace were making him the target of every eye there. Half-way down he spotted Burger standing near the bar, in earnest conversation with Chris Bell, and felt better. If he could just get over there . . .

"Well—Quintain."

Sanderson was standing at the foot of the stairs, smiling up at him. Quintain hurried down the last few steps, and stood beside him. He was surprised to find that he and Sanderson were about the same height, a fact he'd never noticed before. He always thought of Sanderson as at least several inches taller than his own six-one.

"I was beginning to wonder . . ."

"Actually," Quintain said, surprised by his own outspokenness, "I timed it this way. I thought I wouldn't be so noticed if I came late." He laughed hollowly. "Seems to have worked out just the opposite."

Sanderson smiled easily, and replied, "I understand. No need to feel nervous, though. These are all friendly people."

Quintain allowed Sanderson to lead him to the bar, and hand him a drink. Then, his hostly obligation fulfilled, Sanderson drifted off. Across the terrace Quintain saw Verna standing with her back to him, talking to a large man who was half sitting, half leaning against a guardrail along the edge of the terrace. He turned and walked to where Burger and Christine Bell stood.

"Hey, Quint." Burger greeted him, with a large smile. "You two know each other?"

Christine Bell regarded him cooly and said she was afraid not. Quintain resisted an impulse to remind her of their meeting about the magazine piece.

Burger waved his drink at the party. "Some bash, eh? This is it, kid. This is what we all bust our tails hoping to achieve, and look at 'em. Aren't they the most bored looking bunch of dudes you ever saw?"

Christine laughed, making Quintain look her way. Her laugh was young, free, bubbling with some wild spirit, and he found it very appealing. She must have sensed something in his glance, because she quickly sobered and turned away. She was wearing a sheath of rich purple velvet, almost black in the lamplight, no sleeves and very little neck. Her arms and shoulders were delicately slender, but strongly modeled in the yellow light. Her dark hair was caught at the back in a loose luxuriant coil that had been pinned high on her head, exposing her long, slender neck. Her skin was close-grained and smooth, without the almost obligatory California tan. He was struck with how small she was, how large and ungainly his own body seemed in contrast to hers.

Burger was pointing out the celebrities at the party. A famous singer-actor-bon-vivant slumped in a bored posture in front of a stunning blonde who was breathlessly trying to hold his attention. The singer looked old and tired, his face furrowed and ridged by too much sun and too many nights like this one, his eyes darting around the party looking, Quintain imagined, for someone or something to kindle the flame of an interest too-long dead. An actress, the long-time star of her own television series, chattering brightly at her escort, her clothes and hair style a good ten years too young for her.

Quintain wondered what terrible stresses to mind and body she had to bear to maintain that perpetual innocent, ingenue image that was her hallmark. He noticed a fat, laughing Buddha of a man, the chairman of the board of an aerospace company lately in the news for its chaotic financial condition, its bribes to foreign governments and its violations of the political contribution laws. And, finally, a towering gnarled old man with a Carl Sandburg shock of white hair, holding court with a dozen respectful guests, who Burger identified as General Frawley.

Quintain stared at the living legend of Continental Investments. His eyes were the color of onyx in the lamplight, deepset under the white ledge of brow, and they seemed to emanate an energy of awesome proportions when he happened to turn Quintain's way. Over the twenty yards separating them, Quintain could feel the old man's power almost like a palpable beating of the air between them.

"Looks like an old eagle ready to unsheath his talons and rip your insides out, doesn't he?" Burger asked, squinting eyes at the old man.

"I don't think I'd like to cross him," Quintain agreed.

"He can be absolutely charming, when he wants to be," Chris Bell said.

Burger drained his glass. "I'm going to get another dose of this liquid courage, and march right over there and introduce myself. General Frawley should know who it is that's holding his company together." Burger winked at Quintain. "Want to come along?"

"No thanks. This is not my night to be suicidal."

Burger went to the bar, and a few moments later Chris and Quintain watched as he marched his little round body up to General Frawley's group and stuck out his hand to the gaunt old man. The General took Burger's hand, listened for a moment to something Burger said, and then threw his head back and let loose a hearty laugh.

80

Chris Bell smiled as she watched Burger. "Your friend has nerve."

"In large doses."

She turned her dark eyes up to his face. "You look quite different from the last time I saw you."

"I thought you didn't remember."

"I didn't, until just now. It was the Datamation story, wasn't it?" She held her glass up. "Would you get me another —scotch rocks?"

When Quintain returned with her drink, he said, "How different?"

"What? Oh. I don't know. I remembered you as shorter, older—"

"I was in my work guise."

"What guise is that?"

"Low profile. Insignificant. Avoid controversy." He thought of Verna Sanderson, and shuddered inwardly.

Chris smiled. "And tonight—?"

He held his glass up in a mock toast. "Man of the world, in my rented dinner jacket and false courage."

"Why didn't you remind me we had met?"

He shrugged. "Maybe I didn't want you to remember the shorter, older version."

Her eyes held him, seemed to pin him with their open honesty. "Why would you want to impress me?"

He stared into his drink. "It was the way you laughed a minute ago. Something about that laugh I liked. Don't ask me to try to explain it."

"Bullshit!"

"What!" Quintain nearly dropped his glass.

"You're very practised, aren't you? With your little-boy-shy act." Her eyes were alive with contempt. Quintain couldn't bring himself to look into them, but looked instead at a neutral point on her forehead. "I see now why Burger calls you Slick."

Quintain laughed bitterly. "Lady, you are about as wrong as—"

"I've been hustled by experts, buddy," she retorted, her voice as hard-edged as a knife. "You're good, but not that good."

Quintain lowered his eyes and spoke earnestly. "Listen, you've got it all backwards. I'm not—" He raised his eyes to see her stiff back receding from him.

Quintain drained his glass and made his way miserably to the bar for another. He was off to a great start, he thought with self-contempt. If he kept this up, he'd be lucky not to have the guests lynching him by midnight.

He took a good gulp of the fresh drink, squared his shoulders, and decided to start over. If Christine Bell was so goddamned touchy and wrong about people, that wasn't his concern.

"Hello there, Quintain."

Quintain turned to find McCormick smiling amiably at him.

"Some party, eh?" McCormick waved his pipe around.

Quintain nodded curtly. He hadn't seen McCormick since the big man had delivered the rebuff about the computer time, and he found he still resented the memory of the cavalier way McCormick had treated him.

McCormick was chuckling and looking across the terrace. "Now there's a model for our waning years."

Quintain looked where McCormick indicated and saw Miss Palmer, her corseted little body encased in a hideous blue and red print evening dress, laughing up at Sanderson as she pinched his arm playfully between thumb and finger.

"She must be pushing seventy," McCormick went on, oblivious to Quintain's hostility.

At that moment Pendelton joined them, with a nod for each man. He chatted amiably with them, being careful to include Quintain in the conversation. As soon as he gracefully could, Quintain excused himself, moved off, and immediately was accosted by Verna Sanderson. For a dizzying moment, Quintain wondered if the party had been held for the express purpose of confronting him with all his past mistakes.

"I've got to talk to you," Verna told him in an intense whisper. "Follow me." She turned and walked to the stairs, and up them into the house.

Quintain stood rooted, watching her go, his face bloodless. He didn't know what she wanted with him, but he was afraid he could guess. More kinky games. Right under the noses of her husband and all those powerful people. Well, by God, he wouldn't do it! He felt a heavy hand on his shoulder, turned, and his knees almost buckled when he stared into the face of Kenneth Sanderson.

"Don't you think you'd better get going?" Sanderson asked in a low voice. "Verna's waiting in the alcove just to the left of the living room. It's terribly important, old man." Sanderson thumped him once on the shoulder and moved away as Quintain stared after him with his mouth open.

On the way up the stairs Quintain told himself that it was all right. Sanderson wouldn't send him to an assignation with his own wife. Verna just wanted to talk. That's what he told himself, but the old paranoid in his head cackled and said it was a game, a plot cooked up by Verna and Sanderson, to trap him in some indiscretion. Sanderson would be lurking nearby, the old paranoid said, with a loaded shotgun.

Quintain entered the brightly lit living room and crossed it cautiously. Ten-gauge shotgun, the old paranoid said, full choke. Quintain peered into the darkened alcove.

"In here." Verna was sitting on a bench under a huge abstract painting, smoking one of her exotic cigarettes. She patted the cushion of the bench.

Don't sit down, the old paranoid said, for God's sake! "I'll stand," Quintain whispered.

Through the cloud of paranoia Quintain saw that Verna was nervous. He had never seen her unsure of herself. It gave him the courage to come a step closer.

"I have to talk to you," Verna said.

Quintain nodded. "Okay . . ."

"Not here. There isn't time."

Quintain cast a nervous glance around. "What do you mean?"

"I'll come to your place tomorrow." She put her hand up and clutched his sleeve. "Will you meet me there?"

Quintain was beginning to sweat. "Jesus. Tell me now."

"No!" She stood quickly. Quintain peered into her face. What the hell is wrong with her? "I'll come in the morning."

He tried to laugh, but it came out as a nervous bark. "You're . . . you're not pregnant?"

"Don't be ridiculous."

"Right. That's ridiculous . . ."

"Your place at nine?"

"Can't you tell me something . . . ?"

"Not here. Don't worry about it. It's just a little problem."

"Listen, if Sanderson finds out, what do you think—?"

"He knows. Sandy knows. Don't *worry.*"

That stopped Quintain. Sanderson knew? Sanderson had sent him up here to meet her. What kind of weird, complicated plot was this? "I don't know . . ." he said. He wanted desperately to be out of there.

"Just trust me. You won't regret it."

He agreed, simply to get out of the situation. "Okay. But make it eleven. I plan on having a king-size hangover."

She laughed, but it sounded forced. "Eleven it is. But be alone, won't you, darling?"

He nodded. What did she expect, that he'd invite the neighbors in to meet his former mistress?

Burger was deep in conversation with General Frawley when Quintain returned to the terrace, the hangers-on standing around trying to hide their jealousy. Quintain got a fresh drink from the bar, and marched up to the group. What he had told Burger before had been wrong—it *was* his night to be suicidal.

"Hi," Quintain said.

Burger turned, grinned, and said, "General, let me present Alexander Quintain. Another one of the sturdy pillars supporting your company."

The General's hand was sere and stringy, but powerful. "Quintain," he said, focusing those avian old eyes on a point about three inches inside Quintain's skull. "Are you as amusing as your colleague?"

"I'm afraid not, General."

"Too bad," the General said, and turned back to Burger. It was as if the heat had been turned off, allowing a freezing frost to come sweeping into the two square feet Quintain occupied.

Quintain muttered some platitude to excuse himself and turned away. He needn't have bothered. The General didn't even glance up when he left. Quintain made his way aimlessly across the terrace, wondering if he really existed. The General gave the impression he did not. The General, Quintain decided, was an Idealist in the metaphysical sense; what his mind perceived existed—when he turned his attention away, Quintain no longer existed. Quintain decided he was getting drunk. He decided to get drunker.

He got a fresh drink and wandered to the railing of the terrace. The big man who had earlier been talking to Verna leaned against the railing, alone, observing the party with what Quintain decided was a disdainful stare. Quintain leaned beside him, and said, "Some circus."

The man turned his head slowly, like a camera panning, and fixed his eyes on Quintain's face. Quintain realized how large the man really was. His head was massive, almost square, topped by short-cropped, curly hair that was receding rapidly at the temples, leaving behind one comma of auburn, high on the crown. The man raised a cigarette to his lips with a hand that looked like it could be used to hold up buildings, and said, "Who are you." Not a question, a demand.

Quintain told him. The man stared at him for a beat, and then turned to look again at the party.

"And you?" Quintain asked.

"Fronck," the man said without changing his gaze.

Quintain was going to ask him if he worked for Continental, when the man placed his hand on Quintain's shoulder, and said, "Excuse me."

The hand felt like a sack of cement resting there on his shoulder. Quintain estimated that Fronck, if he were so inclined, could pick him up easily without shifting his grip.

Fronck rose, walked to a group of people, and then the group went up the steps and into the house. Quintain stared after them balefully. He was beginning to feel like a pariah.

"I just met Quintain," Fronck said.

"I don't know that that was wise," Diamond answered.

"When the time comes," Fronck replied, "it won't matter. What chance has he got?"

Cutter eyed Fronck's big body. "Against you, not much. Unless he is in the habit of carrying an elephant gun."

Fronck twisted his head around and stared angrily at Cutter. "You have an unhealthy habit of giving out those little digs."

Cutter returned the stare cooly. "Unhealthy for whom, Fronck?"

They were standing in the only fully enclosed room of the house, a room that had been converted to a gallery displaying the Sandersons' collection of sculpture. Fronck stood by a large Picasso casting of a goat.

"We'll see," Fronck said, his eyes riveted to Cutter's.

"Fronck," Cutter replied in a weary, patronizing tone, "try to remember that you are our employee. We have hired you, and gone to the trouble of importing your considerable physique for one purpose. Try to keep that in mind."

"You hired me because I am the best," Fronck replied, his eyes shifting to Diamond for confirmation.

Cutter laughed unpleasantly. "We hired you because Prince is dead, and wouldn't work for us even if he were alive. We hired you because Felix has been delayed—"

"That's enough," Diamond said, as Fronck started to move toward Cutter.

Cutter gave ground. Fronck was surprisingly quick on his feet for such a big man. He cut off Cutter's retreat, herding him back toward a pedestal with a Marini bronze standing on it.

"*They* are the best," Cutter said, no panic showing in his face. He was slightly crouched, measuring the distance between himself and Fronck very carefully. "You are second-rate—"

Fronck made his move in the only way he knew how. He feinted to his left, and brought the rigid fingers of his right hand thrusting toward Cutter's lower abdomen. Cutter didn't try to match his strength. He turned quickly, causing the blow to glance off his hip, and then spun and crouched waiting for Fronck's next charge. During the time his body had been turned away from the others a knife had appeared in his hand, a slim, deadly blade of carbonized steel.

"Enough!" Diamond stepped between the two. Fronck continued to stare into Cutter's eyes for a moment and then backed off. Cutter laughed and the knife disappeared into his coat so quickly that the group behind Diamond didn't see it go. "Wait outside," Diamond said to Fronck.

After Fronck had left, Diamond turned furiously to Cutter. "What are you doing! Is your ego so bloated that you have to jeopardize our operation with your childish posturing?"

Cutter shrugged and casually lit a cigarette. "That Cretin irritates me."

Stone spoke for the first time. "So let him irritate you."

Cutter smiled at Stone. "Okay, oh wise one." Stone laughed. The tension in the room eased.

"All right," Diamond said. "We haven't got much time. We've got decisions to make." He turned to the others. "Cutter and Stone and I went ahead with this as soon as we found out about Felix. We need unanimous consent—"

"To burn Quintain?" a man asked.

Diamond nodded. "Yes—but in a different manner than we planned before. It would be better if Felix were here, but he isn't. Why he's gone to cover again we don't know. We do know there was a bloody awful mess at Heathrow, and that Felix never got on the plane."

Diamond carefully looked around the room, trying to judge the common mood. Of the twenty members of The Council, twelve were present—enough for a quorum. He recalled the heated debates when they had taken on the OPEC assignment. The assignment had evolved from a scheme by the United States government to hold the line on Arab oil.

A fanatical Arab organization had approached the government through diplomatic channels in Switzerland with a deal. The Arabs would supply the names of certain OPEC ministers that were susceptible to a variety of pressures—bribery, blackmail, and, in one case, a predilection on a minister's part for certain perverted and hard-to-come-by sexual diversions. In return, the Arabs wanted unofficial assurance that the United States would put pressure on Israel to resolve the Palestine question in a way favorable to the interests of the Arabs.

The CIA had in turn approached The Council. The United States couldn't handle the delicate problem of applying the pressure to the OPEC ministers to vote their way. If they were caught doing that they would lose their credibility with every Middle East country, including Israel. The Council was hired to do the work, but they couldn't be contented with just doing the job and collecting the sizable fee. With the information about how the OPEC ministers would vote they had a chance to speculate in oil—a chance too tempting for their considerable avarice. And in order to make the largest profit, they had had to rig the meeting so prices would rise, instead of hold the line, as they had been hired to accomplish. Naturally, the United States government wouldn't support the Arab position after the prices rose. The Council made it seem as though the Arabs' information had been bad. The Arabs weren't fooled. They found out about the double-dealing, and had tried to burn Felix when he went to pick up the information in Arizona.

"I told you," Diamond said, "that this would happen. But now that it has, your Chairman will bail you out, as usual."

"Cut the electioneering," Cutter said, "and get on with it, won't you?"

"The plan is to take Quintain tomorrow," Diamond said.

"Felix isn't going to like that," Atlas said.

"Felix will damn well have to like it," Diamond retorted. "We gave him his chance to get Quintain."

"*That's* talking like our leader," Stone interjected.

Diamond flushed. "Look, if you think you can do any better—"

"Get *on* with it!" Cutter demanded.

"*All right*," Diamond barked. "Stone will get Fronck in. Quintain trusts Stone, so no sweat there. Quintain is an amateur. Fronck can be damn quick and efficient when he doesn't get any resistance."

"He'd better be," Stone said. "I'm going to be right in the middle if anything blows up."

"Yes," Atlas replied. "I'd like it a lot better if there was a back-up for Stone."

Diamond nodded. "Who do you suggest?"

"Cutter," the man answered. "I'd sleep easier tonight if I knew you and that blade of yours were going to be around."

Cutter grinned at Atlas, pleased by his words. "Okay with me. In fact, I would've been delighted to do the job in the first place."

"We've been through that," Diamond said. "He'd run like a rabbit—"

"All right," Atlas interrupted. "We're agreed then. Stone and Fronck, Cutter along as back-up. I dont know about the rest of you, but I would like to get back to the party."

As they were walking back to the terrace, Atlas and Diamond trailed behind the rest.

"Can we rely on Fronck?" Atlas asked quietly.

"For this, yes," Diamond replied. "It is a mechanical thing. He is simply the decoy."

Atlas shook his head. "I hope you're right. If Cutter ever gets a chance with that knife, Fronck is dead."

"I told you," Diamond replied testily, "strictly mechanical. The car is fixed, and with the way Cutter drives—"

Atlas held up a hand. "Please. No details. Assuming this succeeds, that still leaves Quintain."

Diamond sighed heavily, as if the burdens of office were getting to be too much for him. "One step at a time. First, Cutter and Stone. Then, if we're lucky, Felix will be back in circulation, and he can find our money and have his revenge."

"I hope you're right. Felix can be very unpredictable when he's crossed. He holds no loyalties except to himself."

"For God's sake," Diamond sighed, "let's get a drink and see if we can't forget business for five minutes."

Burger found Quintain slumped alone against the railing, staring morosely into his empty glass.

"Hey, Slick! Hold down the shouting and laughing, you want to have the cops on us?"

Quintain held up his glass. "I've been drinking these things like I've got a fire inside, and no effect."

Burger squinted at him. "What happened to you and Christine? I set you up with a lovely little fox like that, and find you here crying in your scotch. Is that gratitude?"

Quintain let go of a bitter laugh. "Mrs. Bell let me say about two sentences and then burned off my eyebrows."

"What! Did you try to move in too fast?"

"To hear her tell it. Burg, I can't even be honest and get anywhere."

"Misread your honorable intentions, did she?"

"Honest to God, all I was *trying* to say was that I liked her."

Burger nodded wisely.

"Then," Quintain continued, "I got turned into a block of ice by General Frawley. Okay. So I'm not in Chris Bell's or Frawley's league—I'll buy that. But listen to this. I then tried to strike up a conversation with a guy about the size of the house there, and, from what I could judge, with about as much intelligence, and you know what happened? After about three words, he got bored and walked away."

"Okay, lad," Burger said briskly, "no more feeling sorry for ourselves." He gripped Quintain by the shoulders, made him stand, and brushed his lapels. "Frawley and your huge friend are not important, right? Who is important is Chris Bell. You are wrong. She is definitely in your league. You two have got a lot in common if you can ever get past each other's stubborn pride."

Quintain stared down at Burger. "I naturally assumed that you and she—"

Burger laughed gaily. "Chris Bell? Are you kidding? The only reason she agreed to get me in here on her ticket is she knows I know the limits and will not trespass. She is definitely not pussy-cat material. She is definitely for the Quintains of this old world."

91

Quintain shook his head emphatically. "Listen! If I was a bug, she'd step on me."

"Let me tell you about Christine Bell, old son. She is winding up a bitter, hard-won divorce from one Frank Bell. She went into that marriage like some people go into convents. Dedicated to making it go. Visions of the golden couple, each with their own successful careers, growing old together collecting good prints of the impressionists, Steuben swans, and getting their photos attractively displayed in the papers. In short, living out the Big Dream. But it went sour."

Quintain nodded. "Professional jealousy. I remember Mary—"

"Nope," Burger cut him off. "Seems old Frankie had an addiction to young secretaries in the Public Defender's office. When she found him out, she bailed out with the Steuben swans and a suspicion that all men are bastards, which of course we are, only some are less so than others, and that's where you come in." Burger paused for breath.

"Me!"

"Look," Burger tapped Quintain's chest with the back of his hand, "you are a big, gangly oaf with a size extra-large heart. You're smart enough, and, although I can't seem to make you realize it, you are devilishly attractive to the kind of woman who goes for the slightly pock-marked Abe Lincoln type. You are taking an ungodly amount of time to get over a busted marriage, and I am about to give up and decide you like wallowing in your own messes. Get over there to Christine Bell and prove me wrong."

"But, what do I say—?"

Burger turned him firmly and gave him a shove.

Quintain found Christine Bell engaged in a quiet conversation with a tall young woman. Quintain moved up to them, blushed, and said, "I'd like to explain just one thing."

The tall girl looked at Quintain, then at Chris Bell, and

said, "I think I'll see how those steaks are coming." She walked away.

Christine Bell looked up at Quintain for a long moment and then said, "All right. Just one thing."

"I was *not* trying to hustle you. I am *not* practiced at anything. I have trouble asking the operator to help me with a phone call."

"That's two things," Christine Bell replied, but she was smiling when she said it. "Look—I apologize for taking your head off. I—I've been under some pressure recently. I'm not usually that way." She held out her hand. "Should we try again?"

Quintain took her hand. "I'm Alexander Quintain."

"Chris Bell. Alexander? Do they call you Alex?"

"Usually Quint."

"Or Slick?" she asked with a wry grin.

Quintain laughed. "Only Burger. I'd like it if you called me Alex."

She frowned. "You mean for the duration of the party?"

Quintain blushed again. "Okay, so I won't hope it will work out to something more than that—"

"Don't push," Chris said sharply. And then, seeing the anguished expression on his face, added, gently, "Alex."

"See," Quintain said miserably. "That's what I mean. I say things wrong. I don't really know if I'd like it to work out to something more. I'd just like the chance to know you better, and find out if I'd like it."

"You know," she said with a thoughtful expression, "this shy, little-boy effect of yours is very appealing to someone like me. And there are men—the practiced ones—who can put it on very convincingly. So my guard goes up."

"I thought we'd been through that. If you want to know the truth, I've always envied Burger his easy way with women."

"Oh, I've come to the conclusion that you're sincere. I

93

D

don't think anyone can make themselves blush the way you do."

Quintain promptly blushed.

They talked. They ate their steaks together, sitting on canvas stools, shoulders touching.

Burger found them, still on the stools, steaks long since finished, oblivious to the party dwindling around them. "Hey, you two." Burger passed a hand between their faces. "Time to wake up and face the ugly realities of the world. The party is over."

Quintain stared up at him, as if trying to place him.

Burger knelt beside them. "Listen," he said earnestly, "the old General seems to have taken a shine to me. Wants me to stay for a little game of poker up at the house. The General can't sleep during the night, like us ordinary mortals, and demands company for his insomnia. Can you get Chris home?"

Of course Quintain could. Quintain would be delighted. Chris, after a suspicious look at Burger, agreed.

She loved the MG and Quintain loved her for loving it. He lowered the top and stowed the side-curtains in the boot. Christine wrapped a scarf around her head. The night was clear, the wind of their passing sharp with the briny smell of the ocean. The old car settled into the road, purring along at sixty. She lived in the valley. He took the Topanga Canyon cutoff.

Her house was a small, neat stucco in the middle of a row of small, neat stuccos. He parked in the drive, and left the engine idling. She sat with her hands folded in her lap, looking ahead at the splash of light the headlamps of the MG were throwing up on the garage doors. They both spoke at once.

"Listen," he said, "I'd like to see you again . . ."

"I can't invite you in . . ."

They laughed. "When?" she asked.

"Tomorrow. I mean tonight. Or Sunday. Or Monday ..."

She stared out the windshield for a long moment. "What would you want to do?"

"Dinner? A movie? I could fix you dinner at my place ..." He blushed. "I mean, whatever ..."

She turned slowly and gave him an appraising look. "Did you and Burger cook this up ... your taking me home?"

"No! Listen, you name it. Whatever you want to do, any night ..."

"Are you a good cook?" She had her hand on the door handle.

"The best. I can get references."

She was out of the car now, standing by the door. "I'll chance your cooking. Tonight?"

"Great!"

She paused and cast a sidelong glance at him. "That poker game just seems so convenient ..."

He leaned across the car and put his hand over hers that was resting on the door. "Truth," he said, "defeats paranoia."

Chapter 9

MONIQUE knew that sooner or later Felix would show up again. She was not one of those lucky, chosen people who escape punishment for their sins. Felix was her own special punishment.

Barely a month had passed since she had made the last payment on the little café in the Montmartre when Felix showed up. Monique was behind the bar, where she liked to be. The weather was good. She had a decent luncheon crowd, well sprinkled with the tourists who would eat a meal and drink a bottle of good wine, instead of nursing a cheap bottle of burgundy all afternoon like her regulars. She was still glowing from the sense of stability that paying off the restaurant had given her.

Fifteen years of struggle and worry, and now the place was hers. Without the payments she could fix it up a little, do some of the things she'd always planned. Maybe even manage a trip next year back to Montreal to find out how many of her relatives were still alive. She was laughing, tossing her big head with the tight, golden curls at the bar customers as she served them, when she saw Felix come through the door. The smile congealed on her face. He nodded toward the stairs that led to Monique's apartment over the restaurant, and walked to them and went up.

She turned the bar over to Gaby, the elderly waitress, and plodded with heavy heart up the stairs. She was a big woman, in her early forties, with a bad heart. By the time she entered the apartment, she was breathing heavily and her big, Flemish face was flushed.

96

"Well, Felix," she said. He stood in the center of the small parlor staring at her. He was dressed in a beautifully cut English suit, and he had done something to his hair. "I wondered if you were still alive." She spoke in her French that still bore the traces of Montreal in its vowels.

"Speak English," he ordered. "Where is Paul?"

Paul. There it was, no preamble. That was Felix. She felt like slapping him, wished she had the courage to do it. "Out. You know Paul. He'll be back for dinner, you can bet."

Felix held up the cheap valise in his hand. She noticed it had an odd hole in one end. "I'll be staying for a while," he said.

She nodded wearily.

"Paul still in the same room?"

She nodded again. He stared at her. "I have the impression you were hoping I was dead."

She shrugged, then laughed suddenly, a wheezing bark of a laugh. "Your hair! You are wearing hair-piece, Felix."

He stepped to her side and gripped her wrist. "I'll be staying for a while, Monique," he repeated.

"You're . . . hurting . . ." she gasped, trying to free her wrist.

He bore down on her wrist, and she gave a little gasping yelp of pain. "I'll need my meals brought up here—is that clear?"

Through her pain her hate showed plainly in her face, Felix smiled. "Remember, Yvonne. The Sûreté is still interested in the little file I have on you. There is no statute of limitations . . ." He released her.

She rubbed her wrist, crouched and tense as he walked casually around the apartment looking it over. He opened the door to Paul's room and looked in. "I'll need a chair . . . where is that desk?"

"In my room," she replied sullenly.

"I'll attend to it," he said with a cruel smile. "We mustn't tax your poor sick heart."

"You're too kind, Felix."

She went heavily back to the café and relieved Gaby behind the bar. Her smile was gone, and she waited on her customers sullenly, speaking to them only as much as was necessary. The sun still shone as brightly as before, but now it depressed her. She wouldn't have minded if one of those sudden, blustering Paris rains had come up. Somehow it would've made her feel better.

Paul came back at five. He bounced across the restaurant and leaned against the bar, wreathed in his sunny smile. He was more slightly built than Monique, with a delicate, thin face, and a small mouth. But he had her crisp curling blond hair and her large blue eyes, and anyone that saw them together could tell immediately that he was her son.

"Mama," he announced, "I am ravenous. What do you have that you can wrap a crêpe around?"

"Felix is here," she said in a low, dull voice.

A worried frown passed like a cloud across his face, and then was gone. "Really! Where has he been?"

She shrugged. "Did you expect he would confide that to me? After all, I am only his hostess, his servant—only your mother—"

"Now, Mama," he reached across the bar and stroked her cheek. "Don't you have a smile for your Paul?"

She smiled. She couldn't prevent herself smiling at him, even though she knew what was coming, knew very well the hell she was in for.

"I guess I'd better go up?" He looked at her anxiously, seeking her approval.

"Yes. I'll bring some food when Henri comes on."

She watched her son walk across to the stairs. He had a bouncing step, a jaunty way of tilting his head, that made even the tourists look up and smile at him. He was twenty-two years old. He was her only child. And she loved him fiercely, protectively. She hated herself for sending him up to

98

Felix. She told herself it was better to get it over with, while she was still down here, the business occupying her mind. If they got it over with now maybe she could get some sleep tonight, and knew she wouldn't even as she told herself.

She asked herself, as she had done so often in the past, what choice she had. It didn't make her feel any better. If Paul were a normal boy, then perhaps she could take it philosophically. But if he had been born normal she probably wouldn't have felt about him as she did. By that time of his life a normal boy would have been out on his own, but since that summer he was five, when she had first noticed that he wasn't like other five-year-olds, she had known their relationship could never be normal. Someone would have to look out for him for the rest of his life, and that someone had to be her. The doctor she had taken him to had been mercifully frank and clear. Your son will never be normal. He will, at best, have a ten- or twelve-year-old mentality. Not as bad as it could be, he added.

If she'd been alone, perhaps she could've faced prison, and thereby freed herself from Felix. But she had to live for Paul. Who else would take him if she were locked up? Felix had been coming for years, coming imperiously, as if her servitude were some natural right of his. He would stay for days, once for over a month, and then he would be gone, without a word, with no notice. It had angered her, at first, but eventually she got used to it, regarded his comings and goings as a slightly painful penalty for her sins. Then Felix had begun with Paul, and she knew she would never be used to that, that she would never rest again until she saw Felix dead, even if she had to do it with her own hand.

Paul threw open the door to the bedroom, and stood on the threshhold with a breathless, expectant look on his face. "Felix!"

Felix rose from the desk smiling. "Come here! Close the

99

door." He took Paul in his arms and kissed him greedily.

Paul slipped out of Felix's grasp, laughed, and bounced down on the bed. "Do we have a game this time?"

Felix sat beside him and took his hand. "The same as always, Paul. Do you remember?"

Paul shrugged petulantly. "You don't live here. I never heard of you. I'm tired of the same old game, Felix. Can't we make up a new one?"

Felix patted his hand. "No, dear. That one is very necessary." He stroked Paul's leg. "Why don't you slip out of those clothes?"

While he and Paul undressed, Felix said, "I have a surprise for you."

Paul's face lit up. "Really? What?"

"Finish that, and I'll show you."

When they were naked, Felix took the strap from the valise, doubled it over, and struck his palm with it.

Paul looked at the strap with shining eyes. "A new one?"

Felix chuckled. "No more old belts, eh? Would you like to try it?"

Paul eagerly took the strap. He held it high over his head, and brought it singing down onto the mattress of the bed. "I'm going to give you such a whack!" He shouted, and then laughed.

Felix slumped to his knees, his head between his shoulders, his back offered to Paul. "Yes."

Paul raised the strap over Felix's back, and paused. "Have you been bad, Felix?"

"Yes!"

"Very, very bad?"

"Oh, yes," Felix moaned. "For God's sake—yes!"

Paul smiled and brought the strap down hard.

Stone was tired. Cutter was slumped in a chair. Diamond paced between them. They were alone in the Sandersons' art room, the grotesque statuary surrounding them like silent sentries. The party was long since over. From the distant reaches of the house they could hear the occasional laughter from the all-night poker game.

Cutter stirred, clapped his hands together. "We're almost home."

"Let's celebrate when it's over," Diamond said nervously.

"How much is the final count, again?" Stone asked dreamily.

"I told you," Diamond said in an exasperated voice, "a little over a million dollars."

"Six hundred for you and I," Cutter said triumphantly to Stone.

Stone sat up suddenly. "The Council will buy it?"

"Sure, baby," Cutter said patiently. "Quintain wouldn't talk. We searched everywhere. We'll tear his apartment, his office, even his car apart, to make it look good." Cutter smiled slowly. "That clever devil Quintain must've opened a Swiss account."

"I wish I had the money in my hand," Stone said, stretching out a hand palm up. "Somehow it would make me feel better."

"You will," Cutter said. "Soon. This time Sunday we'll be in Brazil. The money is right there in the Banco Nacional waiting . . ."

Stone stared up at Diamond. "I still don't see why it's in a joint account."

Diamond sighed heavily. "Because we couldn't split it into separate accounts, since we didn't know how much we'd be able to take. We had to have one place to put it."

"Let's just make sure we all go to the bank together," Cutter said ominously.

"A million dollars," Stone said, chuckling throatily. "My, that Quintain was greedy."

"I've been thinking about that," Cutter said. "I must look

101

like a pretty sloppy administrator to let him get away with that much. Has there been any ... unofficial talk in The Council?"

Diamond looked carefully at Cutter before answering. "A little," he replied. "I've managed to squelch it before it spread."

Cutter shrugged. "Well, it only reaffirms my opinion of The Council. If they buy this, they'll buy anything." Stone looked alarmed.

"Take my word," Diamond said quickly. "They bought it. Why shouldn't they? Quintain had access, opportunity, and he sure as hell could've used the money."

"And Felix—" Stone asked. "What about him?"

"He's gone to cover. Don't worry about him."

"He'll be back," Stone said with a small shudder.

Cutter rose and stretched mightily. "Don't worry about Felix. I'll handle him." He offered a hand to Stone. "Come along, darling. Bed calls."

Verna smiled up at her husband and took his offered hand.

Felix took two days to locate the Jew, and another week to set up the meeting. The Jew was being unusually cautious and Felix, who had confined himself to Monique's apartment had had to use Monique to set up the meeting.

Finally, it was arranged. They met at three on a morning of icy, misting rain, on a bench overlooking the Seine just outside Boulougne-Billancourt. The Jew was sitting on the bench huddled into an old army great-coat. Felix observed him from the shelter of an arcade of shops a block away until he spotted the Jew's bodyguard in a stand of trees fifty yards west of the Jew's position.

When Felix sat beside him, the Jew did not look up, but kept his chin deep in the great-coat. "This weather," the Jew began, as if it had not been two years since they had seen one another. "I keep telling myself I will move south, but I never do."

Felix took a breath lozenge from his pocket and put it in his mouth. "You could afford it." He knew better than to try to hurry the Jew.

"It's this city," the Jew replied. "It's an addiction." Then, with hardly a pause or change of tone, "You will have to convince me not to have you killed, my friend."

Felix kept his face immobile. "So? I have no argument with you."

The Jew sighed, and began to pack a pipe with strongly aromatic tobacco. Felix tensed, mentally calculating the distance to the bodyguard, laying out a course of retreat and another for attack. The Jew took a large kitchen match from his coat and sheltered the end from the rain with his fist. "No. In fact, our accounts are out of balance in your favor. That is why you are still alive. I also appreciate your not mentioning old debts."

Felix shrugged. "We have always been more useful to each other alive."

The Jew sucked on the dead pipe. "Until now."

Felix stared at the Jew's impassive face. "I know it's not money."

"We haven't much time. What we need to discuss now is what happened to you in America last year. Assume I know nothing."

Felix could feel the weight of the gun in his coat pocket. "You haven't changed," he said to the Jew. "And I'm glad to see it. Why should I tell you anything?"

"The man you spotted from the Arcade," the Jew replied, "is a decoy. The other two are quite close . . . in fact, within hearing of my voice if I but raise it a bit. Believe me when I say that unless you start talking immediately, I will have no choice."

Felix felt a bead of sweat break on his back and roll down

his spine. "The concern I was working for had a pick-up arranged. The fellow was selling information. Routine operation, normally. But the information was very sensitive, so it was decided I would plan the pick-up, and make it. There was a betrayal. I had a contingency plan and had to use it. Everybody on my team was burned."

The Jew chuckled. "Apparently you hadn't bothered to tell your team about the contingency. So like you, Felix. I'm afraid you're going to have to do better than that."

Felix nodded. His body was now sweating profusely under his heavy clothes. "I assumed as much. I've given you the outline. Ask what you will."

"What was the information?"

"A tally of how each minister was going to vote at the OPEC meeting in Vienna."

"Reliable?"

"Very. A man on the permanent staff."

"Let's see . . . that would've been before the actual meeting when, as I recall, they raised oil prices ten percent a barrel. Pretty valuable information, I should say."

"Yes. My concern bought and sold shipments of oil, while in transit."

"Rather like a futures market, eh? And if they had known it was going up ten percent they could've gobbled up a lot of shipments, with a guaranteed ten percent profit?"

"More like five. That much buying would put pressure on the price."

"Still . . . five percent guaranteed isn't bad."

"The return was more than five percent, since you can buy invoices for oil with a letter of credit and a small cash deposit."

The Jew chuckled. "Stories like that could almost bring me out of retirement, as old as I am. Tell me . . . who set you up?"

Felix composed his answer carefully before speaking. He

104

could tell by the off-hand way the Jew asked the question that they had come to the critical point. "I wish I knew for sure. The concern I work for gave me the names of three people. But since then I have had reason to question that information."

"These three . . who are they?"

"All Americans. Two of them are . . . members of the concern I work for. They're called Stone and Cutter."

"I've heard of Cutter. Bad actor. An amateur that likes to cut people up, eh? And the third?"

"An outsider named Quintain."

"And why haven't you dealt with these three?"

"I had to go to cover. The Arabs tried to burn me last week in London."

"Why would these three Americans turn the Arabs on you?"

"They were taking money that wasn't theirs. A large amount. They wanted me out of the way. They also wanted the confusion of my being burned to cover their escape. That is the story I've been given."

"But why would the Arabs care? Why burn you . . . ?"

"My organization double-dealt them. The Arabs made it possible for us to get the OPEC information. We were supposed to use it to get the oil ministers to hold the line on the prices. In return, the Arabs had reason to believe that pressures would be put on Israel to effect a Palestinian settlement."

"You knew this?" the Jew asked quietly.

Felix shrugged. "You know me. I have no interest in politics. I do my work."

The Jew chuckled drily. "Instead your organization used the information to make a killing, the prices went up, and pressure wasn't applied to Israel. I can imagine the Arabs would be a little upset about that. But why didn't they go

105

after your organization? As you say, you were only doing your job."

"They didn't know who I worked for . . . not then . . . their only contact was in the American Government."

"And now . . . ?"

"I'm not sure. I know they still want me. They proved that at Heathrow."

The Jew was quiet for a long time, staring out at the river. Finally, he said, "I believe you."

"Felix," the Jew continued, "I no longer need money. I'm too old to get into operations any longer, although the spirit is still there. So I am reduced to dealing in my little intrigues and manipulations."

"The Arabs came to me and said they wanted you dead. I owe them a favor and would've helped them if I could. But I owe you a favor too. So I assess. As I see it, you are guilty of naivete, but then we've hardly expected political sophistication from the professionals in this business, have we? In fact, it is discouraged. So, as I see it, the Arabs are after the wrong man. You were doing a job . . ."

"Can you help me?"

The Jew put his pipe away. "What do you imagine I can do?"

"The Arabs trust you. Talk to them. Tell them they are after the wrong man."

The Jew shook his head slowly. "Felix, they trust no one. True, I have a certain standing with them. But trust—?"

"I have to get back to the United States," Felix said fiercely. "I have to jump cover. I don't want those damnable Arabs at my back. You said you owed me something."

"Don't misunderstand me, my friend," the Jew replied solemnly. "I honor my obligations. I will try. But don't expect miracles."

"That is all I ask."

106

The Jew stood. "In any case, I will be back to you in a day or two."

"Thank you. And thank you for not lighting that pipe."

The Jew laughed. "You haven't lost it, Felix. God, what I would give to be your age again. Of course, you're right. One second after I had struck that match, you would've been dead."

The following afternoon, the Jew called Felix at Monique's.

"I have done as agreed," the Jew said.

"Yes?"

"They nodded, and smiled, and said of course they understood. A terrible misunderstanding, they said."

"But?"

"Perhaps I believe them and, then again, perhaps I don't. In any case, keep a sharp lookout on the trail behind you, my friend."

"Always," Felix said, and hung up. An hour later he was on a plane bound for the United States.

Chapter 10

FRONCK tried to keep up with the Sandersons' Porsche, but it was a futile effort for his rented Ford. All he could manage was to keep them in occasional sight on the hairpins of State Highway One ahead of him. He flipped the radio on and tuned it blindly until he found a classical station and settled back in the seat to let the sounds of a Rachmaninov piano concerto soothe him for the job ahead.

Getting the Sandersons to take their own car had been simple. Diamond had pointed out that otherwise Fronck would have to deliver them back to Malibu to pick up their car afterward. And obviously the bitch Verna had not wanted to ride alone with Fronck, although if she had any brains she would've leaped at the chance to ride with a real man who, given the opportunity, could make her forever dissatisfied with that poor excuse for a husband she had that everyone called Cutter.

Fronck looked at his watch. It was a little past ten in the morning. If the device worked as it was supposed to, Sanderson should by now be in trouble, perhaps already crashed. It was a simple procedure, easy to prepare, but devastating in effect. Fronck had chiseled a small gash in the copper tubing leading from the master cylinder for the Porsche's brakes. Each time Sanderson applied the brakes, fluid would spurt out onto the highway, until the brakes would finally fail.

If, by some miracle, either of them should survive the crash, Fronck would be there to finish them off with blows of his big hands that would inflict injuries hard to distinguish from those received in the crash.

108

Fronck negotiated an s-curve, and as he pulled the Ford out onto a straight stretch running beside the beach, he saw the Porsche. It was lying on its top in the surf, burning furiously, the waves rocking it and slowly turning it. Someone lay in the surf beside the car. Fronck pulled over, skidded to a stop, got out quickly and ran for the car, his big face set in a frown, acting to the best of his limited ability the role of the concerned passerby.

As he neared, he could see that it was the woman in the surf, lying face down. Then he saw Sanderson in the car, his limp arm extended out the window, where the surf was flopping it in a grotesque kind of a beckoning motion. The flames were already reaching the cockpit, and Fronck knew he wouldn't have to worry about the man. As he shifted his direction and ran toward Verna he marveled at how furiously the car was burning surrounded by all that water, and then he saw that the waves themselves seemed to be on fire as burning gasoline spread across them from the ruptured tank.

He reached Verna, and flipped her body over by her wrist. Her face was a slate-grey, and there was a dark blue bruise on her temple. Her lips were slightly parted, and he caught a glimpse of white under one eyelid. He knelt beside her, unmindful of the surf tugging at his clothes, and raised his hand for a blow to Verna's exposed throat, when he heard a shout that seemed to come from the waves in front of him. He stared, wondering if he were hearing things, and a face appeared over a wave not fifty feet ahead and he heard the shout again. He relaxed his hand and stood. Then he saw the boy, slicing toward him on his knees on a surfboard. The boy rode the wave out, and leaped from the board and ran to Fronck. Fronck became aware of other voices, and turned to see a man and a woman splashing through the surf toward him, their blue Chevrolet parked beside his Ford on the highway.

"What happened!" the boy shouted.

"Accident," Fronck said. "I was just going by."

The boy looked briefly at the car, and then bent over Verna. "God . . . she doesn't look good."

No, she doesn't, Fronck thought. She must be dead. Probably a broken neck. Certainly drowned. He turned and began to walk back to his car. The man and the woman drew up to him. "Need help?" the man asked, trying to catch his breath.

"Yes," Fronck said. "I'll get the authorities." And he ran to his car, got in, and sped away, back to Malibu to report to Diamond on his success.

The man bent over Verna, and then motioned to the surfer. "Help me get her up on the beach . . . hurry!"

They placed her limp body on the sand and the man bent over her and began mouth-to-mouth resuscitation. Verna coughed.

"She's alive," the man said to his wife. He turned to the surfer. "You saved her by getting her head out of the water."

"Not me," the boy said. "It was that big guy that turned her over."

Quintain waited in his apartment until eleven-thirty before he decided that Verna definitely wasn't coming. He considered whether he should call her and then decided it was her problem. He would be quite contented if he never saw her again.

He surveyed his apartment with distaste. Until then he had hardly paid it any attention, and that was the problem. He had furnished it with odds and ends picked up from garage sales and cheap furniture stores, so that now his living room resembled a storage room for some family's discarded possessions. He spent a desultory hour trying to find a more attractive arrangement for the furniture, and finally gave it up as hopeless.

He caught himself looking at his watch several times an

110

hour, and forced himself to stop it. Chris was coming at seven. He had been so pleased by her acceptance of his invitation that he had completely forgotten to discuss time and transportation with her. As soon as he had gotten up that morning he had called her.

"Seven is fine," she had said in a sleepy voice.

"I'll pick you up."

"No, Alex. I'm not ready for that. I want my own transportation."

He would've agreed to anything, a chaperone even, just to see her again.

He cleaned his apartment, borrowing the landlady's wheezing old vacuum cleaner. Then, on an impulse, and allowing himself no time to think it over, he got in the MG and drove out to Wilshire to a middle-class men's store and bought a sand colored twill leisure suit and a burnt orange shirt made of a silken polyester material. The bill came to over a hundred dollars; and as he wrote the check it occurred to him that, aside from the expenditure for the MG, this was the largest amount of money he had spent on himself in nearly three years. He left the store humming tunelessly to himself. He drove to a grocery store and bought food and wine for the evening.

When he returned to the apartment he still had an hour and a half until Chris was scheduled to arrive. He showered, and shaved very carefully with a new blade. He didn't want his face marred with unbecoming nicks. He put on the pants of the leisure suit and the new shirt. They felt luxurious against his skin. He considered himself in the mirror for a moment, wishing his face wasn't quite so angular, that his mouth didn't have such a sardonic twist at the corners, and that his eyes didn't look like they were cut from faded denim. He arranged his hair with his fingers and a brush, hoping it would for once stay in place longer than five minutes, and realized that he hadn't had a paranoid thought all day, and

111

he laughed out loud and did a little two-step dance into the kitchen to get the bottles of liquor out and arrange them on the counter. He surveyed the kitchen for a moment, thinking through his plans for dinner, and then clapped his hands and went into the bedroom to slip into his jacket.

Chris arrived promptly at seven. She seemed nervous, looked quickly around the apartment and made polite comments without really seeming to see it. He knew *he* was nervous. He got through the initial greetings as quickly as he could, and went in the kitchen to make them drinks.

"Something smell's good," Chris said as he handed her a scotch and soda.

Quintain settled down in a chair across from the couch Chris was sitting on. He lifted his martini. "Let's wish the chef luck. He needs it."

She looked at him with grave eyes. "Did you hear about Kenneth Sanderson?"

The unexpected mention of Sanderson's name startled him. "No."

"He was killed this morning."

Quintain stared at her. "Killed . . . !"

"His car went off the highway just below Malibu. Verna was with him . . ."

"My God! Are you sure?"

She nodded. "It's been on the news. I thought you would've heard it."

He didn't tell her that he had been so consumed with the anticipation of this evening that the outside world hadn't existed for him. "Is . . . is Verna . . . ?"

"She's in the hospital. I tried to see her, but they aren't allowing visitors. Apparently she's going to be all right."

Quintain passed a hand across his eyes. "God. Just last night . . ."

"I know," she said. "I've been thinking the same thing. They both were such vital people. Are you okay?"

He nodded, and took a large drink of his martini.

"Were you close to them?" Chris asked.

"Not really. Of course I worked for him, but it had only been a few weeks." He couldn't tell her about Verna. No matter how long he and Chris might know each other, he doubted he could ever tell her about that strange affair. "And you ... were you close to them?"

"No. Oh, I've known them for years. I've been to parties there. But I really didn't travel in their circle. It was a pretty fast crowd." She paused, and stared into her drink. "It's strange. I never would've guessed that Kenneth Sanderson would die the way he did. He was an excellent driver."

Quintain nodded. "He seemed so ... so damned competent."

Chris sighed. "I'm sorry I had to bring such grim news ..."

Quintain didn't let it spoil the evening. He had planned and anticipated it all day, and he wasn't going to allow anything to mar it. He mixed fresh drinks, and changed the subject. Soon the alcohol and some natural affinity they had for one another, that Quintain had noticed at the party, took over and they began talking about themselves.

Chris told him about her marriage. Five years to a man that she had thought was in every way her ideal partner. He had a good intellect, was ambitious, successful, interested in things outside his own profession—but, and this she said with a little catch in her voice that told Quintain she wasn't as recovered from the effects of the split as she pretended, a liar. A practiced deceiver.

"God," Chris said, "he was so *good* at it. For almost the whole time we were married, he was carrying on affairs. And I still wouldn't have known if I hadn't stumbled onto it."

She had stopped at his office unexpectedly one afternoon to find her husband and his secretary on the couch. Chris took the rest of the day off and went home, and when her husband arrived that night he found all his belongings neatly stacked in the carport.

"You're a tough lady," Quintain said, not without a certain amount of awe.

"I had no choice. I knew if I had to go through that again I'd lose some essential part of myself."

Her husband had pleaded with her by telephone and through letters, but Chris remained adamant. In the meantime she found out about the others.

"When people know you're in trouble," Chris said bitterly, "they are all too eager to tell you things you should have known years before."

Quintain nodded, remembering the so-called friends of his who had gone to pains to keep him informed of Mary's love life after they had separated.

"That's why you thought I was giving you a line at the party?"

"Yes," Chris agreed. "I guess I lost faith in my judgment of men. He fooled me for so long . . ."

Quintain excused himself, and went into the kitchen to see to the dinner. When he returned Chris had her shoes off and her slender legs tucked under her.

"Okay," Chris said with a smile, "your turn."

He told her about Mary.

"She sounds like quite a woman," Chris said, her eyebrows arched in an unspoken question.

"It wasn't my idea to break up," Quintain replied. "But I guess she'd had enough . . ."

"Enough?" Quintain could sense Christine stiffening when she asked the question.

He waved a hand wearily. "Oh, it wasn't anything like your deal. I was faithful and so was she."

He told her about the year with the analyst, and the final, inevitable, break.

"You seem fine to me," Chris said.

114

"I'm getting better. In a strange way, I think the split with Mary was good for me. It made me begin to examine some things about myself. It hasn't all gone, but at least now I can recognize my paranoia and try to deal with it instead of going off on wild fantasies."

"*That's* what you said to me when I got out of the car last night."

"Truth defeats paranoia? It's my motto for living."

The dinner was a success. Chris saved her compliments until they were back in the living room with their coffee and brandy. She lit a cigarette, sighed with deep satisfaction, and made him believe he was a master chef. He was so self-satisfied and comfortable in her presence that he got his paintings out of the closet and showed them to her.

He had begun painting after he arrived in Los Angeles, while the wounds were still open. The paintings represented a kind of therapeutic log of his psychological progress. He showed them to her in the order of their creation. She shuddered over the first few, dark, twisted nonrepresentational excretions from the torment that had possessed him then. But she began to brighten as he went along, shuffling paintings to the rear of the stack.

"I like that! Is it a sunset?"

He looked at it. "If you say so."

She told him about her writing. "I started out with a degree in creative writing and the conviction that all I needed was a little quiet time to become another Virginia Woolf. My money and my delusions ran out at the same time."

She abruptly told him she was twenty-seven and asked his age. When he said thirty-three, she asked, "How does it feel?"

"What? The thirties? To tell the truth, not much different."

"That's a relief. I'll stop worrying."

"You shouldn't worry—right now you look about nineteen."

In the light from the one lamp Quintain had on, she did.

Finally, he sighed, and said, "Do you know you are the

first person besides Burger that I've really talked to in three years?" Christine was on the couch, Quintain facing her in the chair, one leg thrown over the arm.

"I'm flattered," she replied and then, after a slight pause, "you and Burger are really that close?"

"I thought you knew that."

She nodded. "Of course, I knew you were friends. He's rather an enigma to me."

"He's a complex guy. But about the best friend you could imagine."

"He's certainly had a varied background."

Quintain put down his brandy glass. "You mean his CIA career?"

She nodded.

"Well—he was doing about the same thing there. Computer work."

She frowned. "Is that what he told you?"

"Sure." He hesitated, and looked closely at her. "What do you mean—*told* me?"

"Well," she replied, "it's no national secret. He did start out in their computer center, but when Continental recruited him, he was with Special Operations. Uncle Luke's made it corporate policy to steal bright young men from the CIA and FBI."

"Uncle Luke?"

"General Frawley. He's really a distant cousin, but I've called him Uncle Luke since I was a little girl."

"What is this 'Special Operations'?"

"I don't know, really. You know—the cloak and dagger branch, that does all that spy stuff."

Quintain stared at her "*Burger?*"

She laughed. "I know. He hardly seems the type. But few of them do. Uncle Luke is the only one I know that fits the stereotype, or did, when he was younger."

"I'll be damned," Quintain said. "I wonder why he never

told me." He felt a little hurt that he had to find this out from someone else.

"Oh, none of them do much talking. They're bound to secrecy for the rest of their lives about what they did. There's some law . . ."

"The National Security Act, or something," Quintain replied. "But he could've at least told me as much as you did."

"I wouldn't worry about it. I doubt that he's told anyone. The only reason I know is that I have to for my job. We do get inquiries from the media about our people. All these ex-spies in an investment company make good copy. It's all I can do to keep the media from running all over the place doing features."

Quintain got them more coffee and brandy. As he poured the brandy, he said, "You know, I've always been curious about who was and who wasn't."

Chris smiled. "Okay. You guess, and I'll score you."

"Sanderson." He immediately regretted saying the dead man's name, but it had been an honest reaction. It was the first name that came to him.

Chris shook her head. "See what I mean? If anyone is type-cast for the dashing spy role, Kenneth is," She didn't seem to notice her use of the present tense. "He's an amateur."

"An amateur?"

"That's what the ones who are call the ones who aren't."

"Then I'm an amateur?"

"And I."

Quintain grinned. "God, what a weird feeling. To know I have a secret standing."

She returned the smile. "More like a low-caste mark. The professionals have a kind of contempt for the amateurs."

"Are they all ex-CIA?"

"No. For example, your boss, Brian McCormick, was FBI. He was a manager in the FBI data center."

"Okay. I've got one."

117

"You'd better," she laughed. "So far you haven't scored."

"Pendelton!"

"Right! But how . . . ?"

"I'm getting the hang of it. He's the last person I would expect to be an ex-spy."

Christine laughed. "See what I mean?"

He nodded. "And McCormick seems too big and clumsy."

She looked at him slyly. "So far, though, you've made the supreme mistake."

He stared at her, thinking hard. "Don't tell me," he ordered her. A moment later he struck his forehead with his palm. "God! Women!"

Chris laughed. "There goes the last stereotype."

"Who?" Quintain asked eagerly.

"You know Miss Palmer?"

Quintain stared.

"She was a very heavy-duty spy, I understand," Chris said, her eyes glinting with mischief.

Quintain shook his head in wonderment at the thought of that prim corseted old lady who looked like nothing more than she did someone's maiden aunt being a spy.

He got up to replenish the brandy and when he returned from the kitchen with their glasses he caught Chris looking at her watch. The effects of the drinks, the success of his dinner, and their easy conversation made him bold. He sat on the couch beside her.

She turned her face up to his, her eyes large with an unspoken question, a warning. He bent down and touched her lips with his own. Her mouth was soft and cool. She didn't push him away, or object, but there was no emotion in her kiss, no response to the quickening of his own emotions. He broke from the kiss and touched her cheek with trembling fingers. He looked into her dark eyes.

"It's too soon," she said.

"No," he said. "No, it's not."

He kissed her again, abandoning his caution, and letting his passion show. She resisted at first, put a hand on his chest and pushed weakly. Finally her mouth responded, opened, her cool hand touched the back of his neck, and then pulled him into her and the fingers pushed up into his hair.

The doorbell rang.

Quintain pulled away, and swore. Chris laughed. "Providence," she said. Quintain stood, and looked at his watch. It was nearly midnight.

The doorbell rang again, insistently.

He smiled down at Chris. "It is *not* too soon." He turned and went to the door.

He pulled the door open angrily, prepared to vent his anger on what he was sure was someone with the wrong address.

He stared, shocked beyond speech, into Verna's face. Her hair was disheveled, falling forward onto her forehead and cheeks. Her skin was a sickly liver color, her blue eyes strangely unfocused. She wore an old cloth coat that was several sizes too large for her, and that, incongruously, had a wilted orchid corsage pinned to its lapel.

Verna swayed, and then collapsed forward into his startled grasp. "Help me," she whispered. "Help me."

Chapter 11

DIAMOND calculated that he hadn't been to bed in more than forty hours, and immediately wished he hadn't. Somehow knowing the number of hours he had been sleepless made him feel worse.

The Council met after midnight, Saturday already gone. They were meeting in Diamond's office at Continental headquarters. Diamond was still in his dinner jacket from the party the previous night, his tie off, his collar wilted and dirty from the sweat of his mental exertions.

Atlas had changed from his plaid dinner jacket into a sport coat and soft shirt. He looked fresh and rested. Now he was staring into Diamond's face and saying, "How could we have been so foolish as to leave it up to an idiot like Fronck?"

Diamond could feel all the eyes in the room on his face, and he resented Atlas focusing this attention on him; but he hid his resentment, and said, in a calm, dry voice, "None of us could do it. Fronck was the only one we could get on such notice. It was simply bad luck that the surfer was there."

"Bad luck?" Palmer asked, her eyes glinting coldly behind her steel-rimmed glasses. "Since when do we rely on luck for outcomes?"

Diamond stared bleakly at Palmer. He didn't like her and felt he never would. She was the only member of The Council who insisted on using her real name. Not just this apostasy created Diamond's enmity: it was her cold contempt that was exhibited for anyone's judgment but her own. And, though he had a cautious wariness for the intentions of every member of The Council, he trusted this little woman the least. He firmly believed that, if the opportunity occurred, she would order him eliminated without any more compunction than she would slap a mosquito.

"Since you weren't responsible for the operation," Diamond said coldly, "I suggest you hear us out before you prejudge us." He had used the collective pronoun deliberately to make the point that he had not been alone in the decision.

Miss Palmer made a face as if she smelled something unpleasant. "Then, *please* proceed."

"Stone was taken to L.A. County Hospital," Atlas continued.

"Is she still there?" someone behind Diamond asked. He turned to find that the questioner was Regan, and it surprised him, because the big, taciturn man was usually silent in Councils until the time for a vote came. Diamond felt a premonition of danger knotting his stomach. If even Regan was joining in, then The Council was really stirred up.

"Yes," Atlas answered Regan. "She's in an intensive care unit. If they move her to a private hospital it won't be before this morning."

"And what have we been doing in the meantime?" Palmer asked, her voice rising on the last word as if she had already made up her mind the answer would displease her.

Diamond shrugged. "What could we do? You don't simply walk into a hospital, into the intensive care unit, and say to all the doctors and nurses, excuse me while I kill your patient."

"Yes," Atlas agreed. "In her present position she is as invulnerable as if she were in jail."

"Then *all* you're doing is a surveillance?" Palmer persisted.

"No," Atlas answered. "There is no necessity—"

"*No* necessity!" Palmer stared at not Atlas, but Diamond, as if her ears had betrayed her.

"She is in shock," Diamond said in a tight voice. "Possible internal injuries. The woman nearly drowned. She is heavily sedated. What are you afraid of, Palmer? That she will leap from her bed, tubes and needles dragging behind, and come after you?"

"She is a danger to us as long as she is alive," Palmer's eyes darted around the room, and Diamond knew she was looking for support among the others. "If she decides to talk—"

"Now, why would she do that?" Atlas asked. "She knows nothing more than that she's been in a car accident. She may know by now that her husband was killed. He always did drive too fast. Why would she suddenly turn against us?"

"We even sent her flowers," Diamond added, and then wished he hadn't.

"Ah! Flowers!" Palmer said. "Congratulations, Mr. Chairman! Your strategies are so clever."

Someone laughed. Diamond flushed. "That is not as foolish as it sounds. We have also let it be known that several of us had inquired about her condition. She isn't allowed visitors, or we would've gone to console her. We are trying to proceed in a normal manner. She was unconscious when Fronck got to the scene, so she has no reason to connect us."

Diamond could see by the color rising in Palmer's heavy cheeks that he had scored points. She waved a hand irritably, turned her head, and stared at the wall.

"Until she's out of intensive care, and in a room of her own, there is little we can do but wait," Atlas went on.

"What are the chances that we won't have to do anything?" a man across the room asked.

"Not very good," Atlas replied. "She's pretty battered, but nothing she can't survive. The doctor I spoke to said her constitution is strong. The prognosis is positive."

"All right," Regan said. "How do we proceed?"

"Once she is in a room of her own," Atlas replied, "it will be simple to get to her. *And*," he raised his voice to preempt the objection Palmer was opening her mouth to deliver, "we have left instructions for a private room with the authorities at the hospital."

"And then?" the man across the room asked.

Atlas rubbed the back of his hand, bending his head to study it closely. "We feel a suicide is in order—"

"She is despondent at the loss of her husband," Diamond added quickly. "Quite usual under the circumstances."

"Good," the man across the room said, and Diamond felt some of the tension in the room ease. "Of course," the man added, "we'll get someone besides Fronck to do the job?"

Diamond allowed himself a smile. "Rest assured. We've already arranged it."

Atlas mentioned a man's name, and said that he was flying in in the morning to handle the job. There was a general murmur of approval in the room.

"He's damned expensive," Palmer said petulantly.

"Would you prefer to cut corners on this?" Diamond asked in a velvet voice.

"No!" Palmer retorted angrily. "But this mess has already cost us a million dollars."

"Quintain will be happy to tell us where the money is," Atlas said, turning to Diamond. "Won't he?"

Diamond resisted an impulse to wipe his brow. All twenty members of The Council were crowded into the office, and the air was stale and hot. "We'll certainly make him want to," he replied.

"How do you know he even knows where it is?" Palmer snapped. "I say get Verna and him together, and see which one cracks first."

Diamond took a careful breath. "He was behind the whole thing. He fixed the computer to steal the money. He *has* to know where it is."

"I wish to God Felix was here," Palmer said.

"No one is indispensable," Diamond replied. "We can handle it . . ."

The private line on Diamond's phone winked on. Diamond picked up the receiver, listened for a moment, and slowly replaced it. He suddenly looked much older than his years. "She's ... she's left the hospital ..."

Instinctively, Quintain caught Verna under the arms as her legs gave way. Chris, with a little cry of surprise, leaped to his side. She helped him half-carry, half-lift Verna onto the couch.

They stood looking down at Verna's pale face. Her breathing was quick and shallow. A fine line of perspiration stood on her forehead. Her eyes were closed, the eyelids a powdery shade of blue.

"My God," Chris said. "She looks awful. Surely the hospital wouldn't let her go in this condition."

"I don't know," Quintain said grimly. "But I know what I'm going to do." He turned and walked toward the phone.

"What?" Chris asked.

"Get a doctor." Quintain had the phone in his hand.

"No!" The force of Verna's voice startled him. He turned, the receiver still in his hand, and looked at her. Her eyes were open and she was struggling to sit up while Chris tried to hold her down.

"Just ... just come here ... just for a minute," Verna panted.

Chris looked at him. "You'd better do it. She's going to hurt herself."

Quintain put down the receiver and walked to the couch. He sat beside Verna and took her hand in his. "Look," he said, "you need help."

The old coat Verna was wearing had fallen open to reveal a short hospital gown beneath. Verna closed her eyes, swallowed painfully, and passed a trembling hand across her forehead. "They tried to kill me," she whispered.

124

Chris gave Quintain a significant look. "She's burning up. She doesn't know what she's saying."

"No!" Verna's eyes fluttered open. She stared directly into Quintain's eyes. "Please ... believe me. I know what I'm saying ... please!"

Quintain patted her hand. "Okay. It's all right. Who tried to kill you? The hospital?"

Verna tried to swallow again. It was painful to watch. "Fronck," she whispered.

"Fronck!"

Chris stood. "Do you have any fruit juice? I'm no doctor, but she needs liquids."

Quintain nodded. "In the freezer." Chris went into the kitchen.

Quintain looked into Verna's pleading face. "I haven't got much time," she said in a hoarse whisper. "I'm going to pass out any minute. Please let me trust you."

The contrast between the cool, beautiful woman that Quintain had known in all her passions, and this babbling shell that lay before him filled Quintain with a deep sorrow, and then a flashing rage at what he did not know. "You mean the big guy at the party tried to kill you?"

She sighed deeply, and for a moment he thought she had gone to sleep. "Yes. It wasn't him, though. He was hired to do it."

Quintain tried to take that in, but his head was whirling with too many incongruities. "Who ... who hired him, Verna?"

"The Council," she whispered. Quintain had to bend over her to hear the next word. "Diamond ..."

"The Council? You mean the Council at Continental?"

She had drifted off too far to answer.

Chris returned with a pitcher of orange juice and a glass. She looked questioningly at Quintain, and he put a finger to his lips, rose and led her into the kitchen.

125

"I think she's sleeping," he said.

"What did she say?"

He frowned and shook his head. "Crazy stuff. Do you remember a huge man at the party named Fronck?"

"The red-haired one that looked like a football player?"

"Yeah. Verna claims he tried to kill her."

Chris nodded. "I heard her say that. I didn't know his name."

"But that's only part of it. She claims Fronck was hired by the Council, and somebody or something named Diamond."

"The Council!"

"Yeah. I don't know if she means the one at Continental. She passed out before I could ask her."

"That's crazy! She is delirious. We'd better get a doctor."

He hesitated, and Chris saw it. "You are going to get help, aren't you?"

"Yes. Soon. I just want to talk to her one more time." He took the pitcher from her. "Let's see if we can get some of this down her."

When they returned to the living room Verna's eyes were open, and tears were standing in them. "You did it, didn't you?" she asked Quintain in a voice so pathetic that it made him ache with compassion.

He sat beside her. "No, I didn't call anyone. I told you you could trust me. Now. We are going to get you to drink some nice, freshly canned orange juice. Think you can manage that?"

Verna closed her eyes once, and then looked at him and said, "I'll try." She drank half a glass before she collapsed back on the couch exhausted. Chris put the back of her hand on Verna's forehead, and gave Quintain a sharp look. "Will you get a doctor now?"

He looked up at her and slowly shook his head. "Not yet."

"Surely you don't believe her? She's out of her head."

"I don't know,' Quintain replied. "If you consider what she

126

said it makes a weird kind of sense. If we get a doctor, what will he do?"

"Put her in the hospital, where she belongs," Chris said impatiently.

"And if someone is after her, where is the first place they would look?"

Chris' eyes widened. "The hospital!"

Quintain nodded.

"But that wreck was an accident. The radio said Kenneth lost control on a curve."

"You said yourself he was an expert driver."

"Yes." She hesitated, and then gave him a peculiar look.

Quintain had seen that look before. From his father, from Mary, from the psychiatrist. He didn't blame Chris for what she must be thinking after all he had told her that evening about his psychological problems. He wasn't sure himself that what he felt was the old paranoia, or healthy caution. All he knew for sure was that Verna had asked for his trust, and he was going to give it to her.

"Look," he said firmly, "maybe I'm crazy, but I'm not calling anyone until I can get her to agree to it."

Chris stared at him for a moment. "All right. But there's no reason we shouldn't do what we can. Do you have any rubbing alcohol? We've got to get that fever down."

Quintain gave her a grateful look, and directed her to the alcohol and towels.

While Chris was gone, Verna opened her eyes. Quintain bent over her and said gently, "It's okay, Verna. We're going to take care of you. No doctors until you give the word."

She squeezed his hand weakly, and dropped off again. He thought she looked more peaceful this time.

With Quintain's help, Chris stripped the old cloth coat and the hospital gown from Verna, and they gave her an alcohol bath. Then, deciding it was best to leave her where she was, they put one of Quintain's pajama tops on her, and covered her with a sheet and blankets. When they had finished, Verna looked better. Some color had returned to her face, and her breathing was deep and regular. Chris put her fingers on her forehead. "Her fever's down."

There followed a tense whispered argument while Quintain tried to convince Chris to get in her car and go home, and she fiercely stuck to her insistence that she was going to stay and help him take care of Verna. He was overcome with an eerie sense of danger and wanted her out of there, in the safety of her little house in the valley, but he didn't tell her that. Finally, he saw argument was futile, and he capitulated.

"Only on the condition that you take the bed. I'll make a pallet on the floor out here."

She agreed and they went off to the bedroom—she to prepare for bed, and he to get blankets and a pillow for his make-shift bed.

He was settled into his pallet that he had placed next to the couch where Verna slept peacefully, when he remembered the door. He got up in his shorts, having given Chris his only other pair of pajamas, and went to the door to make sure he had locked both the bolt and the safety chain. When he turned, Chris was standing in the doorway to the bedroom. He felt as if he had been caught at something deceitful.

"I just came to say goodnight," she whispered. "How's the patient?"

"Okay," he murmured. "Good night."

Chris turned back into the bedroom, and then hesitated. She turned toward him. "Alex," she whispered, "I feel better with the door locked, too. I want you to know that." And she disappeared into the bedroom.

He lay on his pallet, listening to Verna's steady breathing and thinking about how Chris had looked standing in the doorway, her hands completely hidden by the arms of his pajamas, her hair a soft cloud in the dim light, and he decided he had never before seen such a beautiful sight.

Palmer leaped up from her seat and thrust her red face into Diamond's. "You *idiot*," she hissed, "is this how you handle an assignment?"

"Slowly," Atlas cautioned, but there was an edge of steel in his voice that made Diamond wary. "How do we know she is out?"

This time Diamond couldn't resist taking a handkerchief from his pocket and wiping his face with it. "It was the man we had watching Quintain's apartment who called. She's gone there."

"Get over there and get them," Palmer shouted.

"Wait," Atlas said. "This may be working out—"

"Working *out*?" Palmer's mouth was rigid with contempt. "They are probably in touch with the police right now."

"Use your head," Diamond said. "They've as much to lose as we have."

"And we can handle the police," Atlas added. "Now let's just calm down and see what must be done."

"Palmer's right," Regan said. He moved to the center of the room. "We've got them trapped. Why wait?"

"Because we have to plan this thing properly," Atlas said testily. "We need to separate them, and keep Quintain alive for awhile. It's delicate."

"I'll handle it personally," Diamond said. "The man we sent for can take care of Stone, and I'll cut Quintain out."

Atlas nodded. "You're the one to do it."

"I agree," Palmer said. "For another reason. It's about time we began to hold someone responsible for this mess."

"Yes," Atlas said softly, looking at Diamond. "If this doesn't come off properly, Diamond, I think we're going to have to reassess the make-up of The Council."

The room was silent, but Diamond could feel the eyes on him, and he could sense their menacing agreement with Atlas. Finally, Atlas sighed, and said, "You'll need a technician for Quintain's interrogation."

129

"I'll use Fronck."

Palmer snorted.

"No," Atlas said. "He's right. Fronck is a good technician."

"He enjoys his work," Regan agreed.

Palmer made a grimace of disgust. "He's the idiot that got us in this mess."

"There is one difference," Diamond stood and leaned in toward Palmer, his eyes inches from her glittering spectacles. "I'll be there."

Chapter 12

QUINTAIN awoke with a start. His eyes felt grainy. The odor of cooking food made his nostrils quiver. He wondered for a confused moment what he was doing on the floor of his living room, and then he remembered. He turned quickly to the couch. Morning light silhouetted it against the windows.

Verna slept in the same position he had left her. He looked closely at her face, gently touched her forehead. Her color was nearly normal, and her skin felt cool. Quintain heard a drawer close in the kitchen. He slipped into his pants and shirt and padded silently, barefooted, into the kitchen.

Chris was at the stove with her back to him. She still wore his pajamas, but she had rolled up the sleeves and pants legs. She looked like a little girl.

He walked quietly to her and stood behind her, while he slipped his arms around her waist. She turned, startled, into his embrace, and then laughed up at him. "I love you in my pajamas," he said.

"I'll always wear them when we go out."

He kissed her forehead.

"Are you hungry?"

He bent and kissed her neck. "Starved."

"I meant for food." She stroked the back of his neck, and then pushed him gently away. "Do you want me to burn the bacon?"

"Yes." He reached for her again, but she side-stepped his arms, and picked up a spatula and began turning bacon that was frying on the stove. "How's our patient? Better, don't you think?"

He nodded and reached past her for a piece of bacon. She made a feint at his hand with the spatula. He tipped his head back and put the bacon in his mouth.

Chris pointed to a plate on the counter. "I made her soft-boiled eggs. Do you think that's all right?"

"I guess so. She has to eat." Quintain didn't want to talk about Verna at that moment. He was too caught in the feeling of warm domesticity that watching Chris prepare breakfast gave him.

"I've been thinking," Chris said as she lay out two more plates on the counter, "why did Verna come here?"

"What do you mean?"

"Well . . . you said yourself you hardly know her, and there must be lots of other places she could've gone. The Sandersons had friends everywhere."

"I don't know," he said weakly. He hated to lie to her, but he hated even more the thought of the contempt she might feel for him if he told her the truth about himself and Verna.

"What are you going to do?"

"Try to talk her into going to the hospital. What are your plans?"

"Oh," she expertly flipped eggs onto the two empty plates, "I'll stick around, if you want. Sundays are lost days for me, anyway."

"Yes," he replied, advancing on her, "I want." He took the frying pan firmly from her and put it on the stove. "I definitely want." He took her in his arms and kissed her very gently on the mouth.

"My," she sighed, "you certainly get over your shyness in a hurry."

"It's all done with wonder drugs," he murmured into her hair. "The miracle of modern medicine."

There was a cough and an indistinct murmur from the living room. Quintain picked up the plate Chris had prepared for Verna, and said, "Shall we make morning rounds, Doctor?"

Verna was sitting up on the couch, trying to arrange her hair with her fingers. Her eyes were clear, and with the exception of the livid bruise on her forehead, she looked almost normal to Quintain. He expected, in the light of day, and with her senses obviously restored, that she wouldn't remember her ravings of the evening before. He felt a twinge of embarrassment as he remembered his own act of checking the locks on the door. With the sun streaming in the windows the night before all seemed like some garish nightmare from his childhood.

But something was still wrong with Verna. While they ate, Chris and Quintain gathered around the couch, Verna was taciturn and strange. She answered their questions with half-hearted, broken sentences, and she would not look directly at Quintain.

Chris helped Verna into the bathroom after breakfast, and when she came back she gave Quintain a questioning little shrug, and began gathering up their dishes. When Verna returned to the doorway, Quintain jumped up to help her to the couch. Chris was in the kitchen.

"I've got to talk to you," Verna whispered against his shoulder as he eased her back on the couch.

He pulled a chair close to the couch, sat in it, and said, "Okay."

Verna shook her head, and glanced toward the kitchen. "Alone."

"Oh, now look ..." Quintain said. He suddenly felt exasperated with Verna, with the whole situation. He had taken her in, had gone along with her ravings, and now she wanted him to get rid of Chris, who had helped her as much as he had.

"You don't understand," Verna whispered tensely. "They want to kill you too."

133

"... I don't know what you imagine is going on, but I think the best place for you ... they *what*?"

Verna looked very solemn. "And they will, too, if you don't listen."

Quintain massaged his eyes with his fingertips. "Why did you come here, Verna? I know we had a ... thing. But you were never really close to me."

She leaned toward him, her face fierce with tension. "Because I don't know anyone else. Don't you see ... everyone I know in this city is a part of it. But I know you're not, because they want to kill you too."

Quintain stared at her. He knew she was mad. He thought he knew how to defeat Verna's paranoia. He felt a flash of irony that he, the patient, was now thinking like a therapist. In the kitchen he could hear the clash of dishes as Chris washed them.

"All right," he began. "Chris. Chris is one of them?"

"I don't think so. But don't you see, she works with them. She could tell them ..."

"Oh, now look, Verna. Chris has been here since last night. She's been trying to *save* your life."

Verna closed her eyes, but Quintain could see by her furrowed brow that it was to think rather than from the weakness caused by her injuries. She opened her eyes very wide, and said, "All right. I'll trust her. I don't have any choice."

Quintain almost made a sarcastic reply, but Verna looked so frightened and vulnerable that instead he got up without a word, went to the kitchen door, and held it open while he said, "Chris, will you come in here? Verna wants to tell us something."

His theory was that if they let Verna get all of her delusions out in the light, they would wilt and die. But as Chris and he took seats around the couch and Verna began to talk, he felt his theory wilting instead of her delusions. She made

134

too much sense, even though what she said was so astounding that it had him and Chris gasping protests.

"The center of the whole thing is The Council," Verna said. "In the beginning it was set up to coordinate between the partnership and the company. It was staffed with middle-management people ... people who were ambitious for top-management power. But the way Continental is structured, the only people who have that power are the partners. And you can't work your way into a partnership ... you have to have the money and the power to begin with. That was a mistake—putting all those hungry, frustrated people into that Council. They weren't content to just coordinate. They began to take power for themselves. They began to get Continental into a business it was never intended for ... espionage. It was a natural ... most of the people on The Council, and a lot of others in the company, were experienced. They had the contacts, knew where to go for jobs.

"At first, they had a rule," Verna continued, "that they would only work for the United States and its allies. And there was plenty of work—things that governments want done but can't do themselves—things that, if they're caught, could bring governments down, lose elections ..."

"But what's the difference if they do it themselves, or hire it done?" Quintain asked, despite himself getting caught up in Verna's narrative.

"Accountability," Verna replied. "That's the big word in The Council. Their product is accountability, or absence of it.

"At first The Council specialized in intelligence ... the tough jobs. Breaking into places and stealing documents, microfilms, taking pictures ... whatever was wanted ...

"And then, like any business, The Council began to feel a need to build on their successes, to diversify.

"... they wanted to get into the big money jobs ... removals."

135

"Removals?" Chris asked, but Quintain guessed what Verna meant.

"Assassinations," Verna said simply. "The big time.

"They had called in an expert, a man who was known only as Felix, and offered him the job of heading up the new endeavor. They made him a member of The Council, and he succeeded very well ... so well that 'removals' became the dominant revenue producer.

"It was exciting. Everyone wanted to work with Felix. He became a power in The Council."

"Murder!" Chris exclaimed with a shudder of revulsion. "Everyone wanted ... ?"

She cut herself off, and Quintain saw that she had realized, just as he had, that they were being drawn into Verna's story, beginning to accept it as fact rather than the fantasies of a distraught mind.

"Oh, it was easy to rationalize," Verna said. "We were in a war against our enemies, the enemies of the free world. We thought of ourselves as heroes. Heroes who were becoming rich from our heroics."

"We?" Quintain asked.

Verna nodded. "Yes. I wasn't in The Council, but Sandy got me work. They needed women with ... certain attributes ... couldn't find enough of them.

"Then someone on The Council had discovered that they could make more money than they had ever dreamed possible, and acquire more power, if they gave a certain reverse twist to their various enterprises.

"That's when the trouble started," Verna said. "They began to play on both sides of the street. We found that the Russians and Chinese were just as eager to employ us as the British and the Americans, but because of our unique position of trust with their enemies, the communists would pay a lot more."

"What happened to all the patriotic rationalizations?" Quintain asked.

Verna waved her hand. "By the boards. Oh, there was a minority dissent in The Council from a couple of the old conservatives who had been there at the beginning. But by that time The Council was dominated by the new breed. So we went into the double-dealing business. The original customers thought they still worked for them, and they did. But they also dealt espionage and removals to the communists. And then, of course, someone had to reverse the reverse, and they began to make their work more valuable to the original customers by trading on their special position with the communists."

"That must've been a little hair-raising," Quintain said.

"It was like roller skating on ice . . ." Verna paused, and a cloud of misery passed across her face. "Sandy used to say that," she whispered. "God! I could use a cigarette."

Chris produced a pack from her purse and handed it to Verna.

Verna inhaled deeply, and blew a hard stream of smoke at the ceiling. "About this time, the competition began to cause problems . . ."

"Competition!" Quintain stared at her in amazement.

Verna smiled sardonically. "It was too good a thing to have a monopoly. The toughest competitor is in England . . . it's called The Group. It was started by ex-British secret service people . . . people who had been retired, or passed over for promotion and quit. And the competition in this game doesn't have any Sherman anti-trust act to go by. They make up their own rules. They burned some of our people . . . we burned some of theirs . . ." She saw their puzzled looks. "Killed. Eliminated. Anyway, we had a period of about a year when we had an uneasy truce, and then it all broke open again just recently when Felix killed a man called Prince that worked for The Group."

Quintain sensed that Verna, now that she had gotten into her narrative so deeply, was enjoying it, enjoying the shock it caused her audience. Her face had taken on an unhealthy flush, and her eyes looked fevered.

"Verna," Chris said, "I know the people on The Council. I work with them on public relations. I just can't believe that they ... that ..."

Verna began a laugh that ended in a fit of racking, convulsive coughs. She lay back on the couch, the back of her hand on her forehead. "I guess I'm not as healthy as I thought."

Chris felt Verna's cheek. "Your fever's started up again. You'd better rest."

"In a minute. I've got to convince you. You say you know the people on The Council, but you don't. There are two councils ... the one you know, that the partners appoint, and the one that really runs the espionage and removals business. There are overlaps. The others don't know any more about what's going on than you did." Her voice trailed off to a weak whisper.

Chris looked at Quintain. "We should do the alcohol bath again ..."

"Wait." He leaned toward Verna, who now had her eyes closed. "Verna," he said softly, "can you hear me?" Verna gave a barely perceptible nod. "Assuming what you've told us is true, why would these people want to kill me? I'm not involved with them in any way."

Quintain had to place his ear close to her lips to hear her answer. "Inevitable. So much double-dealing ... someone would get the idea to double-deal The Council. So much money ... special accounts ... unreported. Sandy needed the money."

"You mean Sanderson stole money from The Council?"

"Sandy couldn't live ... without ... all his life, rich. He and I and Diamond ..."

"She's going out," Chris said. "We've got to ..."

138

"You get the alcohol," Quintain said.

When Chris left the room, Quintain bent over Verna and took her hand. "Verna. Verna!" Her eyelids fluttered, but didn't open. "You and Sanderson and Diamond stole the money?"

"No ... no. You did ..."

"I ...!"

"We set you up ... the investment program ..."

"How?"

"I don't know, exactly. Sandy handled that." Her voice was fading.

"And you handled me," Quintain said, surprised at his own bitterness.

Verna smiled˙wanly. "No, darling. That was strictly my own idea. But when Sandy found out, of course he used it ... to get you to the party ... to get you alone here yesterday morning." Her hand gripped his with surprising strength. "To ... to kill you. Forgive me ..."

Her hand fell from Quintain's grasp. He sat and stared at her until Chris returned and roused him to help her with the alcohol bath.

After they had bathed Verna and wrapped her in a blanket, they left her sleeping on the couch and went into the kitchen.

"God," Quintain said, running his fingers forward through his hair. "She says she and Sanderson and this Diamond stole money and made it look like I did it."

"But how could they?"

"The investment program ... the computer program I ran for Sanderson. So she says."

"But is that possible? Wouldn't you know?"

He shook his head. "That's what scares me. Sanderson gave me the constants and I just ran the program. I didn't even write it. He got it from the program library at Continental. I don't *know* what it did."

Quintain sat heavily at the table. "Jesus, Chris, if this is true, I've got to straighten it out."

"But is it true? It's incredible!"

"Why would she make it up? And in her condition, to tell it the way she did . . . Wait a minute! Why would Sanderson need money? He was rich, wasn't he?"

Chris looked thoughtful. "He inherited money, I know that. But there had been talk . . ."

"What talk? Tell me everything you can remember."

Chris sat opposite Quintain, a frown of concentration on her face. "Well, once when Uncle Luke and I were at the Sandersons' Malibu place, I made some envious remark about their house to him, and Uncle Luke said something like I wouldn't envy them if I had the mortgage they had."

"A lot of wealthy people have mortgages, for tax write-offs . . ."

"There were other things, too. I'm trying to remember who said it, but somebody once made a remark to me about Verna selling some jewelry . . ."

"Jewelry! Christ, that's not good . . ."

"What are you going to do?"

"I don't know." He stared at the table top. "First I've got to find out what the truth is." He stood. "Can you stay with Verna?"

She nodded. "What are you going to do?"

"I'm going down to the office and tear that program apart. I was a fool not to do it in the first place. Then we'll know if what Verna said is true . . . if I've been used to steal money."

Chris stood. "Do you think that's wise, to go down there . . . ?"

"It's Sunday. With a little luck I can get in and out with no one but the guard knowing . . ." *The guard!* Quintain hesitated. What if the guard was one of *them*?

"I wish I knew where Uncle Luke is," Chris said. "I know he could help us."

"See if you can find out, while I'm gone," Quintain replied. "But don't talk to him until we know what the truth is." He went off in search of his shoes.

Quintain left the MG in the garage he rented for it, and took the bus down Wilshire to the office. He didn't want the MG, with its conspicuous paint job, anywhere near the office while he was in it.

He had decided he would have to trust his luck about the guard, and it seemed to be a good decision. The man hardly glanced at him as Quintain signed in. He went up the empty elevator to the executive floor, and got into his office without seeing anyone.

He took the program from the bottom drawer of his desk. It was in the form of a deck of punched cards. Wrapped around the cards was a program listing that displayed in printed form the original programmer's instructions. He spread the listing on his desk, took off his coat, locked the door of his office, and sat down to figure out what the program did.

Two hours later he turned the last page of the listing, drew a line under a program statement with a red pencil, flipped back through the listing and found the constant table the statement referred to, and, after studying the table for a moment, very quietly closed the listing and sat staring at the wall behind his desk.

It had all been so easy, so painless for Sanderson. The constants he had given Quintain to run the program against had simply reduced the profit Continental made from currency exchanges by fractional percentages, and then transferred the resulting monies to an account labeled only with a number. The money that had been skimmed had only been fractions of pennies per unit of currency, but there had been millions and millions of those units. Quintain did a rough calculation in his head. In the weeks he had been operating the program, they must have transferred hundreds of thousands of dollars

141

into the dummy account. He couldn't tell from his information where the money went. Probably directly into a liquid bank account where it could be easily withdrawn in cash.

The whole scheme was so transparently simple that Sanderson couldn't have hoped to conceal it. Of course, he had never intended to. He had given Quintain the constants verbally, while Quintain wrote them down. All the evidence pointed at Quintain as the embezzler. Even the tablet with the daily lists of constants in his own handwriting were still in his desk.

He was in trouble. Everything that Verna had told him and Chris now took on the light of truth.

He considered going to the police. But what could he tell them? Verna's story, no matter how much Quintain might believe it now, could only seem like a wild diversionary tactic to a policeman. The only hard evidence that Quintain had to take to the police lay before him on his desk, and that evidence all pointed to him as a thief.

He needed more information. He needed to find where that dummy account led. He needed to ask Verna why The Council wanted to kill him, when it seemed to him all they had to do was turn him over to the police. The money that had been stolen was taken from the legitimate business of Continental. Why wasn't a long jail term adequate punishment for embezzlement? If Verna had told him everything, The Council had no interest in the legitimate side of the business. It didn't make sense.

He also needed to find out from Verna who the people on The Council were, and most important, who Diamond was.

He began to make a list of questions to ask Verna. When he finished, he tore the list from the pad he had written it on, put it in his coat pocket, put on the coat, and left.

He saw no one but the guard on his way out. He walked a block down Wilshire to catch the bus, rather than catching it in front of the office. Within fifteen minutes after he had left his office, he was standing in front of his apartment door, inserting his key in the lock. He had been gone almost three hours.

The living room was empty. Verna's bed on the couch had the blanket thrown back. Quintain assumed she had just gotten up to go to the bathroom.

He went into the bedroom, expecting to see Chris there waiting for Verna to come out of the bathroom. The bedroom was empty. The bathroom door stood open. The bathroom was empty. The first alarm rang in his head.

He ran back through the living room and into the kitchen. Empty. Now all the alarm bells were going full tilt. He shouted Chris' name, and ran back to the bedroom. He stopped on the threshhold, numbed by what he now saw. The closet door was open only a few inches. From this angle he could see on the floor of the closet the dim outline of a bare foot. He knew immediately that that foot belonged to Chris. He ran to the closet door, his mind reeling with shock, not realizing he was repeating over and over, "No, no, no . . ."

Chapter 13

DIAMOND and Fronck watched Quintain walk along the street two blocks away and turn into his apartment building. Diamond put the car in gear, and eased it into the street.

"We'll take them both," Diamond said.

Fronck looked at him. "The girl?"

"We can use her," Diamond replied. "She should still be unconscious."

"Who is that guy that took Verna?" Fronck's little eyes narrowed.

"Outside help. He's an expert on suicides."

"I could've taken Verna," Fronck said. He was seething that he had this end of the assignment, instead of being allowed to take Verna. Thirty minutes alone with her before he killed her was all he would've taken, with no one being the wiser.

"You're not an expert on suicides," Diamond replied patiently. "Concentrate on this job. Bring them down one at a time. Make sure they're out for a while. If anyone sees you . . ."

"My friend is sick. Have to get 'em to a hospital."

"Right. Bring Quintain first. If anyone spots you, we'll go around back for the girl." Diamond pulled the car to the curb in front of Quintain's apartment building. "Don't screw this one up," he said to Fronck as the big man got out of the car.

Diamond watched Fronck lumber through the door to the building and disappear from sight in the small unattended lobby. The street was deserted. Two blocks away a man was doing something to a bed of plants that grew along the sidewalk, too far away to be a problem.

Diamond was tense. The next few hours would tell everything about his future, if he was going to have one. It would be all right with him if Fronck screwed up this job in a certain way . . . if he killed Quintain. It would save Diamond a lot of anxiety. He'd brought Fronck because the man was as dumb as he was large. He hoped that Fronck would not be subtle enough to deduce anything from whatever Quintain might say. Diamond had to play this charade out to its end, to get The Council off his back. Unless he got lucky, and Fronck actually did kill Quintain. But Diamond had learned not to expect anything but bad results from luck in this business.

For example, it was lousy luck that Verna had survived the car wreck, and had later escaped from the hospital and gotten to Quintain. Diamond didn't know what Verna might have told Quintain. That was where the danger lay, that Quintain might say something during the next few hours that would penetrate even Fronck's thick head. Then Diamond would have to kill Fronck. More complications. The Council was already straining at its leash, threatening to leap at Diamond's throat. He doubted he would survive many more complications.

He thought of what he would do with the money when it was over, to take his mind off the ordeal ahead. Nearly a million dollars. He had thought out his future very carefully. He would stay on The Council for another month or two. By that time Felix should have returned, intriguing to get the chairmanship. Diamond would feign a battle, but he would let Felix win in the end. Then, pretending wounded pride at his demotion, Diamond would quit. It had been done before. The Council's policy on retirement was firm. A majority vote in favor. But after his sham battle with Felix, he knew he would be able to muster the vote. The Council understood the debilitating effects of loss of prestige. Most of them were where they were because of mutually shared lust for power, coupled with an obsession with danger.

Then, after he retired, he would quietly drift away to Italy. There was a spot on the Mediterranean, just south of Livorno, that he had in mind. Small villas surrounding a picturesque fishing village. Close enough to Rome for an occasional weekend there, when the lassitude became too much. He would live unpretentiously, but well. He would have the food and wine that he needed, the women. He was weary, tired of this business. He'd been in it so long that he couldn't remember any other life. The future he had planned all lay in the balance over the next few hours. Was, even now, beginning to be decided inside that building.

Diamond experienced a spasm of impatience. What was keeping Fronck? He looked at his watch and was surprised to discover that Fronck had only been gone for a few minutes. He slumped behind the wheel, trying to relax.

Quintain threw open the closet door. Chris was slumped against the back wall, one leg under her body, the other thrust in front of her. Her head had fallen forward onto her chest, and her hair cascaded over her face, hiding it.

He knelt, brushed the hair back, and looked into her face. Her eyes were closed and her jaw was slack, her mouth open, but she was breathing.

He picked her up easily, carried her to the bed, and lay her gently on it. He knelt on the bed beside her and looked at her face. "Chris," he whispered.

A scratching, metallic noise came from the direction of the living room . . . a noise that registered just at the edge of his consciousness. The noise was familiar. He looked up, toward the living room, trying to remember what it was. The noise had stopped. Then he realized what it had been.

Someone had put a key in the lock on his door.

146

He got off the bed, and went quietly to the bedroom door and looked across the living room at the front door. It was still closed. Then the noise came again. Whoever was out there was trying keys in the lock. He heard the lock turn, and then stop. He held his breath. The key was withdrawn, and another inserted.

Quintain took a deep breath and let it out slowly. Then, pushing off from the edge of the doorway, he ran to the door, and carefully secured the chain lock in its keeper. His hands trembled, but he managed to do it quietly. He looked desperately around the living room. He needed time . . . time to get Chris out of there. His eye fell on the overstuffed chair . . . an old, heavy frayed specimen of nineteen-fifties design that he'd picked up at a garage sale. In a series of heaving lifts and frantic skids he managed to get the chair to the door. He pushed the back against the door panel and started back for the bedroom.

As he passed through the bedroom door he heard the bolt withdraw from its keeper and the door thump hollowly against the chair. He scooped Chris up. Her eyes fluttered up at him, and she put her arms around his neck and settled her head against his chest with a little whimper.

He ran into the kitchen with Chris. The door was open against the chain, the chair still in place. Fingers the size of blackjacks curled around the edge of the door. He put Chris gently on the floor, her back propped against the cabinets, and put his palms against the frame of the window over the breakfast table. Outside the window was the fire escape. The sound of wood splintering came from the living room.

The window at first refused his exertion, and then gave with a screech of old paint. He turned to get Chris, and found Fronck standing in the doorway of the kitchen.

Fronck seemed larger than Quintain remembered. His bulk filled the doorway. Quintain glanced at Chris, whose eyes

147

were now open but clouded. She put a hand to her neck, and moaned.

Quintain was breathing heavily from the exertion of opening the window and from fear. He could feel adrenalin burning his nostrils. He crouched, his head thrust toward Fronck like a trapped animal.

"What do you want?" he croaked.

Fronck smiled, his teeth were stained with tobacco. "You," he replied, and began to move slowly toward Quintain, his arms outstretched in a herding attitude. Those arms looked like log rails to Quintain. Fronck's fingers flexed as he moved toward Quintain, flexed in and out, in some evil anticipation. Quintain sidled to his left, and put the table between himself and Fronck.

Quintain's hands gripped the edge of the table, and Fronck's eyes flickered down to take that in. Quintain gave up the idea of shoving the table into Fronck, but he kept his hands there, his arms tensed, as if he hadn't.

"Take it easy," Fronck said, "and you won't get hurt."

"Sure," Quintain whispered. If ever someone meant him harm, this giant did.

He shoved the table at Fronck, who was waiting for it. Fronck dropped his hands to catch the edge of the table, and as he did, Quintain launched himself headfirst across the table.

He felt his head slam into the big body, heard Fronck's grunt of surprise and anger, and then they were down on the floor, the table on top of them. Quintain brought his right elbow up, and smashed it toward Fronck's face as he doubled a knee into the point in space he estimated was occupied by Fronck's crotch.

The elbow hit Fronck on the cheek. He brought his knee up again, and was rewarded with a grunt and a fleeting grimace of pain across Fronck's face. Quintain was on top of

Fronck, but the table was on top of Quintain, restricting his movements.

Fronck found a very simple solution to his situation. He stood up. As he did, he brought Quintain and the table with him. The table fell against the window, shattering a pane. Fronck had his forearm under Quintain's right armpit. Quintain was suspended on his toes, but he managed to bring his left fist around in a sweeping arc and it bounced off Fronck's forehead with a force that sent a jolt of pain all the way to Quintain's shoulder. Fronck didn't even blink.

Fronck shifted his position, bringing Quintain's right arm up in a hammerlock. Quintain could feel the power in that grip, and he felt that Fronck could break that arm off if he wanted to. Quintain was as helpless as a child, dancing on his toes, his chin jabbing his chest. Peripherally, Quintain saw Fronck's free hand drawn back, and then sweep toward the back of his neck, edge-first. He didn't feel the blow. He sank down into a dark place where someone was putting on a demonstration of elemental electricity. Jagged lines of white and blue flame probed the space. An electron raced around the edges, tracing its path in a shimmering line of yellow light. A voice tried to describe the show, but it was lost in its own echo, which was lost in its echo ... echoing, on and on, like some aural hall of mirrors.

Quintain was aware of being roughly lifted and dropped face down. Then he felt his pants being lowered, and he fumbled for consciousness. He felt embarrassment at the thought of lying there with his pants lowered and he drifted up to a level on the verge of consciousness, but he couldn't get his body to move.

He was lying with his head turned, his cheek grinding into the linoleum. Got to clean that floor, he thought, and then he saw Chris. She was still slumped against the cabinets, her head down, but her eyes were open in horror. He couldn't get his head to move, but he rolled his eyes in the direction

Chris was staring until he thought they would fall out of their sockets. Dimly, he could see Fronck's big hand dwarfing the hypodermic needle. Fronck. He remembered. Partial command over his body returned. He waited, gathering himself for one desperate leap, trying to clear his head. He decided rolling would be best. Roll like the matadors when the bull has them down. Roll to his left, away from Fronck, and then there was a stab of pain in his hip. He started his roll. He got his body up on its side, and then the wave of warm lassitude hit him. He fell back on his face, but he never felt the impact.

Diamond got the car through the interchange and onto the San Bernardino Freeway and tried to relax for the long drive to Lake Arrowhead. He looked at his watch, took the traffic into account, and estimated they would be at the cabin in an hour and a half.

"An hour and a half,' he announced. "What did you give them?"

"Half a load apiece," Fronck replied from the back seat. "They'll last."

Half a syringe for each. Diamond looked in the rear view mirror. Fronck's head filled it. Quintain and the girl sat slumped on either side of him, Fronck's big arms around them holding their heads against his chest. They would be out for two hours Diamond estimated. The girl probably half an hour longer, she was so small. Plenty of time. And if they did start to come around, Diamond had a spare vial in his coat pocket.

The cabin at Arrowhead had been acquired by The Council several years before. It had belonged to a member of The Council, so the transfer of title had been easy to arrange. The cabin was located in the woods north of the lake, on three acres of property. The closest neighbor, a dentist, who used his A-frame on weekends and vacations, was two miles away, with a ravine cut by a seasonal creek intervening between.

The cabin was an expensive necessity. Not that the purchase price or the maintenance were exorbitant, but the precautions necessary to keep the cabin "safe" were.

Diamond glanced in the mirror again. He took a perverse pleasure in the sight of the livid bruise on Fronck's forehead. He didn't like Fronck. He didn't like the look on the brute's face as he had lowered Chris Bell into the car, his hand lingering on her breast a moment too long to be accidental. He particularly didn't like the fact that Fronck had screwed up the assignment with the Sandersons and, conversely, hadn't screwed it up with Quintain. Diamond knew Fronck's reputation for a blinding, quick anger, and he cursed his luck that Fronck hadn't killed Quintain in the apartment when he attacked him.

"You're going to have a pretty face," Diamond said malevolently, and was rewarded by seeing Fronck's face flush.

"Stupid bastard," Fronck growled. "Thought he could take me."

"Seems he gave it a good try," Diamond persisted, remembering the stiff legged way Fronck had walked when he had appeared from Quintain's apartment. "He's not even a pro. Maybe you're getting old, Fronck."

"No," Fronck said thoughtfully. "I'm as good as ever. He's a funny bastard, is all."

"Funny?"

"Yah. You know . . . throwin' himself around like he'd gone nuts."

Diamond chuckled mirthlessly. "Didn't play by the rules, eh, Fronck?"

Fronck's face turned ponderous with thought. Diamond gave up trying to needle him. The man's mentality was beneath anything more subtle than a club over the head. He didn't even recognize Diamond's sarcasm.

"Yah," Fronck said, finally. "You could say that. Say . . . turn on some music, will you?"

Diamond flipped on the radio. "By all means. What'll it be, Fronck . . . top forty? The Children's Hour? Or, if you're in a classical mood, how about Teeny Boppers Tune Time, with Mad Dog Fletcher?"

"Yah, that's it. Classical . . ."

Diamond stared at him in the mirror. "You mean *classical* classical?"

"You know . . . Chopin, Bach . . . those guys."

Diamond shook his head in wonderment, and tuned in a classical station.

The cabin was situated two hundred yards back from North Shore Valley Road. The drive was a narrow, graveled trail through the trees, large enough for only one car. Diamond stopped at the gate and got out to unlock it. On three sides the property was surrounded by a steel cyclone fence, eight feet high, with three strands of barbed wire extending it another two feet at the top. On the fourth side the deep ravine formed a natural barrier. Diamond unlocked the gate, drove through, and got out to close it, but a man appeared from the woods, a Doberman at his side.

"I'll get it, sir," the man said. The Doberman stared at Diamond. He was in a heavy harness, and the man held him by a leather handle rising from the harness. The Doberman dug its claws futiley into the ground as Diamond got back in the car, its lips silently curled back to expose its heavy fangs. This was part of the expense of keeping the cabin a safe place. Six men with Dobermans constantly patrolling in shifts of two. Each was armed with magnum revolvers, and each was an expert marksman and dog handler, which made their salaries high.

Diamond herded the car slowly down the gravel drive, broke into the clearing at the cabin, and parked in front in the turnaround. A blue Dodge was parked off to one side, in

152

front of a storage shed. Diamond frowned. No one was supposed to be there. He knew the car didn't belong to the guards. They kept a heavy four-wheel drive vehicle parked in back of the cabin.

Diamond went up on the porch, the door opened a few inches, and the black muzzle of a Doberman thrust through the opening. The dog growled menacingly deep in its throat.

"Get that goddam dog away," Diamond said.

The door opened all the way, revealing another guard. "Of course, sir. *Flat*, Satan."

Diamond stepped through the door. "Help Fronck," he said to the guard. The guard hurried out with the dog.

Atlas and Miss Palmer stood in front of a fire in the field-stone fireplace.

"Ah, Diamond," Atlas said. "How did it go?"

Diamond tensed. Something was wrong. He remembered that he had left his gun in the glove box of the car. It was too late to get it. "Fine," he said.

Fronck and the guard entered, carrying Quintain. They silently took him in one of the bedrooms at the rear of the cabin, and returned and went outside.

"We've developed a little hitch," Atlas said. He broke off, as Fronck and the guard carried Chris Bell's limp body through to another bedroom. When they returned to the main room, Atlas smiled at them.

"Wait outside for a while, you two, will you?"

After the two men had gone, Atlas said, "I'm afraid The Council needs you back in Los Angeles."

"I have work to do here," Diamond replied softly.

"Yes, of course," Atlas agreed. "Miss Palmer has graciously volunteered to step in for you."

"This is too important . . ."

"*Too* important!" Miss Palmer exclaimed, her blue eyes glinting balefully at Diamond. "Who do you think you're talking to . . ."

153

Atlas interrupted with a chuckle. "Now, now. No profit in squabbling, is there? Diamond, you haven't forgotten that Miss Palmer's speciality is interrogation?"

"If that's what you want to call it," Diamond said curtly.

"She gets results."

"So did the Inquisition."

"Oh, dear," Atlas replied, taking Miss Palmer paternally by the arm to cut off the protest that she was about to deliver. "I never thought our chairman would be squeamish. The fact remains, Diamond ... The Council needs you. It is not a request."

"In what capacity?"

"Why," Atlas raised eyebrows over eyes wide with innocence. "As Chairman, of course."

"You'll have to give me a reason. This is too important to us, for me to walk away from it without a damned good reason." Diamond's stomach was knotted with tension. Palmer was not Fronck. The chances were poor that she could interrogate Quintain without deducing the truth about Diamond. Diamond knew she would be the most implacable, dangerous enemy he'd ever faced. He hoped he could bluff it through with Atlas, hoped that Atlas hadn't been given permission to reveal the reason for this sudden summoning by The Council, or that the reason would be too weak. After all, Diamond thought, I am the Chairman ...

The hope was in vain.

Atlas immediately gave him a very good reason. One he couldn't ignore.

"Felix," Atlas said easily, "is back."

Chapter 14

QUINTAIN was floating in a warm ambiance, his body gently massaged by it. He wanted to sink deeper but he kept bobbing to the surface, and the more he struggled to sink back, the more he bobbed.

He became aware of a voice, a soothing, gentle voice. He opened his eyes. Above his head was a pattern of light and shadow. It fascinated him. He stared into it, his mind merging with the pattern. The voice gently urged him back. A hand turned his head. He looked into Miss Palmer's eyes. Kind eyes. He smiled at her. She returned his smile. He decided he loved Miss Palmer very much.

"Well, Mr. Quintain. You've had a nice rest."

He nodded. He smiled. Fronck's head came into view beside Miss Palmer's. He smiled at Fronck. He decided that Fronck was, like so many big men, very tender-hearted. That was why he was now bending over Quintain with a concerned expression. Quintain wanted to reassure him that he, Quintain, had never felt better in his life, but he couldn't summon the energy. Instead he smiled and smiled.

Miss Palmer nodded at Fronck, and Fronck moved in closer to Quintain, his big body blotting out the patterns above, his hands moving quickly. Quintain became aware of his body being lifted. Something slid across his legs. Fronck held him up in a sitting position, turning his torso this way and that. Quintain frowned. Something was wrong. Fronck let him fall back. Quintain shivered. Then he knew. He was naked. He looked for Miss Palmer's face, found it, and tried to communicate silently his embarrassment, his apology for his condition. Miss Palmer smiled. She understood it wasn't his fault.

"Now," Miss Palmer said.

Fronck moved to Quintain's feet. Quintain watched as if from a great distance as Fronck picked up his legs and quickly made three turns around his ankles with a nylon rope. Quintain watched as Fronck knotted the rope, admiring the professional way he did it. Fronck stepped back. Quintain let his eyes travel from his ankles, up the rope to the shadows above. Fronck stepped under the wheels, gripped a piece of the rope that dangled from one, and pulled. Quintain slid forward, his ankles rose.

"Wait," Miss Palmer said, and Quintain was glad she had noticed. She would get this straightened out. His head hurt, and he put a hand up and massaged his forehead. Miss Palmer made a breaking motion, there was a soft pop, and she held her hand to Quintain's face. Fire erupted in his nose. Something exploded inside his head. He jerked violently away from Miss Palmer's hand, but it followed him. He gasped. The fire stopped. He sat up suddenly, and stared wildly around the room. "Chris!"

Miss Palmer nodded at Fronck. Fronck began to pull the rope. Quintain slid slowly forward with each pull. He realized he was on a bed. He gripped the bed, carrying sheets forward with him. He remembered now . . . remembered his fight with Fronck. "Wait . . ." he croaked. He had questions that needed answers. Where was Chris? Where was he? Why was Miss Palmer there? What . . . ?

Fronck went on pulling the rope, a bored look on his face. A simple workman, doing his job. He went on pulling it, until only Quintain's shoulders were on the bed, the sheets now bunched around them by his clawing hands. Fronck went on pulling. Now only Quintain's head was on the bed. He stretched his neck, trying to stay on the bed. His feet were above him, pointing at the ceiling. Fronck pulled. Quintain's head came off the bed. He swung free, the sheets he still

156

gripped trailing after him. Fronck caught his body around the waist, ripped the sheets from Quintain's hands, and threw them on the bed. Quintain's body twisted. He let his arms fall, stretched them. He could just touch the floor with his palms.

"Arms," Miss Palmer said.

Fronck stooped, pulled Quintain's arms up behind his back, and bound them tightly just above the elbows. Quintain's shoulders were pulled back by the force of the bonds, and his arms began to ache. The room revolved. Miss Palmer's inverted legs and feet, clad in black heavy shoes, swung by. A chair. Fronck's thick legs, enormous shoes. The casters on the bed legs. Held on that for a moment, and then Fronck's legs again, the chair . . .

The room braked to a stop. Miss Palmer's face hung in front of him upside down. He saw that she wore false teeth. "Let's talk," Miss Palmer said. "Shall we?" Her breath was atrocious.

Quintain watched Miss Palmer's legs retreat to a chair, turn behind it, and the chair advanced toward him. Miss Palmer came around and sat in the chair. She looked down into his face. Her neck was wattled and red. Her head a cone haloed with white spidery hair etched against the shadow of the ceiling.

"Leave us."

Fronck's heavy tread receded. A door opened and closed.

"Now," Miss Palmer sighed. She produced a black thin cigar, lit it, and exhaled a satisfied pencil of smoke. "We might as well be comfortable."

"What . . . ?"

Miss Palmer's hand darted out, the fingers formed in a claw. She grasped a nipple in that pincer and twisted. Quintain's breath left him. He made a hoarse, sucking noise in his throat. The pain stopped.

Somewhere in the distance a radio was switched on and

157

F

tuned rapidly through stations, fragments of music, voices, until it came to rest on a station playing a symphony orchestra.

"You'll talk when I say you can," Miss Palmer said. "Do you understand?"

Miss Palmer settled back comfortably in her chair. As she talked Quintain could see her mouth open and close like a turtle's beak, and above that her thick, rouged cheeks hid her eyes.

"There are three basic principles in interrogation," Miss Palmer began pedantically. "First, you must make the subject helpless, and you must convince him beyond doubt that he is helpless . . . that he is in your power, and as subject to the interrogator's whim as a newborn baby. Second, you must develop a theory of his character. Character is the proper subject of the interrogator . . . the strengths and weaknesses, the little prides and vanities, the hidden terrors. Each subject has his own profile, like a set of fingerprints. And third, you must make the subject understand everything you plan to do, share with him your techniques, your discoveries about his character. Here many interrogators make their mistake. It is the anticipation of pain, tempered with the realization that there is not one blessed thing he can do to prevent it, not the pain itself, that makes the subject pliable."

Miss Palmer leaned forward in her chair, her nose inches from Quintain's chin. "Let me explain your situation," she said in a confidential tone. "You are of course aware that you are naked, and trussed up like a prize turkey. What you don't know is where you are. Oh," she said quickly reading the anticipation in Quintain's eyes, "I don't mean geography. Dear No . . ." she chuckled, and her teeth made an unpleasant clacking sound. "We won't tell you that. Suffice it, that you are not on your home territory. You have been removed to an alien place. We could've flown you out of the country, or to another state, or most anywhere . . . you don't know, and you won't. What I will tell you is this . . . you are at a place that is controlled by us. Its grounds are patrolled by men armed with guns and vicious dogs. It is surrounded by high fences and invulnerable natural barriers. It is remote. You could scream until you were hoarse, and no one would come to your aid. And . . ." she paused and leaned so close that for a moment Quintain was revulsed by the thought that her face might touch his. "And . . . I am in complete charge. I hold your fate in my hands. I am the monarch."

Miss Palmer leaned back in her chair, and took a drag on her cigar. "Where is the money?" she asked in a pleasant voice.

Quintain stared up at her, his head was roaring with blood. He was sure that he could bear the pain in his ankles not one second longer. "Money . . . ?" he rasped.

Miss Palmer smiled. She stretched an arm up and touched his genitals very gently. "You are familiar with novocain? We can easily deaden this part of your body . . . your maleness, eh? And then we can begin cutting. You see, the terror there is that you can't feel the pain, but you can feel the cutting, so you don't really know how much damage we're doing. That way, your imagination is free to roam. Do you have a good imagination, Mr. Quintain? Ah. I see you do." She dropped her hand. "Where is the money?"

"Listen," Quintain gasped. "It wasn't me. Sanderson set me up. He gave me the constants. I didn't even know . . ."

"Dear me," Miss Palmer sighed wearily. "This is tedious, Mr. Quintain." She stood, and moved out of his sight. "You think it over while I'm gone." The door opened. The sound of classical music soared. The door closed.

Quintain arched his back, trying to relieve the pain in his arms. His ankles had stopped hurting and were now as numb as if they had become a part of the rope that suspended him. Arching his back didn't relieve the pain in his arms, but it did make him begin revolving again. He discovered, through painful experiment, that he could increase the arc of the revolutions by arching his body at their midpoint. He tried to examine the room he was in to establish some orientation. He was in a rustic building. Wooden floors. Open ceilings traversed by rough beams. Knotty pine walls. One window that he could see. Covered with some kind of heavy wire mesh. Through the window he glimpsed the top of a tree. It was a fir. He was in a cabin or a lodge some place where firs grew.

The chair Miss Palmer had been sitting in was a foot from his head. By swinging his shoulders as he revolved, he could brush the edge of the seat with his forehead. What good that would do him, he didn't know. He looked up at the block and tackle. A hook extending from the top block had been thrust through a rope tied around one of the ceiling beams. He began to formulate a plan. A weak, improbable plan. But the only one he had. He had to have time. He had to find out where Chris was.

"Enjoying yourself?" Miss Palmer wanted to know as she sat in the chair again. She held a glass in her hand that was filled with ice and a cool, inviting liquid. As she sat there she sipped from it occasionally, making sure Quintain could see her do it. She never mentioned the glass, but it worked its effect. Quintain began to feel that his mouth and throat had been lined with felt.

"Where is the money?" Miss Palmer asked.

Quintain made his voice as weak and indistinct as he could. "All right, I'll tell you. Just tell me where Chris is."

Miss Palmer remained in her relaxed posture. Quintain cursed himself for not having made his voice weak enough. She had understood him perfectly. "You are not making the deals here, Mr. Quintain. I am going to ask you only once more, before I take measures. Where is the money?"

Quintain mumbled some sounds. Miss Palmer leaned forward, bringing the chair a few inches closer. "What! Speak up!" Quintain gauged the distance to the chair. It seemed close enough. Now he had to get her to leave. "I said," he replied distinctly, "that you would revolt any real man."

Her face pinched into a red, vicious mask. Her hand darted out to his nipple, and he tried not to scream as her fingernails dug into the tender flesh. Sweat stood on her upper lip, and her eyes had a mad, uncontrolled glaze. Quintain wondered if he had gone too far, if she could control herself. Finally her eyes cleared, and the pain abated. She wiped her lip with a trembling finger. "Very well," she said, "we'll do a little cutting, shall we?"

She stood with an angry motion that pushed the chair back several inches, and Quintain's heart sank. After he heard the door close, he tried to swing to the chair, but found that it was now farther away than it had been before. He could not touch it.

Fronck accompanied Miss Palmer when she returned. He carried a black cloth in one hand.

Miss Palmer sat in the chair and slowly filled a hypodermic syringe from a rubber capped vial. "Novocain," Miss Palmer said, her voice now free of its former madness. She finished filling the syringe, and held a surgeon's scalpel inches from Quintain's eyes. The scalpel had a serrated blade. "This," Miss Palmer said, "is used for small bones, gristle, things like that. We're going to use it on you, because it will create a sawing sensation after we've deadened you. You'll be able to follow the proceedings with part of your senses."

She made a motion with her hand, and Fronck wrapped the black cloth around Quintain's eyes and tied it at the back of his head. "Senses," Miss Palmer continued, "are little understood by the average person. We close our eyes, to avoid pain. Have you ever done that in the dentist's chair, Mr. Quintain?" Quintain felt his genitals lifted, and then felt the sharp stab of the needle. "But in reality that increases the awareness, the other senses – touch, hearing—are heightened

161

when we are deprived of sight. Can you feel that? Good. I believe we are ready."

Quintain heard Fronck's heavy steps, heard the door open and close. Don't let her do it, he prayed silently. God. Not that.

"Can you feel that, Mr. Quintain? I have your testicles in my hand . . ."

"*I'll tell you* . . ." Quintain shouted.

As Miss Palmer chuckled, Quintain heard the clacking of her teeth. "Too late, Mr. Quintain. Too late. You will learn to take your chances when you have them. Can you feel that? I am making the initial cut . . ." she grunted. "Tougher than it looks . . ."

Quintain could feel it. Oh, he could feel it . . . the rasping, tearing sensation. And he could hear it. Could hear the traverse of the knife, the grinding, rending noise of tissue parting. He screamed. The darkness of the blindfold was invaded by another, deeper darkness. The knife continued to cut. He screamed again. Then he fainted.

Quintain heard a brittle plinking sound that went from a high tone to a low tone, and then repeated. He opened his eyes. Miss Palmer smiled at him from the chair. She held a comb in her hand, passing her thumb slowly over the teeth. He groaned, blinked his eyes, and then rolled them upward.

"Still there, Mr. Quintain. See . . ."

She stood, lifted his genitals away from his body so he could see them, drew the teeth of the comb across them, and then laughed. His genitals were still deadened from the novocain, but he could feel the tearing sensation of the comb, hear the sawing whisper of the teeth.

"You're a very lucky man," Miss Palmer said, as she sat down again. "You are still a man." She held up the scalpel, and her eyes grew cold behind their glasses. "Let me assure you that next time I will alter that."

"Okay," Quintain whispered. This time he did not have to

feign the weakness in his voice. Miss Palmer scooted the chair closer and put her face down to Quintain's.

Quintain had a last, desperate, inspiration. "Don't ..." he hissed. "Don't touch me ..."

Miss Palmer stared at him with wide, pleased eyes. "Don't touch you ... like this?" She placed her cheek against his, and as she did, he heard the chair scrape on the floor, felt her leg brush his ear. "When you've told me, dear, I'll remove my face ..."

He could feel the brittle skin against his, smell the strong odor of rouge. "Safe deposit box," he gasped.

"Where's the key?" she said quickly.

"My apartment ..."

"Where ... ?"

"Under ..." he forced his brain to think. Under what? "Under the sink. Bathroom. Taped ..."

Miss Palmer stood, and turned, then returned to kneel by him. *Don't touch that chair*, Quintain commanded her with his eyes. "You know," Miss Palmer said, "we can check this out very quickly. A phone call. Fifteen, twenty minutes." She stood, and gathered his genitals in her hands. "If you're lying ... next time it won't be a comb, and I'll let you watch."

After he heard the door close, Quintain closed his eyes and tried to steady his mind. Only then did he allow himself to look at the chair. The edge of the chair seat was inches away, much closer than it had been.

He arched his back, flexed his knees, and his body swung back, then toward the chair. His forehead struck the edge of the seat, and the chair moved away. He had no time to judge how far before he was swinging back. At the top of the swing he twisted his body upward, felt pain shoot through his legs and back, and then he was swinging for the chair again. He pulled his body up by flexing his knees, and rolled his head as far forward as he could, his neck muscles stretched to their limit. From the top of his eyes he saw the edge of the chair swing under him and he dropped. His head hit the chair seat, slid forward as his body started the swing back, and held.

His head was now supported by the chair, his body angled between it and his ankles. By flexing his knees, pushing his head in a nodding motion, he managed to walk his head to the edge of the seat. He slumped forward, felt the edge of the chair seat take skin off his forehead and then his nose, and as he swung free of the chair, he made a lunge and got the seat in his teeth. He could taste the sweaty grain of the wood. He flexed his knees, and with a repeated jarring effort, managed to drag the chair forward. The scraping of the chair legs against the wooden floor seemed as loud as explosions to him. He let go of the seat, doubled his body up as it swung forward, and then let it extend. His head hit the middle of the seat. The chair was now directly under him, his head on the seat. He rested for a moment, listening. The radio was broadcasting a frenzied piano solo.

He found that when he extended his knees, he could roll forward on his neck, his chin pressed into his chest. From this angle, he could just see the block and tackle above him. He stretched his legs upward, and could see his dead feet come under the bottom wheel, support it, and then put slack in the ropes around it as he lifted it. But it wasn't enough to make the hook at the top move.

He relaxed his straining muscles for a moment, and this time kicked violently with his feet at the block and tackle and saw the hook shift. Again he rested, letting the ropes take his weight. If he could get the hook to fall free, he knew the hardest part would begin. In that split second of equilibrium when the hook was free but before he fell, he would have to throw his body toward the bed. If the block and tackle fell anywhere else the noise was bound to bring someone. He oriented himself to the bed, and then started kicking. On the third kick the hook fell free.

164

For a moment he thought the momentum of his kicks was going to take him over the back of the chair. He kicked out with his legs, and took the full weight of his body on his straining neck. He seemed to balance on the chair for a breathless moment, and then the force of his kick was transmitted to his tipping body, and he fell toward the bed. The block and tackle plummeted onto the center of the bed, followed by his feet and legs. The bedsprings squeaked. His head fell violently from the chair and his face struck the floor. His nose felt broken, and as he lay there, panting, trying to marshall his strength, blood welled from his nostrils.

Quintain turned over slowly, painfully, onto his shoulders, his legs on the bed. His arms were hurting fiercely now, the rope bond cutting into the flesh of his upper arms. He pulled his feet toward him. He could see the bottom wheel of the block and tackle inching toward the edge. He pivoted until his chest and stomach were beside the bed, creeping along on his elbows in a rocking motion. Then he closed his eyes, and let his feet fall from the bed. The block and tackle landed on his tensed stomach. The impact wasn't as bad as he feared. He rolled his body and let the block and tackle slide gently to the floor.

He sat, thinking. He had to get the rope off of his arms. He tried flexing his shoulders back. It relieved the pain of the rope, but didn't move it. He looked around the room for help. The door to a closet stood ajar. He inched across to it on his buttocks, using his legs to propel him, letting the block and tackle drag after. He shut the closet door slowly with his forehead, holding his breath as the latch clicked in place. He looked fearfully at the other door. It was made of thick slabs of pine, cross braced with one-by-fours. He quieted his breathing, and listened. He could hear nothing but the music. He hoped that meant that those on the other side of that door couldn't hear him, either.

By bracing his shoulders against the door, he managed to

165

force himself into a half-standing, half-crouching position. He slid down until he felt the door knob with his arms. He stooped, and hooked the rope under the door knob, and straightened his legs, straining against the resistance of the rope. Blood was coming back into his feet, and they were afire with needles of pain. He flexed his shoulders, ignored the pain, and put more force against the rope. He was sweating profusely now, and that helped him. The rope slipped a fraction of an inch down his wet arms. He flexed, and heaved, and the rope was over his elbows. He let it fall on the floor as he slumped against the door, panting.

He massaged his hands and arms to get some feeling back in them, and then he tackled the rope around his ankles. The knots were tough. Very professional. But, finally, his feet were free. As he massaged his feet and ankles, he tried to estimate how long it had been since Miss Palmer left the room. He found that his sense of time was so warped that he had no idea if it had been minutes or hours. Everything that had happened in that room since he had awakened there seemed to be thrown back into a long tunnel-like perspective of time. He looked at the window. Light slanted through it, throwing a weak orange stain across the wooden floor. It was either late afternoon or morning. He didn't know which. Nor did he know what day it was. The last day he remembered was Sunday, but it seemed a long time ago ... a long time since he had stood at the stove in his apartment holding Chris in his arms.

The thought of Chris stung him out of the hypnotic reverie he'd fallen into. He struggled to his feet. His feet and ankles still hurt, but they supported him well enough. His nose was clotted with dried blood, making him breathe through his mouth. It occurred to him that the door could open any time and Miss Palmer and Fronck could walk in, and he fought back the panic that threatened to choke him. He saw his clothes in a pile by the bed and limped to them and quickly

166

put them on. His crotch felt like a large, nerveless growth. He couldn't find his shoes, only one of his socks. He dropped the sock, and padded across to the closet and opened it. It was dusty with disuse. Three empty hangers on the cross-bar. A blanket on the shelf over the bar. No help there. He shut the door, thinking.

Miss Palmer had said next time he could watch. That meant no blindfold. His genitals were still dead, so that meant perhaps no more novocain, either. She had brought Fronck with her only when she needed help. He had to gamble that Fronck wouldn't be with her when she returned. What he thought of doing revulsed him for a moment as he picked up the actual instrument of his plan, the rope attached to the block and tackle, and began to pull it through the wheels. Then he thought of Miss Palmer's vicious red face, her calm, clinical manner while describing his mutilation, and hate goaded him on. He had never seen anyone dead in his life, but he realized, with a cold, calculating fury, that he would relish seeing Miss Palmer dead.

When he had the rope free from the block and tackle, he coiled it over his arm, bent one end into a loop and fastened it in a slip knot. He took great care in adjusting the loop's circumference, and in making sure the slip knot worked freely.

He moved the chair against the wall beside the door, and stood on it for a moment, got down, shifted the position of the chair a few inches, and stood on it again, finding it this time in a satisfactory position. The chair was placed so that it would be behind the door when it opened. He threw the un-looped end of the rope over the roof beam nearest the door, took that end in his hand along with the loop, and stood on the chair. He stared for a moment at the light streaming in the window, then got down, went to the closet, got the blanket, and draped it over the window, securing the ends through an old curtain rod across the top of the window.

Then he got on the chair, and waited.

The wait seemed interminable. Quintain breathed deeply, trying to steady his trembling hands. He thought of Chris, of their brief, happy time together. Thinking of her brought calm, and steeled him for the ordeal ahead. He felt he had something momentous to live for. When the door finally opened, an icy calm had descended on him, had focused his every instinct and thought into one powerful objective . . . to survive, to kill if that's what it took to survive . . .

Miss Palmer hesitated in the doorway, craning her head forward into the gloom. She had a small leather satchel in one hand. Over the top of the door Quintain looked down and saw the pink part in her white head. He dropped the loop over her head, and jerked it tight around her neck, pulling forward so that she stumbled into the room. He kicked the door shut, and grasping the other end of the rope near the ceiling, swung off the chair. Miss Palmer was dragged on the toes of her shoes under the beam. Her hands came up to her throat, and the satchel skidded across the floor. Quintain hung with his whole weight on the rope. Miss Palmer's body rose, her feet stretching to maintain contact with the floor, her eyes bulging hideously behind the glasses that magnified them. She opened her mouth, and began a choking, bubbling scream. Quintain screamed with her, his hoarse voice rising over hers. He had screamed before. If Fronck heard him now, Quintain hoped he would think it was more of the same. He continued to pull Miss Palmer toward the beam. She opened her mouth again, and he screamed again, but needlessly, because now she could make no noise but a low gurgling. Her fingers clawed at the rope that had bitten into her wattled neck, so deeply that Quintain could only see a thin strip of it.

He got her up until her toes could just reach the floor, and then his resolve failed. He couldn't bring himself to take her the next fatal few inches. She was immobilized and, with the exception of the gurgling sound, mute. He backed to the closet door, playing out the rope as he kept it taut, and took two half hitches around the door knob. Miss Palmer danced on her toes in a grotesque parody of a ballerina doing a fifth position point.

Quintain knelt and opened the satchel. The scalpel was there, along with hypodermics wrapped in cotton. He took the scalpel, went to the bed, picked up the wheel of the disassembled block and tackle with the hook attached to its top, and holding the wheel by the hook, stood beside the door and banged it with the wheel. Nothing. He banged again. Abruptly, the radio was switched off.

There was a ponderous knock on the door. Fronck's muffled voice came through it. "Miss Palmer. Miss Palmer . . ." Silence.

Quintain readied the scalpel, letting the wheel hang from his left hand. The door knob turned, and the door opened a few inches. "Miss Palmer?"

Fronck's hand came through the door first. There was a gun in it. Quintain drew the scalpel back and drove it through the back of Fronck's hand. Fronck grunted, the gun fell to the floor, and Fronck jerked his hand away before Quintain could withdraw the scalpel.

Then Fronck was in the room. His hand drew back level to the floor, the edge toward Quintain, the scalpel still sticking through it. Quintain brought the wheel around in a short arc and struck Fronck on the side of the face with it. Fronck's head rebounded against the door frame, and he dropped to his knees. Quintain swung the wheel over his head with both hands and brought it down on the back of Fronck's head. Fronck pitched forward, his chest striking the edge of the bed, and then slowly slid off the bed, his hand leaving a vivid crimson trail across the mattress.

Quintain ran to the gun and picked it up. He dropped the wheel, and examined the gun. He knew little about guns. He hadn't fired one since he was twelve, and his father had taken him to a shooting range in one of his disastrous attempts to make a "man" of him. The gun was a heavy revolver, with a barrel of awesome bore. Quintain found the safety in the trigger guard, determined that it was off, and turned toward the door. He stood at the edge and inched his eyes around it. A large room, lodge-like, great stone fireplace with a fire blazing in it, leather couch and chair ... Across the room was an archway into a kitchen. All was silent and empty of life.

He stepped around the wall, and found there was another door farther down. He went to it, pressed his ear against the panel, and heard nothing. He eased the door open, the gun in front of him at his waist. It was a bedroom, similar to the one he had just left. On the bed, her hands and arms bound in adhesive tape, and another wide strip across her mouth, was Chris. Her eyes rolled to his face, and tears sprang up in them. He went to her quickly, and tore the tape from her mouth and started working on freeing her hands. She lay on her side, sobbing with relief and fear.

When he had her free, she threw her arms around his neck and cried against his chest in deep, racking sobs. Her body trembled violently. He let her cry until the trembling abated, and then he held her by the shoulders and looked into her face.

"Chris. We've got to get out of here. I need your help. Can you do it?"

She bit her lower lip, and nodded. She touched his cheek with gentle fingers. "Your poor face."

Chapter 15

AS DIAMOND entered the office ahead of Atlas the faces in the room turned to him, but he saw only one . . . thin, lined, with the deep-set, dark eyes that stared at him coldly, devoid of even the warmth of the recognition.

Diamond sat at the table across from that cruel face, and said, "Hello, Felix."

"You betrayed our agreement," Felix replied.

"*I*? How did I do that?" Diamond appeared relaxed, almost nonchalant, but inside his nerves were tightly coiled.

"I was supposed to interrogate this Quintain. Not you."

"But, Felix," Diamond spread his hands in a gesture of reasonableness, "you weren't here. You had disappeared, again." He added the last for the benefit of the others, to remind them of Felix's recent penchant for going to cover.

"The Arabs tried to burn me in London. You know that."

Diamond smiled mirthlessly. "I'm beginning to wonder if we can afford the luxury of all your enemies, Felix."

Felix ignored the rejoinder. "I intend to get to the bottom of all this. I have the right . . ."

"The *right*?" Diamond allowed the edge of his anger to show as he leaned across the table. "There are other rights involved here, too . . ." There was a low murmur of assent at the table, and Diamond settled back, triumphant.

"I'm sure," Atlas said, "that we can satisfy everyone. We know what happened, Felix . . ."

Felix settled back in his chair, and stared at Diamond. "Tell me . . ."

"Is that an order, Felix?" Diamond stared back. If it was a showdown he wanted . . .

"Tell me . . . *please*," Felix said, his thin mouth curling into a cold smile.

"Go ahead," Atlas said wearily. "Tell him, Diamond."

"For God's sake," Regan exploded. "Yes. We've got better things to do than sit around listening to you two squabbling."

Diamond held up his hand. "All right. Here's the story, Felix. Quintain, along with Cutter, and with Stone's knowledge and approval, took the Investment Company for close to a million dollars. They were going to split it up, and then I guess go to cover somewhere. The auditors are coming next month so we had no choice but to replace the money out of The Council's funds and to destroy all traces of the embezzlement. As you well know, we can't have auditors launching a full-scale investigation. They could expose our whole operation."

"The government would get you off the hook," Felix replied. "They've done it before."

"Yes," Diamond said softly, "they have. But lately we've done quite a bit of business with their opposition. Would you want to take the chance that they would find that out—all that we've been doing?"

Diamond let the silence grow, not taking his eyes off Felix. He knew his advantage, and he intended to press it. Felix was a field man, perhaps the best there was, not an administrator, not accustomed to the intrigues and manipulations of organizational policy.

Finally, Felix waved a dismissing hand and said, "No. I see what you mean."

Diamond relaxed a little. He felt he had passed the crisis point. "We have taken care of Cutter and Stone," he added. "And we will get Quintain to tell us where the money is."

"I hear," Felix said, his eyes glinting, "that you botched the Stone and Cutter job."

"You hear wrong," Diamond said angrily. "We had a little trouble, but it's been resolved. Cutter was killed in a car accident, and Stone has taken her life over losing her husband."

"Why would Cutter set me up to be burned by the Arabs?" Felix asked.

"He thought that would put you out of the way." Diamond said. "You were the one he worried about."

"It's reasonable," Atlas said placatingly. "Cutter wasn't ... er ... fond ..."

"He hated your guts," Diamond said acidly.

"Yes," Atlas said. "They knew you, Felix. They knew how formidable ..."

"Don't patronize me," Felix said contemptuously. He stopped and reflected silently. The room grew quiet under the spell of waiting for Felix, waiting for him to reach a conclusion. Diamond could feel his control slipping away and he was powerless to stop it.

Finally Felix chuckled aridly. "You know, I ran a double agent once in Belgrade. He got so intricate, he doubled back on himself. He had to keep notes to remember what to say to whom." He paused and looked carefully around the room, as if searching for a familiar face. "Somehow this has the same smell. What you tell me has a cosmetic plausibility. But there is one problem ... if *I* were doing what you say they were doing, I wouldn't have done it that way."

"Nor I," Diamond inserted quickly. "But that doesn't mean they didn't."

Felix ignored him. "Miss Palmer is interrogating Quintain now?"

Atlas nodded.

"And her objective is what?"

"Find the money," Diamond replied.

Felix's eyes swung to Diamond's face and studied it. "That's all?"

"Yes."

"I want to interrogate him."

"Miss Palmer is the best we have," Diamond said, his eyes locked with Felix's.

"Granted. But I want to widen her objective, and be there when she asks the questions."

Atlas looked at his watch. "It may be too late. Miss Palmer does not waste time."

Felix didn't take his eyes from Diamond. "Call her. Tell her to wait until I get there."

"Is that another order, Felix?" Diamond asked in a soft, dangerous voice.

"A motion," Felix said.

"Seconded!" Regan bawled. "And let's be done with it."

There were noises of assent. Atlas didn't wait for a formal vote. He didn't even glance at Diamond for approval before he picked up the phone.

Quintain sat on the bed, holding Chris' hands, and told her what had happened, leaving out the details of his torture.

"Verna was telling the truth," Chris said. Her trembling had stopped. She still wore the pajamas that she'd had on when she was taken from Quintain's apartment.

"Do you remember anything?" he asked her.

She shook her head. "I was waiting for Verna to come out of the bathroom." She touched the back of her neck tenderly. "They must have hit me. I didn't see anyone."

Quintain pushed up the hair at the back of her neck. There was a small bruise at its base.

"And here ... did anyone ... ?"

"No," she said quickly. "I woke up the way you found me. The big man ... Fronck ... came in a couple of times ..."

"Did he ...?"

"No. He looked like he wanted to. But I got the feeling he'd been told to leave me alone. He just checked the tape."

174

Quintain told her what Miss Palmer had said about guards and dogs. He showed her the gun he had taken from Fronck. She took it in her small hands, and examined it.

"Thirty-eight magnum," she said.

He looked at her, surprised. "How did you know that?"

"Uncle Luke insisted that all the kids know how to handle guns."

"Have you ever used one like it?"

She nodded. "Similar. It's a cannon. Blows the whole center of a target out."

"Do you think you can use it now?"

She stared at him, comprehension dawning in her eyes. "All I've ever shot is a target."

"That's better than I've done. The only time I tried, I missed everything." They looked at each other. He didn't ask her the question, he didn't have to. She knew.

"The men outside?"

He nodded. "Well," she said with a little shuddering sigh, "Uncle Luke always said I was a better shot than my brothers."

They spent time, too much time, Quintain realized, trying to decide their next move. They had no idea where they were. The mountains, they thought, because of the trees, the cabin. The sun was definitely on its way down. Shadows were beginning to stretch across the floor. Soon it would be dark.

At any moment an armed man might walk in. They needed a plan. They both seemed innervated by their release, by the warmth of being together. He held her for a moment, the gun lying beside them on the bed, staring over her shoulder, trying to get his mind working.

Somewhere in the cabin a phone rang.

They stared at each other. The phone rang again, insistently.

"Shouldn't we . . . ?" Chris asked, her voice rising in alarm.

175

He stood, handed her the gun, and pulled her to her feet. He wasn't going to allow them to be separated.

The phone was mounted on the wall of the kitchen beside an old refrigerator. He lifted the receiver carefully, as if it were a bomb. He held it between their heads. They heard breathing. Then:

"Palmer. Fronck."

There was a scraping noise from the receiver. Then a voice from the background, tinny and small. "What's the matter ... ?"

"Don't know. Who is this?"

Then silence. The hum of the connection. A liquid click, and the dial tone. Quintain let the receiver dangle under the phone. He stared at the dial of the phone.

"The phone book!" he said.

They found it on top of the refrigerator. It said, "San Bernardino, Riverside," and under that, in smaller type, "Mountain Resorts."

They smiled at each other. They were still in California. Somehow they were comforted.

"We could call the police," Chris said.

He nodded absently. His imagination was racing ahead. The police would come. They would find Fronck and Miss Palmer. They would take him. What if Fronck was dead?

"I ... let's think about it," he said. Then he turned in a violent motion. Miss Palmer!

"Wait there," he said to Chris. He was already halfway across the main room. He threw open the door to the bedroom.

The shadows had climbed up Miss Palmer's skirt, over her white blouse, and now lapped at her neck. Her face and hair were bathed in orange light from the open door. She had put up a tough fight. One shoe had been kicked across the room in her struggle for life. She had finally lost.

Her head hung forward on her chest, the rope making an

176

obtuse angle of her neck. Her glasses had slipped forward on her nose, and her eyes stared over the tops of them, as if she had been startled by something, and had lowered her glasses for a better look.

Fronck still lay face down on the floor, and the back of his head was a spongy mass. Quintain closed the door gently, and walked slowly back to the kitchen.

"What is it ...?" Chris peered up into his face. "You look ..."

"Dead," Quintain managed to say. He felt like he was choking. "Both ... dead."

She put her arms around him and held him. He could feel the weight of the gun in Chris' hand at his back. He shuddered violently, and pulled away. He had made up his mind.

"We can't call the police. Not now. I've got to find out what's going on."

She looked at him for a long moment and then said, "All right," in a small, brave voice.

He went to a window in the main room that looked out on the front of the cabin. He pulled the drape back until it exposed an inch of the window and put his eye to the opening. Trees, their trunks blackened with shadow, stood twenty yards away. The upper branches were struck with the yellow rays of the dying sun. A graveled road cut through them and disappeared in the shadows. There was a smoky ambiance above the trees, caused by particles of dust turning in the sunlight. He could see no sign of life.

"Maybe she was lying about the men," he said. It was a faint hope. She had spoken too firmly, with too much of the reality of what she was saying conveyed in her tone. Soon, it would be dark. He let the drape fall back, and went to the rear of the room and repeated the ritual. A truck stood in a clearing just beyond the stoop of the kitchen door.

"Look."

177

He held the drape while Chris looked. He heard her catch her breath. "Do you think . . . ?"

"I don't know," he said quickly, before the reality of what he was going to do could descend on him and smother him with fear.

He took the gun from Chris, opened the kitchen door, and stepped out, hugging the wall of the cabin. He waited for an agonizing moment. He heard nothing. Only the sighing and popping of the trees. The shot he half expected to hurtle out of the shadows at him didn't come. He crouched, and ran to the door of the truck. It was locked. He looked in the cab. He could see that the lock on the other door was down. He ran back to the house.

"Locked," he said, trembling. Chris' face fell.

"Wait!" he said. He ran back to the bedroom, and avoiding looking at the bodies, went through the black valise. Nothing. Steeling himself, he went over to Fronck and went through his pockets. In his pants he found keys. They were on a metal bead chain, with a plastic tag that advertised a car rental agency.

He ran back to Chris, and showed her the keys.

"The truck?"

"I don't think so. There has to be another car around here."

Chris found the car. By looking at an oblique angle out of the window in the kitchen over the sink, they could just see the bumper protruding around the corner of an old shed.

Somewhere in the distance a dog barked, and they looked at each other.

"Let's go . . ." he said.

They went out the kitchen door, around the shed. The doors of the car were unlocked. It looked comfortingly new, gleaming in the dusk that had descended. Quintain opened the driver's door, had Chris slide through, and got behind the wheel. He put the key in the ignition. It went in smoothly. He turned to Chris.

178

"I'm going to leave the lights off. I don't know where that road leads, but I'm not going to waste any time. Hang on and stay down." He put the gun on the seat between them. She picked it up, and tried to smile at him. He turned the key. The engine caught, and seemed to fill the forest with its noise.

He pointed the nose of the car at the road, slammed the automatic transmission in gear, and floored the accelerator. The car fishtailed, and inched forward, throwing up a noisy white plume of gravel. Quintain finally realized what he was doing, and eased off on the accelerator. The car shot forward into the shadows of the trees. Somewhere a man shouted.

He found he could see the white contrast of the road against the dark shadows easily without the lights. The dangers were presented by the twisting curves, where, for unnerving moments, the road ahead was lost. He managed to negotiate them by slowing down more than he wished.

The car broke out of the trees. Ahead the road was straight, traversing a meadow, and ending at a gate. Beyond the gate they could see a highway. A figure was silhouetted by the gate, something leaping at its side. A flash lit up the figure like lightning, and they saw the man, his gun raised, the dog straining beside him.

Something hit the front of the car with a tearing sound and a thump. But it kept going. Quintain floored the accelerator. There was a roar in Quintain's ears. The whole windshield seemed to explode outward, hang in space for a moment, and then collapse inward, spraying their legs and laps with shards of glass. He saw, peripherally, the gun in Chris' hand pointed out the windshield.

She fired again. The man at the gate fell on his face, the dog now loose, and leaping toward the car, its fangs bared. The man had his arm extended, the gun in his hand, trying to sight the car. The dog ran straight at them, and for one frozen moment, Quintain thought it would leap straight

179

through the shattered windshield. At the last moment, it turned out of the way, and spun, snapping at the tires. Chris fired twice, the shots very close together, at the man on the ground. As they went past him, Quintain saw him cover his head with his hands.

Quintain tried to hit the gate in its precise center. It bulged forward for an instant, then gave, flattening under the onrushing car. Quintain spun the wheel, and the car skidded up the grade, and onto the highway. He fought the wheel, got the car straightened out, and pushed the accelerator to the floor again.

"The lights," Chris shouted above the wind.

He pulled on the lights just as they rounded a curve that put a low hillock of trees between them and the gate. The wind was making it hard for him to see. He looked at the speedometer. It was above eighty, creeping toward ninety. He eased back on the accelerator until he could see fairly well. He turned toward Chris and tried to smile.

She dropped the gun on the seat and put her hand on his shoulder. He couldn't tell which was trembling more, her hand, or his body beneath it.

Chapter 16

THE NIGHT was nearly gone when Diamond left the building. There was a lowering of the sky on the western horizon, a premonition of violent weather unusual for Southern California. Hurricane Martha had slammed itself against Baja opposite Gauymas two days before, mauled the coast like an angry terrier with a rag in its teeth, and then had spun off into the Pacific, spent from its efforts, and unwound itself northward, scudding along a mile off the coast as it passed San Diego, marshalling its strength. Now the storm hovered off Santa Monica, eyeing the Los Angeles basin as if making up its mind if it presented a worthy opponent.

The still, threatening tension in the air suited Diamond's mood. He struck off down Wilshire on foot, his tie loosened, collar open, and coattail flapping behind him, as if challenging the brooding storm to come out and fight. He was in a combative mood.

But frustrated. He couldn't fight shadows. That was what The Council had conjured themselves into with their convoluted deliberations: shadows. When the guard at the cabin had called, only fifteen minutes after Diamond's disturbing attempt to reach Miss Palmer, The Council had nearly fallen apart with panic. He and Felix had formed a strange alliance to get them settled down.

"My God," Regan had bellowed. "How the hell could *he ...* ?"

"Are they *sure*?" someone else had shouted. "Both Miss Palmer *and* Fronck?"

Regan jumped to his feet, pointing his big finger at Diamond. "*Do* something. Get after him."

Now that Diamond remembered, he was amused in an acid sort of way that Atlas had been struck into babbling incoherency by the news. At the time he had not been amused at all.

Diamond and Felix had been the only ones to remain calm. Finally they became the eye of the storm, the others brooding and muttering around them, waiting to be told what to do.

"*You* are responsible," Regan accused Diamond.

"Certainly not," Diamond retorted. "It wasn't my idea to leave them up there with Miss Palmer."

"I spoke against calling you back," Regan muttered, absolving himself.

"You *voted* for it," Atlas said, finding his voice. "It was unanimous."

Regan subsided into brooding silence. Felix had not spoken. He remained as he had been when Diamond gave them the news—erect, his face a mask of stone. Now he said, "Do you want to solve this problem, or do you want to go on babbling like schoolchildren?"

"Felix is right," Diamond said. "We've got work to do."

"I propose ..." Felix said quietly, and then waited until there was absolute silence in the room. "I propose to take over the operation."

There was general and relieved agreement. How soon The Council caved in, Diamond couldn't help but think. Anything to get the disaster off their backs.

"Under our instructions," Diamond said flatly.

"Of course," Felix agreed, giving Diamond a sardonic smile and a nod of his head.

"He's got to be killed!" Diamond announced. "We can't take any more chances."

"I don't understand," Atlas lamented. "Quintain is an *amateur*, is he not?"

"What do we know about him?" Felix asked.

Diamond went to his desk, unlocked a drawer, removed a Manila file, and returned with it to the table. He opened the file.

"Came to us three years ago. Divorced. A loner around the company. History of psychological problems . . ."

"What kind of problems?" Felix leaned forward, his eyes sharp with interest.

Diamond consulted the file. "Paranoia, borderline schizophrenia . . ."

"My God!" Regan interjected. "Is this company hiring nuts now?"

"They have no choice," Diamond replied drily "It's illegal to discriminate against someone simply because he's been to a psychiatrist. Quintain's record indicated a satisfactory discharge from therapy. He had a good work history . . ."

"What position?" Felix asked.

"Systems Analyst. Then special assistant to Cutter the last few weeks."

"Ah," Felix said.

"Funny duck," Atlas mused. "Did you ever see him around the hallways? Always looking this way and that, furtive, like an animal."

"I guess he had something to be furtive about," Regan grumbled. "A million dollars of the company's money."

"How does someone like *that* . . . ?" Atlas asked. "I mean, *both* Palmer and Fronck."

Felix pressed his fingers together and touched his lips with them. "Yes. How? They are the worst kind, these near psychotics." He looked up at Diamond. "Do you remember that one in Paris, what . . . five years ago?"

Diamond nodded. "Larsen. The Swede, they called him." Larsen had been one of The Council's first operational jobs

183

from the CIA. A big man, wealthy enough to have his history of psychotic breaks too deeply hidden to prevent his being appointed to the Swedish NATO mission.

"He had some twisted idea about his politics . . . shoveling NATO secrets to the KGB as fast as he could . . ." Diamond reminisced.

"Very influential family," Felix added. "The CIA couldn't touch him, for fear of getting the Swedes mad. Couldn't get him recalled, because the Swedes insisted on hard evidence."

"I remember," Atlas said. "Our first big job. Larsen went berserk."

"Had an automatic weapon of some kind in his apartment," Diamond added.

"A Shephard-Turpin," Felix said. "He'd carried it for years. Shot up his apartment, and two of our men. I had to go in after him myself."

Diamond stared at Felix. He was the only man he knew who would call a Sten gun a Shephard-Turpin, after the men who had designed it.

"The point being," Felix went on, "that Larsen had the gun long before he got mixed up in espionage. These people, certain of them, are prepared for violence, because they imagine they are threatened even when they aren't. If Quintain is one of them, then the thought of violence is not new to him. It is an old companion. And the worst of it is, they are unpredictable. I'd rather go against a professional any day."

Atlas, who was not a professional, and who had been in his former life a Certified Public Accountant, shuddered noticeably. "Yes, well, what do we do?"

"Find him. Kill him," Diamond said. "On sight."

"What about the money?" Atlas asked.

"We'll have to eat the loss," Diamond replied. "The whole operation is threatened as long as Quintain is alive. We can't afford an investigation."

184

"Felix," Regan asked, "do you agree?"

"Perhaps," Felix said. "Let me propose my charter on this matter."

In the end, the best Diamond could do was a weak compromise. Felix was to use his discretion. He wanted to interrogate Quintain for his own reasons, and The Council still entertained hopes of finding out where its money was. Felix was to interrogate if it was absolutely safe.

Diamond stopped walking to light a cigarette. He stared unseeingly at the flame before he blew the match out and flung it to the ground. Cars whispered past in the street like animals making for shelter against the impending storm.

Quintain had hardly looked human when they had arrived at the motel. The proprietor's face had immediately told him that. They had parked the car out of sight of the motel office, to avoid explanations about the smashed windshield and Chris' strange costume. The rain was already pouring through the open windshield when he had left her huddled in the front seat to dash into the office to register.

The man behind the desk looked up from his *L.A. Times*. His eyes took in Quintain's bare feet, and then, rising to his face, widened with alarm. In their exhaustion and relief, neither he nor Chris had thought of the effect his bloody face might have.

Quintain had improvised a story about getting rained out on a camping trip. It had been weak, but the proprietor, after a moment of staring suspiciously at Quintain's credit card and his driver's licence photo, had silently pushed the registration pad over to him.

Quintain lay on the bed in the motel room, staring at the ceiling that was echoing with the drum of the rain. He was too tired to move, and yet his mind was alert and strangely exhilarated.

Chris came from the bathroom carrying a towel and damp washcloth. She knelt on the bed beside him and gently bathed his face, and patted it dry. She got down from the bed, and went back in the bathroom.

Quintain groped toward the nightstand by the bed without turning his head, felt the cool, oily metal of the gun lightly with his fingertips, and let his hand drop wearily. He wondered at his need to touch the gun. Reassurance? That seemed reasonable enough, but he knew it was rationalization. He had touched it out of a sense of power, a confirmation of his potency.

He thought of the two people he had killed. The remorse had come swiftly at the cabin when he had found them dead. It had vanished swiftly, too. Now, thinking about it gave him an unaccustomed feeling of warmth, of security—similar to the emotion an open fire on a cold night evoked.

Chris stood in the doorway of the bathroom facing him. The only light in the room came from the bathroom, spilling through the dark hair on her shoulders, silhouetting her body through his pajamas that she still wore.

"You look almost human again," she said in a shy voice. "I'm going to take a hot shower."

"Sounds good. I'll take one after you."

While he listened to the whine of the pipes in the shower mingled with the drumming of the rain, he recalled the events of the past hours as he might recall a story he had read. It hardly seemed possible that he had been a participant in those events.

After they had broken through the gate and gotten safely onto the highway, they had driven under the spell of traveling away from a place at which they didn't remember arriving. They didn't know precisely where they were until they had come to the village of Arrowhead. Then Chris, who had been there, directed them down the mountain, and into San Bernardino. They had driven on until they had come

186

to Colton, and Quintain had looked at her and she had nodded. The motel was the first one they had come to after they left the freeway, a squalid little gathering of green board-and-batten cottages grouped in a U around a graveled parking area.

He heard the squeal of the shower being turned off, and he switched on the bedside lamp. The room contained a weathered overstuffed chair slumped against one wall, a scarred chest-of-drawers, a chromo painting of Jesus praying at Gethsemane above it, a luggage stand made of webbing and chrome, and a shrunken, ugly area rug. In the window above the bed was a new air conditioning unit, its brushed chrome face, and multi-colored switches looking out of place in the general ambiance of hopeless poverty the room offered.

Chris opened the bathroom door, letting a billow of steam escape at its top. Quintain got off the bed and went to her. He held her shoulders but she turned her head away.

"Look," he said, "I'll sleep in the chair. The guy was suspicious enough, without my asking for two rooms."

She nodded dumbly, still not looking at him, and he went into the bathroom to take his shower. He let the hot spray play over his body, letting it soak out his tension. His crotch still felt like it belonged to someone else.

When he returned to the bedroom, feeling relaxed from the shower, and dressed only in his pants, she was propped up against the headboard of the bed, her arms crossed over her chest, looking intensely thoughtful.

She looked up at him. "You still don't want to call the police?"

"Not now. Let's see how we feel tomorrow."

"One thing," she said.

He was taking a spare blanket from a drawer in the chest. He turned and looked at her.

"Whatever you do about the police, I want to call Uncle Luke."

187

He hesitated. The old paranoid creeped out of hiding and whispered ugly things to him.

"We still don't know who they are," he said cautiously.

Her small jaw tensed. "Uncle Luke is about the most honest, kindest man ..."

He smiled. "Okay. I can't think of a man who comes better recommended."

She continued to glare at him for a moment, and then her face relaxed into a smile. "Truth," she said.

"Defeats paranoia," he responded. And they laughed.

He threw the blanket on the chair, and went to the bed to get a pillow. He stood hugging the pillow and looking down at her.

"It's strange," he said.

She gave him a look of such pure suspicion, that he laughed. "Don't worry, I'm not building up to anything."

She relaxed a little. "What's strange?"

"Well ..." he hesitated. "Maybe I shouldn't bring it up. It's about the two ... those two ..."

"Fronck and Miss Palmer?" She looked at him with fear in her eyes.

"Forget it." He turned toward the chair.

"No! Talk about it!"

He thought it over for a moment, and then said, "Okay. I ... when I found out they were dead, I thought I would never get over it. Never get over feeling sick, and, well ... despising myself for it."

"And?"

He sighed, and hugged the pillow closer. "I'm over it."

She sat up, and folded her legs under her Indian fashion. She patted the bed. "Come here."

After he sat in front of her, she said, "What do you mean ... over it?"

He couldn't look at her. "I feel a kind of ... oh, pride, I guess."

"About kill . . . about their dying?"

He shook his head wearily. "No. I'll never feel proud of that. More about having survived . . . about us getting out of there."

She hugged her stomach and bent forward, her hair falling across her cheek. Finally she said in a small voice, "I know. When I shot at that man . . . I tried to miss, to scare him off. But . . . I was prepared to . . . to . . ." She sighed and brushed her hair back. "What they'd done to us, it gave me a kind of awful self-righteousness. A power . . ."

"That's it!" He was excited now, excited to discover that she had felt what he had. "Power! I knew that whatever I did was justified by what they'd done to us. Whatever!"

She raised her head slowly and looked into his eyes. A recognition, a realization of something that bound them together and at the same time frightened them, passed between them. He put his hand on her knee, and she covered it with her own. She reached up with her other hand and touched his nose lightly, like a curious child.

"Does it hurt?"

He shook his head.

"It's broken."

He nodded, and lowered his eyes. "I didn't tell you the reason I don't want to go to the police. I mean, all the reasons . . ."

She waited silently, her hand on his.

"Its true I'm afraid of what they'd do to me . . . two people killed, and these people . . . whoever they are, they're powerful." He laughed weakly. "The old paranoia. I can see myself in prison for the rest of my life . . ."

"What's the other reason?"

"I want to settle it myself. I guess I got to thinking I could do it."

She nodded. "You've got to go to the police," she said softly. "You know that."

189

"Yes." He sighed wearily.

"Uncle Luke will help us. I won't let them put you in prison." She gripped his hand tightly.

"I'll do it in the morning." He smiled suddenly. "After I get some shoes."

She laughed softly. "And I some clothes. We can't walk into a police station in pajamas and barefoot . . ."

"Our dignity!" he said with mock outrage.

She laughed again, put her hand on the back of his neck, and drew his head down to her shoulder. He could feel her breath warm on his cheek.

"Love me," she said.

He lay her gently on the bed. He lay beside her and took her face in his hands.

"Chris," he said, "I love you." He suddenly realized that the novocain had worn off, and that that area of his body was now very much alive. They made love in a driven, desperate way, as if by their act of joining they might transport themselves to a place apart—a place where only they and the present existed.

The elements continued to drive the rain relentlessly down over them, as if they had seen too many of man's puny attempts to make himself God to be much impressed with one more.

Chapter 17

THE SAN BERNARDINO County Sheriff's substation in Colton was a low dirty-grey building next to a fire station. A green and white cruiser was parked at the side. The storm had blown itself out, and the sky was streaked with stratocumulus clouds. The streets were wet, and there was an aftermath of heavy chill in the air.

Shortly after eleven, Quintain parked in front of the substation. He was wearing the same pants and shirt he had the day before. The shirt was torn at the buttons and stained with his own blood. His nose was swollen, the flesh around his eyes livid. He wore a new pair of low-cut suede shoes. Chris was dressed in jeans and a white long-sleeved blouse. They had bought the shoes and clothes in a department store in Colton that morning.

A young deputy sat behind a counter at a battered radio set in the anteroom of the substation, chewing on an unlit large cigar and sipping coffee from a styrofoam cup. Behind him Chris and Quintain could see a burly man in deputy's uniform bent over a desk in a glass-walled office. From a speaker on the radio came the occasional squawk of a radio transmitter.

After Quintain had answered his greeting by saying he wanted to report a crime, the deputy swiveled his chair to the low counter, and pulled a form toward him and poised his ballpoint over it.

The deputy only completed the first line of the form, one that demanded the name of the citizen making the report, when he stood suddenly and walked briskly into the office.

Quintain and Chris could see the young deputy bending over the desk talking rapidly to the burly man. Then the burly man was out of the office, walking toward them. Quintain noticed uneasily that he had a hand casually on the butt of his gun as he approached, and he hoped that it was just an unconscious habit. In the office the young deputy was speaking into a telephone.

"Alexander Quintain?"

Quintain nodded, and the man's eyes went to Chris briefly. "Miss Bell? Christine Bell?"

Quintain found himself looking down the barrel of the deputy's service revolver.

"Hands on top of your heads. Turn slowly . . ."

He frisked them expertly and rapidly. "Where is it?" he asked.

"Out in the car," Quintain replied. Chris was sidling a scared look at him. "In the glove box."

The big man kept them facing the wall with their hands on their heads while he sent the young deputy outside. In a moment the deputy reappeared with the thirty-eight, carrying it by the ballpoint pen that he had thrust into the barrel. He went to the counter, pulled a plastic bag from under it, and dropped the gun in.

"Now," the burly man said, "you two just stay put. Someone will be here in a few minutes and tell you all about it."

Five agonizing minutes passed before the door was thrust open, and Quintain, over his shoulder, saw a squat, compact man in a deputy's uniform with captain's bars on the collar enter.

There was a brief low exchange between the captain and the burly man, and then the captain said, "I'll take Perk. We'll send someone over to man the radio."

The burly man mumbled his assent, and the young deputy and the captain herded Quintain and Chris outside and into the back seat of a cruiser.

Soon, they were on the freeway, the cruiser speeding toward the mountains, its red light flashing, the Captain using the siren sparingly to clear the road ahead, the young deputy sitting cocked in the seat, his eyes on them. There was a wire mesh screen between the front and back seats, and the back doors had no inside handles.

Quintain cleared his throat, and said, "Aren't you supposed to give us our rights . . . ?"

"You just keep quiet," the captain replied without looking away from the road. "And nobody's rights will be any the worse."

Quintain did as he was told.

As they climbed the mountains above San Bernardino, Chris held tightly onto Quintain's hand. There was no doubt about where they were being taken.

The gate had been removed from the road and was lying in a ditch of weeds. A sheriff's deputy, standing where the gate had been, waved the captain through and he eased the car along the twisting gravel road, and brought it to a stop in front of the cabin's porch. Two green and white sheriff's cruisers were parked at the side of the porch. A pale blue Plymouth with a whip antenna on the roof stood behind the cruisers.

The captain drew his gun as he opened the back door and waved them out. In the living room of the cabin a deputy was on his hands and knees sifting the ashes in the fireplace with what looked to Quintain like an ordinary kitchen strainer. Across the room a man in civilian clothes was delicately sweeping the door knob of the room where Chris had been a prisoner with a long bristled brush. A deputy squatted in the center of the room packing camera equipment into a leather case. He looked up, nodded at the captain, and inclined his head toward the bedroom where Quintain had been held. The door stood half open.

"You through?" the captain asked the camera man.

193

"Yessir."

The captain motioned Chris and Quintain through the bedroom door.

The bedding had been stripped from the bed, and lay in a pile on the floor beside two still forms covered with canvas sheets. The block and tackle and ropes were laid out neatly along one wall. A deputy knelt on the floor, carefully rolling objects in a plastic sheet. Quintain saw that one of them was the scalpel. A man in civilian clothes squatted beside him, his back to Quintain. The deputy looked up as they entered.

"Cap'n," he said.

The man in civilian clothes slowly turned his head, looked up into Quintain's face, and grinned.

It was Burger.

Quintain became aware that the captain and Burger were talking, but it took his reeling mind a moment to register their words. The captain stood stiffly, almost in an attitude of attention, and Quintain could tell that he was barely controlling his anger.

"I do what I'm ordered," the captain said. "You sign the receipts . . ."

"Of course, Captain," Burger said sweetly. He was standing now, smiling into the captain's rigid face, his short round body and cherubic bespectacled face in distinct contrast to the captain's rugged, military exterior. Yet it was apparent that Burger held the authority.

"I've also been ordered," the captain went on, as if reading his words from a manual, "to assist in transport."

"Won't be necessary," Burger replied, taking some forms from the young deputy and scrawling his name on them.

"It's my duty to inform you," the captain said, as if he wished it weren't, "that they were armed."

Burger looked up with benign interest in his eyes as he handed back the forms to the captain. "What with?"

"H and R thirty-eight magnum."

Burger whistled. "Jesus. Heavy stuff." He looked appraisingly at Quintain, and gave him a wink that the captain couldn't see.

"We've impounded the gun and the car," the captain said.

"I'll take care of it," Burger replied mildly.

The captain flushed. "You do that. You just do that." He turned on his heel and left the room.

Burger put an arm around each of them, and led Chris and Quintain from the cabin. On the way through the living room, Quintain started to ask a question, but Burger squeezed his shoulder and gave him a warning look.

Burger led them to the Plymouth with the whip antenna, put them in the front seat, and went around and got in the driver's side.

He smiled at Quintain and Chris. "Let's save the talk until we're out on the highway." The deputy waved them through the gate, and Burger pulled out onto the highway, and headed the car down the mountain. He pulled out a pack of cigarettes, gave one to Chris, and took one himself.

"Give me one of those," Quintain said, "and tell me what this is all about."

"I didn't think you smoked, Slick," Burger said, holding out the pack.

"About time I started," Quintain replied. His hand trembled as he took the cigarette.

Burger glanced at Quintain. "Your face looks like one of the more unbelievable Hallowe'en masks."

"Listen!" Quintain shouted.

Burger laughed, and held up his hand. "Okay, okay. I'll talk." He became serious, his little eyes squinting at them from behind his glasses. "We went by your apartment last night, and found you gone and the place torn up. You must've put up quite a battle. Who was it, Fronck?"

Quintain nodded. "We?"

Burger gave him an admiring glance. "Jesus," he said, "Fronck!"

"*We*?" Quintain persisted.

Burger sighed. "I work for the government, Quint."

"The government? Who?"

Burger slipped a plastic card from his coat pocket and held it out for Quintain and Chris to see.

"I report to a man in the Department of Agriculture. The Office of Soil Conservation."

Quintain stared at the card. "But this says CIA."

"Never mind what it says," Burger said earnestly. "More than that, you don't want to know, believe me."

Quintain thought that over. He sucked a stinging lungful of smoke from the cigarette, and then nodded. "Okay."

"Where are you taking us?" Chris asked.

"A place we have," Burger said. "You can't go back to your own places for a while. I'm sorry this happened, but we didn't know you were involved, Slick, until yesterday. By the time we got there it was too late. We found Chris' clothes and purse, and knew they'd taken her, too."

"You were looking for us?" Chris asked.

Burger nodded. "We knew they had a place somewhere. We alerted the highway patrol, sent out a bulletin to surrounding counties. When the sheriff found the bodies up at the cabin, he at first didn't connect it. Then they got a positive identification of Palmer and Fronck, and called us."

"Palmer and Fronck," Quintain asked. "You knew ... ?"

Burger nodded. "We've known about them, and a couple of others, for quite a while. The Sandersons ..."

"Verna ..." Chris gasped.

Burger gave her a sad look. "I'm afraid she wasn't as lucky as you two."

Chris gave a little moan. "How?"

"Overdose of sleeping pills. From her own prescription."

"She didn't kill herself," Quintain said heatedly.

196

"Of course not," Burger replied. "But right now that's what the police think, and we're going to let them think it for the time being."

"You can't let them get away with that," Chris said.

"We won't. But we need to lull them a little. If they start scattering, it would make our job a lot tougher."

"Just what is your job?" Quintain asked, and when Burger gave him a warning look, added, "I don't mean you personally. But what are you . . . what is the government after?"

Burger stared at him a moment, and then shook his head. "You have got some nose, there. Fronck?"

"I did it myself. Getting out of Miss Palmer's little swing."

"I saw the gear. Naked? By the ankles?" Quintain could feel Chris' eyes on him.

"Yes."

"Her favorite, Jesus, Slick. You're either an awful lucky fellow, or tougher than hell." Burger looked at him speculatively.

"You didn't tell me," Chris said.

Quintain took her hand. "And you didn't tell us," he said to Burger.

"Okay," Burger replied. "You can tell me what you know, and I'll fill in the blanks that I can. I can't tell you everything right now, for your sake."

"Our sake?"

Burger nodded solemnly. "Miss Palmer isn't the only one of that bunch who has rather peculiar ways of posing questions. Listen, Quint. We are playing with some very scary people."

Quintain touched his face. "You don't have to convince me."

"Let's get you set up in your new place, and then talk it out over a drink. Okay?"

Burger took them to a hotel at L.A. Airport. He led them through the corridors of the airport, and to an elevator that connected directly with the hotel lobby. As they walked across the lobby to another bank of elevators, Burger, in response to Quintain's questioning look, said, "Next to a jail, the area around an airport is one of the securest places in any city. It's loaded with security police, MPs, customs agents. It sure as hell isn't worth the price, but a few nuts with guns and bombs have turned our airports into armed fortresses. Added to all that, we'll have our own fellows around to make sure you're looked after."

Quintain looked around the lobby. "Kind of a luxury jail. I'm not sure I'm going to like it much better than the real thing."

"You won't be here for ever. We still have some channels into The Council." Burger grinned impishly. "We'll see if we can't stir Diamond up a bit."

"Burger," Quintain said wearily, "I hope to hell you have a good explanation for how stirring up that maniac is going to get us out of here."

Burger led them to a suite on the top floor of the hotel. It was made up of a small sitting room, and a bedroom to either side connected to the sitting room through doors.

Burger went to a phone and ordered drinks.

"I want to call Uncle Luke," Chris said.

"He already knows," Burger said. He looked at his watch. "Right now he's on his way to Dulles Airport in Washington. Should be back late this afternoon."

"I want to see him," Chris said.

Burger nodded. "Sure. Just as soon as we have a chance to brief him, I'm sure he'll be up to see you."

At a knock on the door, Burger opened it, and let in a tall, cadaverous looking bell hop, who wheeled in a tray of bottles, glasses and a silver ice bucket. "Thought I might as well set you up for a while," Burger said, as he signed the check.

The waiter left, and Quintain stared after him. "Don't worry, Slick," Burger said quietly as he mixed drinks. "He's one of ours. While you're here, anything you want, just pick up the phone. One of our men will bring it up."

He handed them their drinks, and sat down on a small couch. "Don't stick your noses outside this suite. When our boys deliver food or drinks for you, treat them like the help. We want everything to look perfectly normal. You're Mr. and Mrs. James Seymour from Seattle, on your honeymoon, stopping over here to catch the polar flight to Paris in two days. It's all on this card." He handed Quintain a three-by-five card. "Memorize that before I leave. I don't want to leave it around."

Quintain looked at the card. The writing was in Burger's neat, small hand. It gave the number of the Air France flight, the time of departure, their false names, occupation . . . Quintain looked up.

"Stock Broker?"

Burger smiled. "We couldn't make you a Systems Analyst. Too close to home."

"But I don't know anything about stocks."

"Don't worry about it. You won't have to, if you stick to this room like the wallpaper. It's mostly for the registration at the desk."

Chris sat down heavily in a chair, her hand on her forehead. "I just realized," she said, "that I'm starving."

"Good sign," Burger said. He went to a desk, took a menu out of a drawer, and handed it to her. "You two look that over, while I attend to some administrative details."

He went to the door. "Remember—stick inside this room. Lock the door after me, and don't let anyone in but room service or me." He turned with a smile, "I recommend the Beef Wellington. This is your chance to get some of your income tax back." And he left.

"Mmmm," Chris said. "The Beef Wellington does sound good . . ."

"He did it again," Quintain exclaimed. "He got out of here without answering any questions."

"Dear," Chris said, smiling at him over the menu, "the Soil Conservation Office is probably a very secretive bunch. Now look at this menu so I can order our food."

Burger returned as they were finishing the last of the bottle of wine. On the table were the remains of their dinners, and scant remains they were. Burger threw himself in a chair and lit a cigar. "Everything's set," he reported. "You two are as safe here as in your mother's arms."

"How long?" Quintain asked.

Burger shrugged. "We're getting close. A few days." He leaned forward to knock the ash off his cigar into an ashtray. "Let's talk. How much do you know?"

Quintain told him what Verna had told them, and about his trip to the office to look at the investment program.

"You were taking chances, Slick—going down there alone."

"Now you tell me."

Burger made an apologetic gesture. "Like I say, we just found out what they were up to with you."

"And what is that? I mean, I know Sanderson tried to frame me. But how did they pick me out?"

"They didn't. I did."

Quintain stared at him. "You ... ?"

Burger nodded. "You remember—I tried to get the job myself. When I couldn't, I got it for you."

"Jesus. Thanks a lot. Why?"

"It was a perfect opportunity to find out what Sanderson was up to. You and I are friends. I knew you'd keep me posted."

"Wait a minute." Quintain stood and paced the floor. "It doesn't make sense. If you didn't know about the embezzlement until just the other day, what did you need me up there for?"

"We had reason to believe that The Council was doing some work for people who aren't exactly our friends."

"Treason? Then what Verna told us was true?"

Burger shook his head. "Can't tell you more than that, Quint. Sorry."

Quintain accepted that reluctantly. "Okay," he said, continuing his pacing. "The Sandersons and this Diamond set me up. They got the money, and I got the blame. How come the Sandersons got killed? Did The Council find out?"

"Something like that," Burger replied. "We think Diamond double-crossed them, and kept the money for himself."

"Verna said they eliminated people," Chris said, "that a man named Felix had killed someone that worked for a British organization."

"Prince," Quintain added. "His name was Prince, and she said he worked for something called The Group."

Burger stared at him. "You didn't tell me that before, Quint."

"I forgot it. I guess I was more interested in the part that involved me."

Burger stared thoughtfully at the end of his cigar for a moment, and then seemed to make up his mind about something. "Okay. The harm's done. I may as well tell you the rest. Felix is a professional from the old school. He is from one of the Balkan countries, and was involved with the resistance in Poland at the end of World War Two. After the war he worked for various governments as a kind of mercenary agent. Because of his years of experience, and because of the high attrition in his profession, he is now the best in the world at what he does."

"Which is?"

"Wet operations. Jobs where blood gets spilled."

"And Prince?"

"Another of the old school. Felix had reason to believe that

201

Prince had set him up for elimination. He called him out . . ."

"Called? You mean like a duel?"

Burger smiled wryly. "These old timers have developed a code—an anachronism. When they have a personal feud, they settle it in a man-to-man confrontation that has as many rules and rituals as an old-fashioned duel."

"And Felix won?"

Burger nodded. "Felix always wins."

"How many . . . ?"

Burger shrugged. "Can't say for sure. I imagine Felix has called out, or been called out, several times over the years. You see, Slick, these old timers are living on the fringes of a dying age. They are quickly being replaced with automation. If you want secret intelligence, it's a lot easier now to tap into the other guy's computer, or set up an electronic listening post, or make an overflight with a high altitude plane or a satellite. The days of meeting scummy little men at the back tables of squalid Parisian restaurants are fading fast.

"Anyway, Felix and his kind, the ones that considered themselves the real pros, developed a kind of defense against all the menial, squalid things they had to do. They evolved this code of honor. It's complicated. But if you step over the boundary you can get challenged. It keeps them thinking that they're special." Burger sighed and stubbed out his cigar in the ashtray. "When the truth is, they're all felons, forgers, murderers."

Chris shivered and hugged herself. Quintain sat by her and put his arm around her. "Okay," he said to Burger, "they want me because they think I know where their money is. But why Chris?"

"Because she knows what you know. She was at your apartment with Verna. Verna was on the run. The Council has to assume she told you two more than it's safe for them to have you know."

202

Quintain tightened his embrace of Chris. "Why don't we get her out of here—out of the state—Washington ..."

"No. You're safer here. They'll be watching for exactly that. For you two to run. Here, we can control events. They'd have to have an army to get in here."

Quintain saw the logic of that immediately. Burger rose.

"I've got to be on my way back to work," he said. "I can't get them suspicious of me."

"I hope this goes fast," Quintain said. "I don't think I'd like to go through any more quizzes."

Burger paused. "It would depend on who got you first, Slick. There are those who wouldn't waste time with questions."

Quintain frowned. "What?"

"Think about it," Burger suggested.

Comprehension dawned on Quintain's face. "Diamond wouldn't want to question me. He knows I don't have the money."

"And he doesn't want anyone else to question you, either," Burger added. "Quite a choice, eh? Diamond or Felix."

"*Felix!*"

"Sure. You can bet he's been assigned your case personally." Burger opened the door and stepped out. Then he stuck his head back into the room, and grinned. "Don't worry. Your government is looking after you. Lock the door."

Quintain got up, went to the door, and locked it.

Chapter 18

THE AFTERNOON stretched on interminably for Quintain. Chris retired to a bedroom and fell instantly into exhausted sleep. Quintain paced the sitting room, tried to watch TV, but couldn't concentrate, and finally called room service and ordered a pot of coffee, newspapers and magazines sent up.

Instead of the cadaverous bellhop, a young, muscular man with surfer-blond hair brought the order. Quintain hesitated over the bill, wondering whether to add a tip, and then, remembering Burger's instruction to treat his men as ordinary hotel help, calculated and added fifteen percent. As he handed the ticket to the young man, Quintain gave him a significant look. The bellboy held his eyes for a moment, and then looked away and hurriedly left the room. He seemed almost embarrassed.

Quintain read the papers while he drank his coffee. He searched the first section of the *Times*, and most of the second section before he found the article. It was buried near the back of the section, one column, next to a Bullock's ad.

Local Woman Dead In Hotel. Verna Sanderson, 34 of 1986 Ocean Point, Malibu, was discovered unconscious in her room at the Freeman Hotel, 2338 Sepulveda early this morning. Responding to a call from the night clerk at the hotel, the Fire Dept. emergency rescue unit took her to L.A. County Hospital, where she was pronounced dead on arrival.

Mrs. Sanderson's husband, Kenneth Sanderson

III, was killed in a spectacular car accident at Malibu Saturday night.

The Coroner's office is investigating the cause of her death.

Quintain set the paper aside to show Chris when she woke up, and went to a window and looked out. Century Boulevard was beginning to jam up with late afternoon traffic. Directly below the window the building fell away to a concrete apron fifteen stories below. In the eastern sky, a jet was letting down for approach to the airport, its engines weaving dirty streaks of kerosene smoke against the storm-washed sky.

Quintain turned from the window at the sound of the telephone. It was Burger.

"How's it going, Slick?"

"Fine. I don't know how long I can stand all the merriment. Your surfer was up a while ago and actually said three words to me."

"Surfer?"

"Yeah . . . blond, tall kid with muscles."

"Oh, yeah, Brown. Listen, Quint, I'm at the office. I'm going to be checking out in another hour, and then the fun begins. I'll keep you posted."

"Have you heard from General Frawley?"

There was a pause on the line. "About that, Quint. He came into L.A. International about an hour ago. The Council is tailing him. They probably hope he'll lead them to Chris. So for now we've got to keep him away from there."

"My God. Is he in danger?"

"Don't worry. We're tailing their tail. It's a real merry-go-round out there. Just cozy down with your girl and let Uncle Burg take care of it. I'll see you at elevenish—have a drink ready for me, and I may have some good news for you."

When he hung up Quintain turned to find Chris standing

sleepily in the door to the bedroom. "Who's 'at?" she asked through a yawn.

Quintain reported what Burger had said. She frowned. "I'd feel better if I could see Uncle Luke."

He showed her the article. She looked up sadly from reading it. "Poor Verna. Is this all she gets?"

They ate a desultory dinner in the room. A flat, depressing mood had settled on them. Quintain tried to read the newspaper he had had sent up, while Chris curled up on the couch with a magazine. Finally, he threw down the paper, went to Chris and pulled her to her feet and kissed her. She touched his face gently. The bruises were taking on a yellowish hue, and the bridge of his nose was swollen and flattened to one side. "You should see a doctor."

"It's all right," he murmured, and kissed her again. There was no passion in her response.

"I need some time, Alex," she said.

"You didn't need time last night."

"It was so different then. I don't know. We'd been through so much."

He released her. "I understand."

She put her hand on his arm. "Don't be hurt. I think I know you. I think the way I felt last night was genuine. I just need a little time to be sure."

He took a deep breath and let it out. He smiled at her. "Okay. I'll wait. You're worth it."

"Are you so sure?"

He nodded vehemently. "Positive."

She gave him a look, a strange look that he couldn't fathom, and sat down again and picked up her magazine.

Burger didn't arrive until nearly midnight. His face was red, his clothes awry, as if he had run up the fifteen flights to their floor. "God!" he announced, "I need a drink."

After Burger was settled in a chair with his drink, his color more normal, he said, "Well children, I bring you mixed news. But the bottom line adds up positive."

"When can we get out of here?" Quintain asked eagerly.

"For you, soon," Burger replied. "If you agree to help us. I think we've come up with a way to wind this whole thing up in one big bang."

"What's the mixed part?"

"You've got to take a small risk. Much smaller than it might seem at first."

"Terrific."

"Just hear me out, and then it's up to you. We want you to call Felix out."

Quintain stared at him. "*Call* Felix?"

"Yeah. We'll set it up. You just do what I say, and everything will go all right." Burger leaned forward, his eyes glittering with excitement. "It's our chance to round up the whole bunch. The code says the challenged gets to choose the site. We think he'll choose somewhere around here. If he does the whole damn Council will be there. You can bet on it. Now don't look that way, Quint. We'll be right there."

"They'll never agree to that," Quintain replied. "They think I have the money. What good . . . ?"

"Ah. That's another little wrinkle we've planned. We'll give 'em the money."

"*Give* it to them?"

"Well, not the actual money, of course. We don't have time to go through all the red tape to get that much. But we've prepared some documents that will make them think they've as good as got their hands on it."

"Why should I do that—if I went to all the trouble to steal it?"

"It's a trade. A chance for your life. You know they're going to kill you. This way, if you beat Felix, you're free."

"They'd actually let me go?"

"Of course not. If something went wrong, and Felix lost,

207

they'd squash you like a bug. But, believe me, they won't be worried about that. I told you—Felix is the best."

"Let me get this straight. If I agree, you'll be there? I won't have to ...?"

"We won't let Felix get near you. We'll let them assemble, and then round them up. Don't you see? This is the quickest way we have to identify all the members of The Council. There isn't a one who would miss a chance to see Felix in action. Otherwise, it might take us months to identify them all. And for all that time we'd have to keep you and Chris locked away somewhere."

"Jesus." Quintain passed a hand across his eyes. "I don't know."

"No!" Chris rose and put her hand on Quintain's arm. "Don't do it."

"Listen," Burger said, "I've talked this over with General Frawley. He agrees that it's the only way."

"It is if you don't try to think of another," Quintain retorted angrily. "You've got it all planned, haven't you?"

"Okay, so we've done a little planning. I don't see any other way to get them all together. And unless we get every last one of them, your lives won't be worth living, assuming they let you live. Do you want to spend the rest of your days locked away for your own protection?"

"No." Quintain massaged his temples. "Tell me exactly what I'd have to do."

"Just go to the rendezvous. We'd be right behind you."

"But, Jesus—what if the timing's a little off? What if this guy shoots me while you're getting there?"

"It doesn't work that way, Quint. These duels are fought unarmed, both men naked."

"*Naked!*"

"So you see, he can't shoot you." Burger stared at him expectantly. "You don't have any problems. How about it?"

"Wait a minute," Quintain answered. "I've got to think."

Burger fell silent, watching Quintain with that expectant light in his eyes. Quintain fought with the fear. It was one thing to react instinctively at the cabin, to fight for his life, and for Chris'. It was quite another to walk deliberately into the battle unarmed. Of course, that wasn't quite true— Burger and his men would be close behind.

"I'd go myself, Quint," Burger said quietly. "But you're the one they want. I'll tell you this, though—I won't be any less careful than if it was me."

Quintain looked into Burger's eyes. In the past hours he had begun to look at Burger almost as a stranger, and in a way he was—at least this side of him was. Now he remembered—it all flooded back—their friendship, the only friend he had. He believed him. He *would* be as careful as if it were his own life at stake. If I can't trust my best friend, Quintain told himself . . .

"All right," he said quietly. "I'll do it."

Burger bounded to his feet. "Great! I'll have to leave you two. I'll be back in the morning to fill you in. And with a letter for you to write, Quint."

After Burger was gone, Quintain fixed himself a drink. He felt remarkably calm.

"Aren't you worried?" Chris asked.

"Why should I be worried? I've always wanted to meet a homicidal maniac in hand-to-hand combat."

They retired to separate bedrooms, saying awkward goodnights. Quintain had difficulty getting to sleep. His imagination painted lurid scenes of himself and a faceless, hideous man locked together in a death struggle. When he finally dozed off his sleep was restless, and filled with strange dream fragments: a large, unidentifiable animal galloping through a raging river, its huge jaws snapping at the waters, then a silken presence, warm and reassuring, an arm across his chest. He turned, still more asleep than awake, and reached out. The dream presence did not vanish, but enfolded him more closely. His hand found the silken ripeness of a hip, and traced it up to the falling away of a waist, slim and firm. A gentle, shallow breath warmed his neck, murmured against his flesh, awakened his passions.

"Chris," he whispered.

Her thighs took him hungrily, and clamped him deeply to her. She inhaled a shuddering breath, and let it out with a series of catchings timed to the rhythm of their passions. Her back arched and lifted them both upward, joining them more deeply. Her arms were under his shoulders, and clamped across his back. She thrust at him and gripped him and moaned low animal noises as her head rolled back and forth, tossing her thick hair across her face. Her release was a chaotic giving, a merging with him, that demanded hungrily of him a need that he met for so long, and with such thrusting, pumping vigor, that when it was over he lay with his cheek against her damp, warm breasts, stunned and as helpless as a child.

"Oh God," Chris whispered. "God, God ..."

He stirred, raised his head, and tried to see her face in the darkness. He put his hand out, brushed against her hair, felt her cheek. It was wet.

She moved suddenly, turning her face away.

"Chris," he repeated, his voice urgent now.

"Don't," she said in a strangled voice. "Don't say anything."

Then she was alive with passion again, a desperate yearning that took him unprepared and at first frightened him. She kissed him frantically, her tongue probing his mouth. She rolled him over, toppled onto him in a spasm of flailing limbs, knees, swinging pendulous breasts. Her thighs caught his hips, and she mounted him, and kneeling, with her head thrown back, the weak light at the window catching her pulsing throat, thrust herself on him again and again, until, with a final wracking plunge, collapsed gasping on his chest. He held her, stroking her, his eyes staring unseeing at the dim wash of light at the window, until she fell into a fitful sleep in his arms.

He awoke first. She was sleeping on her side, her arm supporting her cheek, one leg doubled under her, the other thrust out, the foot arched as if trying to touch something solid. Her eyes were shadowed, her mouth chafed and tender-looking. He propped himself on an elbow and watched her. Then, he bent and kissed her gently on the forehead. She stirred, murmured, and doubled her other leg up and wrapped her arm around her knee.

He got out of bed quietly, went in the bathroom, and showered. When he came out with a towel wrapped around his waist, she was in the same doubled-up position, but her eyes were open. He stopped by the bed, uncertain of her mood, and said, "Hi."

She smiled. "Hi, yourself. Did I scare hell out of you last night?"

"No. Well, maybe a little."

"I scared hell out of myself."

He sat on the edge of the bed, and she put out a hand and touched his waist, as if testing to see if he were real. "Chris. I'd like to ask you something."

"Sounds important."

"It is."

She sat up, took cigarettes from the nightstand, and lit one. "Okay."

"Last night, you . . . you were really there. For me."

"That's a question?"

"Was I, for you?"

She exhaled heavily. She was propped up against the head-board, her legs stretched out, her ankles crossed. Her hair dipped across her forehead and covered one eye. She peered at him from that eye. "You ask hard questions, don't you, Alex?"

He took the cigarette from her fingers, took a deep inhalation, and handed it back.

"The last time," she said slowly, "no, and, yes."

"And the first?"

"Yes. All the way."

"Do you want to talk about it?"

She nodded. "I owe you that."

He flushed. "You don't owe me a damn thing. I don't want your indebtedness."

"I'm sorry. I didn't mean it that way. Look," she leaned across to him and touched his face with gentle fingers, turning his head toward her, "I tried to tell you before—I've been through a lot. Not that what I've been through is unique, or, for that matter, any worse than what you went through. It's just that the wounds are fresher."

"I know. Was he . . . ?"

"Don't ask that. There are no comparisons. You were the first man since him. Which is not an advantage, believe me."

"I wouldn't say that."

"But it's true. You asked if I knew who you were. Who you were got all mixed up with what I was, what I'd been through. That last time was a kind of exorcism."

"Did it work? Are all the demons gone?"

"I think so. And for that, I really do owe you a lot. If you were another kind of man—the kind only interested in chalking up one more on the score card—it wouldn't have worked."

"You think I should open an office?"

"Don't be bitter, until you hear it all. That night in the motel—God! Was it only night-before-last?—after what we'd been through. I had a hard time separating out reality. We've really started out with the most incredible handicaps. This situation—Burger cheerfully sitting there and talking about things that I've only seen in nightmares, the whole thing at the cabin—don't you see? We haven't had the chance to know each other in an everyday, mundane way that

212

doesn't include people trying to kill us. On top of all that, I don't know—didn't know—if what I felt was just a kind of reaction to my marriage breaking up."

"Didn't know?"

"I'm a lot surer this morning of how I feel."

The surfer brought their breakfast. This time Quintain treated him like an ordinary bellhop, although the blond giant kept eyeing Chris sitting curled up on the sofa as if he would need little encouragement to linger.

Burger came shortly after noon. He was dressed in a dark suit, and was carrying a briefcase. He sat on the couch, unsnapped the briefcase, and removed a sheaf of official-looking documents.

" The applications for numbered accounts at three different Swiss banks." He gave them a self-satisfied smile. "A little touch of realism on my part. If you divide the money up among three banks, they're less likely to ask questions than if you put the whole lump in one. It's an old tax-evader's trick."

He spread the documents out on the couch. "All backdated to the time the embezzlements started." He held up three thin booklets with plastic covers. "Bank books with deposit records covering the period of the embezzlements."

He held up a last document. "And the clincher. Power-of-attorney, with a blank designee."

Quintain took the power-of-attorney and read it. "So I sign this, and they think they've got their money back. What's to prevent them from killing me any time after that?"

"Two things. You don't sign it until you get to the site of your little rendezvous with Felix. They'll have a notary there, one of their own members. And, second, The Council wouldn't miss this chance to see Felix and you go at it. They're drooling like Roman citizens with front row seats at the Coliseum."

"They'll *have* a notary there?" Chris asked.

Burger nodded. "We've already been in touch with them on your behalf, Alex. I thought I'd have you write them a letter, but as long as we were getting all this other stuff forged, we went ahead and did the letter, too. Saved time."

He flipped to a page in the bank application. Quintain stared down at his own signature. "You did all *that* since last night?"

"At the Office of Soil Conservation," Burger said with a wink, "office hours are a mere formality." Quintain could see that he was enormously pleased with himself.

"You've been working on this case a long time, haven't you?" Quintain asked.

"Years—literally. And after tonight, we'll have it wrapped up."

"Tonight?" Something caught in Quintain's throat.

"More precisely, two o'clock tomorrow morning. Just before I came up here, we got their answer."

"Where?"

Burger shrugged. "We'll find out tonight, when they pick you up."

"You mean you don't know where they're taking me ... ?"

"Couldn't you have asked them?" Chris asked.

"Not likely, we couldn't." Burger paused, looking appraisingly at them. "Sometimes I forget that everyone in the world isn't mixed up in my work. We can't ask them anything. And we couldn't ask Quint to simply walk up there. He wouldn't have lived long enough to say hello, even if he'd been dumb enough to do it."

"Then, how *did* you do it?" Quintain asked.

Burger spoke patiently, as if explaining elementary arithmetic to children. "We put the letter in the ingoing mail of a certain man we *know* is on The Council. That was this morning. In the letter we included the instructions for the reply.

214

We put some time pressure on so they wouldn't have too long to think it over. We told them to have their courier take a cab at a certain stand at eleven o'clock this morning, and for him to take the cab to a certain address. On the way, he stuffs their reply, sealed in an ordinary business envelope, behind the seat, well out of sight."

"What if they followed the cab?"

Burger grinned. "We fully expect that they tried to. We followed it, too. Incidentally, it was a legitimate cab, one that happened to be next up when their man arrived at the stand. Now, we let the cab pick up fares twice more, following at a discreet distance. Then our man hopped out, walked into a hotel at another entrance, sat and read a paper until our cab was next in line at the stand we'd trailed him to, and then casually walked out and got in. He pulled out the envelope and stuck it in his pocket, got out at his destination, where we were waiting ... simple."

"Simple!" Chris said, her eyes wide with disbelief.

"I see," Quintain said. "They couldn't very well kidnap every passenger he picked up."

"Exactly. Besides, they were probably looking for you to pick it up personally. So right now you have undoubtedly risen in their estimation."

"But, if you don't know where they're taking me, how the hell do I know they won't pull something similar on you?"

"Take it easy, Slick. We're going to have them in a moving net. Four cars. Two ahead, and two behind. All in radio communication. If they break the net at one point, it folds back on them at another. Take my word for it."

"Do I have a choice?"

Burger put his hand on Quintain's shoulder and looked solemnly into his eyes. "I guess not. Try to get some rest. I'll be back at midnight, sharp, to give you your final instructions."

"Burger," Quintain said, matching Burger's solemnity, "do me a favor?"

"Anything I can."

"Don't say, 'final'!"

Chapter 19

BURGER returned precisely at midnight carrying a brief-case. He was taut and excited. His eyes were distant, as if focused beyond the walls of the room.

Quintain felt a sense of detachment himself, as if he stood apart and observed the three of them disinterestedly. His mind floated on a layer of lassitude.

He hadn't been able to follow Burger's suggestion and rest. He had paced, tried to read, talked in staccato bursts to Chris. Chris had been a marvel. Steady and calm. She had soothed him when he needed it, left him alone when he needed that, with an instinct for his moods that was quick and sure. Now, as Burger rattled off instructions, Quintain felt fatigue drain him. His eyelids drooped, his limbs felt leaden.

Burger interrupted himself to stare at Quintain lounging across from him on the couch. "You all right, Quint?"

Quintain nodded and yawned mightily.

Burger's look was admiring. "You are the coolest amateur I've ever run across."

"Reaction," Quintain mumbled. "I'll be up for the main event."

Burger went through the documents in the briefcase. He rehearsed Quintain in amounts, names of banks, procedures for opening accounts in Switzerland. "Be prepared," Burger admonished. "But don't worry about it. I doubt there will be many questions. These papers speak for themselves."

Burger stored the documents back in the briefcase and put it on the couch beside Quintain. Then he took a small card from his coat and handed it across. Quintain stared dully at it. Typed on the card was a Los Angeles address.

"It's out in East L.A. in the old industrial section. A machine shop that Continental invested in and then had to take over when aerospace business went to hell. That's where they'll pick you up to take you to the site. Remember, don't sign that paper until you're sure you're at the site. It's your life insurance policy."

Burger told him to go to the lobby of the hotel at twenty of two, take a cab to the address in East Los Angeles. "We'll be with you all the way," Burger said. He took a small photograph from his coat pocket, and held it out for Quintain to look at. It was a photo of a thin, weathered man dressed in an ill-fitting dark suit, standing on a terrace of some kind with trees behind him. It had the slight distortion and out-of-focus background that telephoto lenses produce.

"It's the only picture we have of Felix," Burger said. "Study it well. This was taken about three years ago. He looks about the same, except now he has a tonsured head just starting to grow back."

"Tonsured?" Quintain looked up at Burger.

"A cover he used recently. Never mind that. Just make sure this man is at the site before you sign the paper."

Quintain bent his head over the photo. Felix's expression was hard to make out. He had an angular, bent nose, a small slash of mouth, but it was the eyes that were arresting. Perhaps through some idiosyncrasy of the lens, the eyes were in clear focus, illuminated by a diagonal shaft of light coming somewhere off-camera. They were peculiarly dead eyes, revealing nothing about the thoughts of the man. They reminded Quintain of the eyes of some predatory animal, not as cold as they were unfeeling in some feral, primordial way.

Burger put the photo back in his pocket. "Don't take anything but the briefcase. Here, empty your pockets now."

Burger and Chris watched him stand and empty his

218

pockets onto a coffee table. Burger took two twenty dollar bills from his own wallet and stuffed them in the pocket of Quintain's jacket that was lying on a chair. "Cab fare," he said.

"Okay," Burger said, squeezing his hands together as he paced. "Remember. Don't say any more than you have to. Only answer questions about the money. That's all they're interested in, anyway."

"That, and killing me," Quintain said in a flat tone.

"Don't worry about that." Burger looked at his watch. "Any problems?"

"What if you're not there?"

"Look, the timing may be off a few seconds either way. Just keep going along with it. We'll get you out in plenty of time."

Burger picked up the card with the address and tucked it in Quintain's shirt pocket, giving the pocket a little pat and looking Quintain up and down. "You'll do fine," he said. He looked at his watch again.

"One minute," Quintain said.

"What?"

"It couldn't be more than one minute since you looked at it the last time."

Burger lowered his arm and shot his cuff over his watch. He forced out a dry, nervous laugh. "I've got to get along," he said. "Remember, we'll be with you . . ."

"All the way," Quintain said.

Quintain and Chris sat close on the couch, her arm twined through his. "I wish I could go with you."

"You wait here, like you've been told."

"Yessir."

"When I get back, we'll wake up Burger's room service and have them drag the biggest steaks in the hotel up here."

"A celebration."

"Right."

219

"I'll have champagne waiting."

He squeezed her hand. It was damp and hot.

At one-thirty-five, Quintain stood and slipped his jacket on. They looked into each other's eyes for a long second. Then he picked up the briefcase and went to the door. By the door was a small table. On top of the table was the key to the room. As he opened the door he automatically picked up the key and put it in his coat pocket. Then he left the room without looking back.

The building was a large quonset structure, set on a half acre of concrete, with a railroad siding on one side, and a row of empty, blasted-looking tenement houses on the other that had been condemned under a city renewal project.

The driver stopped the cab along the chain-link fence that enclosed the machine shop. "You sure this is the place?"

Quintain got out with the briefcase, handed the driver a twenty, and took the change blindly while he stared at the building. He stuffed the change in his pocket and started to walk away.

"Thanks a lot, fella."

Quintain turned, stared at the angry face of the cab driver for a moment, then walked back, took the change from his pocket, found a dollar bill, and handed it through the window of the cab.

The cab pulled away. Quintain stood looking at the dark building. It appeared deserted. The concrete apron was empty. He looked up the street toward the tenement houses. No traffic stirred, no cars were parked on the street. In the other direction, the street ended at a dead end at the railroad tracks. The tracks were rusted from disuse. Beyond them, a weed infested field lay dim and motionless. There was no sign on the building, only the address spelled out in flaking black paint beside a small door, the only opening in his side of the building. The channeled walls were blank. Streaks of rust leached from the siding joints made bloody stains down its face.

He assumed he was to wait where he was. He wondered where Burger and his moving net were. They certainly couldn't risk driving their cars down the dead-end street. He understood that. His hope was that they lurked nearby. Perhaps behind the factory, or on the next street over, behind the houses. He had seen no sign of them on his way there in the taxi. He was uneasy, even though he realized if he could spot them, it wouldn't be difficult for others to. It was a kind of negative affirmation of their competence that didn't reassure him much.

In the door to the factory was a small, dirty window, and as he glanced in that direction a flash of light through the window arrested his attention. It was a brief flare, as if someone inside had switched a flashlight on and off. As he stared at the door across the intervening gloom, it opened and a man came out. He was dressed in a tuxedo, and he walked briskly to where Quintain stood.

"Ah, Mr. Quintain. So glad you could join us."

"You!" The man was McCormick.

"I can appreciate your surprise. The papers are in there?"

Quintain nodded dumbly. McCormick held out his hand, and Quintain passed the briefcase to him.

"Now, Mr. Quintain, if you will just walk ahead of me at a normal pace to that door."

Quintain stopped at the door, and looked over his shoulder. McCormick reached around him, pushed the door open, and gestured with his palm up for Quintain to enter.

A velvet darkness filled the building. Quintain took hesitant steps, his hands feeling in front of his body. A light came on so suddenly that it momentarily blinded him.

As his eyes adjusted he could see a low metal shade spilling a cone of light down onto a rough table that was oil-stained—some kind of work bench. Two men stood by the

H

table looking at him. They were also dressed in tuxedos. One of the men was Pendelton. Quintain glanced back and saw McCormick adjusting a heavy curtain over the window of the door.

"Step over here, please," Pendelton said.

Quintain walked to the bench. He became aware of other presences in the building. He could see little beyond the cone of light; but vague shadows, the scrape of a foot, a low mutter, a whisper of movement told him that he was surrounded by people.

McCormick strode to the bench and swung the briefcase up on it. Pendelton opened it, withdrew the papers to the bench, and carefully went through them. Then he picked up the bank books, and read each one. Finally, he looked up and nodded toward the dark upper reaches of the warehouse.

Pendelton took a gold pen from his pocket, and extended it toward Quintain. "If we could get you to sign . . ."

"When we get to the place," Quintain said. His throat felt parched.

Pendelton didn't lower his pen. He stared into Quintain's eyes. "This is the place, Mr. Quintain."

"I thought—"

"Obviously. But now you know differently, so please sign."

"Not until I see him."

Quintain's mind was spinning. He felt panic threaten to take it over completely, and he struggled to maintain control. He had to think. Pendelton was staring at him with icy contempt. If this was the place, how would Burger reach it in time. Would he keep his network at a safe distance, while inside here Quintain had to face Felix.

"Quintain," Pendelton said, "You have caused us a great deal more trouble that you warrant. Sign the paper."

"Not until I see Felix," Quintain replied. He was surprised that his voice was so calm. He could feel sweat breaking from his armpits and making scalding tracks down the side of his body. He knew he had to stall to give Burger time to figure out what had happened and move in.

Pendelton held Quintain's gaze for long seconds, and finally lowered the pen. He looked over Quintain's shoulder, and said quietly, "Felix."

Quintain turned slowly, as if to meet a blow. The man stood just inside the edge of the cone of light. He was taller than he looked from the picture, his face eroded with lines, his long arms and legs corded with taut sinew, his eyes cast in darkness. He was naked.

Felix stood perfectly still. Then, in a movement so imperceptible it seemed to Quintain that he had disappeared before his eyes, he stepped back into the darkness.

"The signature, Quintain."

Quintain turned back to find Pendelton offering the pen once again. Quintain took it, and Pendelton peeled back the documents to one, and indicated a line on it. Quintain put the pen down to it, and then deliberately let his nerves take over. His hand trembled violently. Pendelton quickly pulled the paper out of range of the shaking pen.

Quintain straightened, and passed a hand across his eyes. "Sorry."

Pendelton produced a silver flask from his hip pocket, unscrewed the lid, and held it out to Quintain. Quintain took the flask in both hands and tipped it up. He held the burning liquor in his mouth, and swallowed it slowly, a trickle at a time. He watched Pendelton's face, and when he estimated the other man's patience was about to break, he tipped the flask up and took another gulp of the scalding liquor.

"Take a deep breath," Pendelton said, "and let it out slowly."

Quintain did as instructed, delaying the exercise as long as he dared. Then he picked up the pen, and dropped it. The man beside Pendelton bent to retrieve it as Quintain found it with his foot and gave it a discreet kick.

"He kicked it!" the man below the table reported. He rose with the pen.

Pendelton's eyes hardened. "Mr. Quintain, if you stall one more second, I will shoot you." He took a gun from inside his coat and leveled it on Quintain's chest.

Quintain bent over the table and quickly signed his name. Pendelton turned the paper and looked at the signature. Then he produced from his coat pocket a small silver case. He removed the top half, and stamped it on the paper. Then he bent over and wrote quickly under Quintain's signature.

Pendelton straightened and once again looked into the darkness.

"Signed and notarized," he reported to the phantom audience.

"Let's get on with it," the voice came echoing, disembodied and ghostly, from above.

McCormick and the stranger led Quintain through the darkness. A light was put on, and Quintain found himself in a narrow room lined on one side with lockers and a bench. As Quintain took his clothes off, the stranger took them and went through the pockets, dropping them in a pile on the bench when he was finished. He stared at the hotel key for a long moment, and then held it up for McCormick to see, put it back in the pocket of Quintain's coat, and dropped it on the bench.

"Right under our noses, weren't you?" McCormick asked with a grim smile.

"Tell him the rules," the other man said. Quintain could see a glint of excited anticipation in his eyes. Quintain now stood naked, shivering more with nerves than cold.

"You'll go in from this end," McCormick began, "Felix from the other. There is only one rule. If you try to break for it before it's over, you'll be killed. Clear?"

Quintain nodded dumbly. He was willing his body to be an antenna that would lead Burger to him quickly.

224

"You can use anything you find lying about," the other man said encouragingly. Quintain sensed the man's eagerness, and he recoiled from it. "It's a machine shop, so you might find most anything. Wrenches, chisels ... Use your imagination, and give us a good go, won't you?"

They took him to the door of the room, and shoved him through. He stumbled out into a blasting glare. The length of the building blazed with light from arc lamps mounted to the underside of a steel walkway that ran along one side of the building twenty feet off the floor. Quintain looked back to see McCormick and the other man clamber up a steel stairway and disappear into the gloom that shrouded the walkway. He looked up into the blackness above the walkway, and knew that he was in a makeshift arena. The spectators were up there. Ringside seats at the coliseum, Burger had said. The building was as long as a football field. Between him and the far wall were scattered machines—lathes, drill presses, arc welders—abandoned artifacts of the dying aerospace industry.

He caught a movement at the end of the building and saw Felix slip behind a row of huge electric motors that were bolted to skids.

His mind searched and found the delicate balance of his predicament. He had to find a strategy that would delay his coming into Felix's range. He had to give Burger time. He wondered how much time had already passed. Perhaps Burger was already moving in. The thought steadied him.

While he employed delaying tactics, provided he could come up with any, he knew he had to avoid the appearance of running from the confrontation. He knew with an icy certainty that his death would be quick and merciless if those watching eyes on the walkway detected any movement toward escape.

One thing was certain. He couldn't continue to stand there like a Judas goat. He crouched and ducked behind a lathe.

He peered cautiously over the edge of the lathe's bed, searching for a weapon, for an idea. Then he saw them. They were lying scattered on the floor by a drill press that stood twenty yards ahead of him. Bolts, with the nuts screwed on the ends. Heavy bolts, perhaps five inches long and an inch in diameter.

He didn't give himself time to think. He darted from the cover of the lathe, and ran hard in a low crouch, and skidded in under the drill press table. He gathered up three of the bolts, and waited, searching the area where he had last seen Felix, crouching like an animal in its burrow. No sign of Felix.

All was quiet, punctuated only by a hollow, echoing cough and the harsh scrape of shoe leather on metal from above. Quintain's spine prickled with the sensation of eyes traveling up it. He spun, striking his shoulder painfully against unyielding metal. No one there. Or had his eye caught the flash of bare flesh at the corner of the lathe he had just evacuated?

He braced himself, rose a little from his cover, and lobbed a bolt toward the lathe. It struck the metal bed and bounced in a slow-turning arc and dropped behind the lathe with a clatter of concrete meeting metal. A fragment of a laugh, choked short by its author into a mocking sound as sharp as the report of a gun, told Quintain of the futility of his action. He spun again with the flesh crawling conviction he was being observed from the rear. Once again only the hulking machines met his darting gaze.

He picked up two more bolts, and with two in each hand, let his knuckles rest on the gritty floor, crouched like a sprinter waiting for the starter's gun. He measured the path to the electric motors, then pushed off in a headlong rush down the factory floor, twisting and weaving between machines, his legs pumping, his chin jerking in rhythm to the slap of his bare feet on the concrete. As he neared the motors he raised both his fists over his head and leaped behind the motors, his body coiled to deliver blows with his weighted fists.

The area was vacant. He crouched behind a motor, panting, sweat stinging his eyes. His charge had been for the benefit of the spectators. He had expected and hoped that Felix would've moved on from the motors. His wild run, though perhaps an indication of poor offensive strategy, couldn't be interpreted as flight. He fervently hoped that Felix was, by now, at the other end of the building.

He squatted on his haunches, and surveyed his surroundings. Down the row of motors was the work bench, and behind it the door. He knew he could never make it to the door; and even if he could, he had no idea what precautions his captors had taken outside. A few feet behind him, near the wall of the building, was a dismantled lathe, its heavy head hanging from a chain over the bed. He had to stand nearly erect to glance over the top of the large motor. A bare expanse of floor ran from the motors to the wall where a row of crates stood.

It was a fluttering around his head, a whisper of air in his ears, more than any definable noise, that made him fall flat under the command of an instinct that he did not know he possessed, and that saved his head from being crushed between the electric motor housing and the head of the dismantled lathe as it swung on its chain over him and clanged into the motor, and then twisted away in a lazy arc.

He rolled to his left, toward the door, and his back struck an obstacle and he was stopped. He looked up into the face of Felix that seemed suspended from the dark firmament of the ceiling. Quintain threw himself with his arms and knees with all the force of his adrenalin charged body, crabbing backward along the floor on his chest and arms. He got his feet under him and rose and faced Felix.

Quintain's violent scramble had put ten feet between them, a separation that Felix was quickly narrowing in a crouch,

227

his hands carried flat at his chest, the rigid fingers pointed at Quintain. Those hands couldn't have looked more lethal if they had held a gun.

Quintain locked his eyes on Felix's and screamed. He screamed with all the force of his fear and anger, a long piercing bellow, his neck corded, his throat and head trembling with its force, but he never took his eyes from Felix's. He saw them flicker and sensed the hesitation in the other man's advance. He brought his left hand up from his side, still screaming, and almost as if he were showing the bolts in his hand to Felix, opened his palm and let them go.

Felix ducked the bolts easily, but Quintain moved in as he ducked and flailed out with his right fist, catching Felix on the ribs just under his armpit. It wasn't a well delivered blow, but the weight of the bolts gave it an extra force, enough to bring a quick surge of surprise to Felix's eyes.

Felix stumbled, and as he did Quintain lowered his head and threw himself at him. Quintain's feet left the ground, and his head struck Felix in the chest. It was a glancing blow, but Quintain's shoulder followed his head, and it made a solid contact that produced a sound like a hammer hitting a ripe melon, and brought a guttural grunt from Felix.

They went down, Felix with his back against the motor, Quintain tumbling past him, his body out of control from the force of his attack. As Quintain felt himself falling helplessly his left shoulder was stabbed with a piercing pain that made him shout. He struck the floor on his chest, doubled up his body, and skidded around in time to see Felix's hand complete its arc. The shoulder where Felix had struck him throbbed. Quintain's arm and hand felt numb and useless, and he realized if that blow had struck him in any vital part it would've killed him.

Quintain was on his good elbow, his feet toward Felix. Felix had fallen in a sitting position against the motor, and he was getting his legs under him to rise, his hands once more at his chest. Quintain lashed out with his heel at Felix's groin, and Felix turned and caught the blow on his thigh. Then he was over Quintain, those hands hovering as Felix bent lower. Quintain looked into Felix's eyes, the eyes from the photograph, indifferent, matte, no flicker of human spirit apparent in them, and knew that death was moments away.

Then Felix's eyes widened, and for an instant the glaze of animal indifference left them to be replaced with a look of outraged surprise. Felix's chest disintegrated, and descended in a bright shower of fragments on Quintain's bare flesh. Felix's body rose, his arms outstretched, and it seemed to Quintain that Felix was flying by his own effort of will, his back arched, his legs thrusting. An explosion filled the factory, thundering against its metal siding. Felix fell across Quintain's legs. Someone shouted. More explosions erupted. The lights went out. Quintain kicked himself free of Felix's body. Gunfire flashed from the walkway over his head, illuminating briefly a ghostly face. Other flashes from floor level answered. The noise became one continuous roar. Quintain rolled on his chest, put his head on his good arm, and tried to merge into the concrete.

The roar subsided. Someone spoke in an ordinary tone of voice. Someone answered. There was an isolated shot, answered with a roar and flash. Quiet. Quintain burrowed deeper into the concrete. More voices. The lights came on, the air was infused with acrid odor of exploded gunpowder. Somewhere a door slammed with a hollow echoing noise. Footsteps ran near him, and he peered over his arm and saw a man running toward the rear of the building. A car engine roared outside, followed by four shots in rapid succession. Tires squeeled, and then the engine noise faded into the distance.

A hand touched his shoulder, the bad one, making him jump with pain.

"Sorry. Nasty looking shoulder you have there." The voice

was clipped, British, with an underlying accent that Quintain couldn't identify.

The man was kneeling by Quintain, looking into his face with polite concern. He was dressed incongruously in a dark business suit and tie. Quintain, with the man's help, sat up. The man's face was dark, the lips full, the nose like a wedge separating his eyes. He cradled a blue automatic pistol in his hand.

A large man with an automatic rifle slung beneath his shoulder ran up and knelt by them, puffing. "Sorry, Colonel. I got a round through the back glass, but he got away." He was even darker than the Colonel, and his accent too was British. "Two of them, I think."

The Colonel cut him off with a rapid burst in a strange language. The man answered, and they helped Quintain to his feet. Quintain swayed, and then got his balance. His left arm hung useless at his side. His shoulder was afire with pain. The Colonel looked closely at it, and spoke to the other man in the strange language, and the man went quickly down the building. Now that he was on his feet, Quintain saw other dark men shepherding men dressed in tuxedos down the steel stairs at the end of the building, their gun barrels urging them along.

A body lay sprawled on the stairs, and the men carefully picked their way around it. The dead man's face was in profile to Quintain, and he saw that it was McCormick. He looked up at the walkway. The lights still shrouded it in darkness, but the head and shoulders of Pendelton hung down into the light, his arms dangling beneath him. His lifeless eyes were open, and seemed to stare directly at Quintain.

The large man returned with a green metal kit, and the Colonel opened it and removed a roll of elastic bandage from it.

"Appears you've got a partial separation, there," the Colonel said. He wrapped the bandage around Quintain's shoulders, bringing a final wrap under his arms and attaching it at his chest with a bandage clip. "Keep your hand tucked in your shirt, when you get one on, and you'll do."

The bandage relieved the pain. "Who are you?" Quintain asked.

The Colonel gave him a strange look, and said, "Never mind that now. Where are your clothes?"

The Colonel followed him to the locker room, and questioned him while he dressed. Quintain answered his questions freely, too exhausted and relieved to feel anything but gratitude for the Colonel and his men.

The Colonel helped him into his shirt, and then carefully placed his left hand inside an open button. "We've heard a bit about you," the Colonel said with a smile. "Didn't believe most of it, though."

Quintain told him the whole story. How he had been framed, the death of the Sandersons, his escape with Chris from the cabin ...

The Colonel's eyes widened. "Fronck? And Palmer? I couldn't believe it when I heard it. Thought you must be some kind of dybbuk, but you look mortal enough ..."

The Colonel questioned him very closely about Burger. When he'd finished, he sighed, and said, "Looks like the yanks handled this with their customary efficiency. Left you in here with Felix while they were probably wheeling around out there running over one another. Good job for you we happened by."

Quintain grinned wanly and said, "It was a good job, all right, although I wouldn't guess you 'happened' by."

"Mr. Quintain," the Colonel replied in a quiet voice that chilled Quintain, "I would strongly urge you to leave off speculating on that score. In fact, it's an awfully good idea for you to forget you were ever here."

"I can go?" Quintain was now completely dressed.

The Colonel nodded. "I'm afraid we're going to have to

231

leave you on your own. Haven't got the time to run a taxi service."

As Quintain turned to leave, the Colonel said, "Oh, Mr. Quintain. Believe me, it will do you no good to report what happened here to the police. By the time you could have them here, there'll be nothing left to back up your story. So save yourself the embarrassment."

"Colonel," Quintain replied levelly, "I don't know what you're talking about. How could I, when I've never met you?'"

Chapter 20

QUINTAIN walked for half an hour before he found a public phone in the lot of a dark service station and called a cab. His shoulder was aching in the night air, and he was stumbling from exhaustion.

He had expected to be picked up by Burger or one of his cars, but after he had walked for nearly a mile he knew that something had gone wrong. Had Burger lost him on the cab ride to the machine shop? Quintain couldn't think clearly. The pain in his shoulder and his numbing fatigue narrowed his mind down to a beam focused on one objective—to get back to the hotel and Chris.

After he called the cab, he looked through the window of the station office and saw by the clock inside that it was nearly four o'clock. He put another coin in the phone and called the hotel, taking the key from his pocket to recall the room number. The phone rang for nearly a minute, and then the hotel operator came back on the line to tell him the obvious news that his party wasn't answering.

"Are you sure you rang the right room?" Fear sent a cold chill up his neck, and cleared his mind. He was suddenly very alert.

"Fifteen-forty-two," the operator said irritably.

He sat in the back of the cab, his mind spinning with questions. Where was Chris? Where could she be at four o'clock in the morning? He felt the dark force of the paranoia closing in on him. He fought to sort fiction from fact, to find the *truth*. But he didn't have the truth. He wouldn't have until he found Chris. Was she gone because she didn't expect him back? He forced that thought from his mind, but it kept struggling to get back in. The Council was gone. Chris couldn't be in any danger now. Why had she left the hotel? He recognized the seductive whisper of the old paranoid. Goddam it, he told the old paranoid, I *love* her . . . !

"What's that?" The cab driver had his head turned toward Quintain, a wary expression on his face.

Jesus, Quintain thought, *I'm talking aloud to myself!* He muttered something about it having been a long day to the cab driver, and the man seemed palpably glad to be rid of him when he dropped him at the United Air Lines terminal where Quintain had directed him.

The United terminal was at the far end of the concourse from the hotel. Quintain walked through the corridor, staying close to the wall, until the elevator to the hotel lobby was in sight. He paused in front of a newspaper dispenser and pretended to read the headlines.

The hallways were nearly deserted. A man in blue overalls pushed a little mountain of oiled sawdust along the floor with half-hearted effort, and gave Quintain a lazy, curious look as he swept past. Quintain realized his appearance was probably little better than that of a derelict, with his dirty clothes, his sweat stained face, and the left arm of his coat hanging empty at his side.

Near the elevator two airport security men were standing and talking, with radios clipped to their belts. He walked to the elevator, got in, and pressed the button for the hotel lobby. The security men gave him a brief examination and went back to their conversation.

Behind the bell-captain's desk in the lobby a man in a bell-hop uniform stood leaning on his elbows, his eyes half-closed. Quintain approached him.

"Is Brown on duty?"

The man looked up slowly, took in Quintain's clothes and

234

his grimy, stubbled face, and decided he was not important enough to change posture for. "Brown?"

"Yeah. Big, blond bellhop."

"No one by that name. You mean Garret?"

Quintain hesitated. "Maybe."

The man turned to a door behind him, pushed it open, and yelled in, "Hey, Garret. Somebody to see you."

The blond surfer came through the door, yawning and buttoning his bellhop's jacket. Quintain saw recognition, mingled with suspicion, dawn in the man's eyes. "You wanna see me?"

The man behind the desk was staring at Quintain with open curiosity. "Is there somewhere we can talk?"

The bellhop finished buttoning his tunic and gave Quintain a long look. "Down here." He led him into a narrow hallway. On one side were swinging doors with porthole windows. Through them, Quintain could see two cooks in chef's hats working over a steam table.

"Yeah?"

"Where's Chris? Miss Bell?"

The surfer's eyes widened. "Who?"

"Listen, I don't have time to play games. Get Burger . . ."

"Sure . . . sure . . ." The bellhop edged along the wall.

Quintain slammed him up against the doors with his good forearm. "Goddam it! You start making sense." Over the man's shoulder he could see the cooks staring at the porthole windows.

"Hey, take it easy." The surfer shoved. He was strong. Quintain stumbled back against the opposite wall.

"Problems, Gary?" One of the chefs stood at the door, his head peering around it. Quintain saw the ugly blade of a heavy knife protruding through the door at waist level.

"This guy . . ."

Quintain turned and ran out of the hall.

The man behind the bellhop's desk stared at him as Quin-

235

tain sprinted across the lobby and into an elevator. He pushed the button for the fifteenth floor. As the doors were closing, he saw the surfer and the chef run from the hall and begin talking animatedly to the man behind the bell-captain's desk.

The hallway on the fifteenth floor was deserted. Quintain paused in front of fifteen-forty-two, and put his ear against the door. He could hear nothing over the throb of an air conditioning unit inside. He put the key in and pushed the door open.

The suite was as he had left it. The items from his pockets on the coffee table, the bed where he had tried to rest rumpled, one of Burger's cigar butts in an ashtray, but it was deserted. He searched for any trace of Chris, a note, some clue to her whereabouts. There was nothing. He considered calling down for messages, but decided it was too risky. He didn't know what the two bellhops and the cook were up to, and he didn't want to find out. He picked up his things from the coffee table, stared for a moment at his key ring, and made a decision. He went down the stairs to the garage level, up a ramp to Century Boulevard, and hailed a passing cab without incident.

He had the cab let him out at an all-night filling station three blocks from the offices of Continental. He went in the restroom, shrugged out of his jacket, and washed his face and neck with his good hand. He arranged his hair, and with one last look at the gaunt, shadowed face that stared back at him in the mirror he left and walked to the Continental building.

The guard gave him a curious look, but let him sign in and go up the elevator. The halls on the thirtieth floor were deserted. He unlocked the door to his office, went in, locking the door behind him. He took off his jacket, pulled the investment program listing from the drawer of his desk, threw it on the desk top, and sat down in front of it.

The program was coded in the Fortran language. It was a language that Quintain was fluent in. Programmers left their mark, almost like a signature, on Fortran programs. The individuality occurred in the choice of labels for the various instruction sets. The programmer could choose any combination of characters or numbers up to six positions in length. Quintain himself, when writing in Fortran, always chose a Q as the first position of his labels to identify the programs he had written. Some programmers even went so far as to create whole sentences with satirical, often lewd meanings, when the labels were read in a certain order. He hadn't paid any particular attention to this program's labels, but now he examined them closely.

After a few minutes of studying the labels a pattern emerged—one he recognized. He put that together with the other facts he had. Two people escaping from the machine shop. The faces of the other spectators as they were led from the building by the Colonel's men—some familiar, some not— and, more important, another face, one that he had seen with those familiar faces many times around the offices and hallways of Continental, and that he had not seen at the machine shop. When he was through thinking, and rose to leave, there was a new grimness about his eyes, a tightness at the corners of his mouth that, had the Colonel been witness to, would've reduced his astonishment at Quintain having killed Miss Palmer and Fronck.

Quintain put the program listing under his arm and left the office without bothering to put out the lights or lock it. He knew he wouldn't be back, ever. As he walked to the elevator the thought struck him that the morning would find the executive ranks of Continental riddled with holes. The Colonel had not indicated to him the fate of his captives, but Quintain doubted that survival was among the choices.

Quintain walked in long purposeful strides along the street. The sky was an inverted pewter bowl, shot with the silver premonition of dawn. A night-owl cab cruised past him on Wilshire, slowing as the driver eyed him speculatively. Quintain ignored it. His mind was fixed on one thing, one destination. The coding sheets were clamped under his arm, and his stride was measured and relentless, ignoring traffic lights on the deserted street. He knew exactly where he was going, and exactly who he would find when he got there. He turned up Vermont, passed the garage where his MG reposed without a glance, shoved through the glass door into the lobby of his apartment building, and went up the steps two at a time.

The door to his apartment was unlocked. He pushed through and stopped in the center of the living room, staring. The only light came from a lamp behind the battered overstuffed chair. Sitting in the chair, her hands gripping the ends of the arms so hard her knuckles were white, was Chris Bell.

Their eyes locked, hers wide with fear. He stood as though under a spell, unable to breathe.

"Hello, Slick."

Quintain spun. Burger sat in shadows, the dark outline of his head against the wall, his glasses two tiny yellow lamps.

Quintain flung the coding sheets on the floor at Burger's feet. He saw the shadow that was Burger's head tilt, and then come up. "Got a little programming problem, Slick?"

Quintain crouched, his head thrust forward on his corded neck. "Goddam you!"

Burger brought the gun up and out into the light. Quintain took half a step forward, his good hand reaching out like a claw. The gun barrel swung in a short arc and pointed beyond Quintain. "She goes first," Burger said in a flat voice.

"Now," Burger said, "suppose you just sit right there on the floor where you are ..."

Quintain stared at the gun barrel, and then folded up to sit on the floor.

238

"I knew you'd be along, Quint. I've learned not to under-estimate you. What did it? The program?"

"No," Quintain said, his voice taut with anger. "It just confirmed it. The clever little labels you always put on your programs. But it started coming together when I talked to Brown." Quintain watched the barrel of the gun closely. He had to stall Burger, get him talking.

Burger frowned. "Brown?"

Quintain laughed mirthlessly. "You don't even remember the name you made up for the bellhop."

"Oh."

"There never were any of your people at the hotel. Those were the regular employees, weren't they?"

"I didn't *have* any people, Quint," Burger said wearily. "But if you figured all that out, why bother to confirm it?" Burger pointed the gun barrel at the program.

"Because I wanted no doubts when I killed you."

Burger chuckled hollowly. "You'd have done it, too, wouldn't you? Or tried, gun or no gun?"

"Yes."

"Except I kept the edge." The barrel swung up and pointed at Chris again.

"Maybe. For now."

"There's a way."

"I doubt that."

"Just listen for God's sake!" Burger's voice was shrill. He paused, and then continued more calmly. "You've got some information I need. If things work out we can all walk out of here."

"Why should I believe that?"

"Because it's the only choice you've got."

"What information?"

"I left the party at the machine shop prematurely. I didn't get to see the finish, to know who the hell it was that was shooting the place up."

239

"I see."

"Oh, I can guess. I just need it confirmed."

"Okay. We'll exchange information."

"No, Slick, I've already thrown enough into the pot."

"What can it matter, now?"

Burger was silent for a long moment. Finally, he said, "Okay. It's funny, but I have this urge to talk to you about it. Can you understand that?"

"I think so. Let's start with the Diamond business."

Burger's sigh was a long, quivering expulsion of breath. "Fifteen years. I am so goddam tired, you don't know how tired. Want to hear something funny? You know why I chose the name Diamond? Because diamonds are hard and they're expensive." He chuckled sardonically. "And right now I feel pretty spongy, and I don't know if I'm worth cab fare."

"Why?" Quintain asked. "We were friends. Why did you set me up?"

"I didn't want to, honest to God, Quint. I fought it, but they said you'd be perfect. Since we *were* friends, I could keep tabs, and control you."

"Verna and Sanderson?"

"Yeah."

"They talked *you* into it?"

"Okay. So it wasn't so hard. I wanted that money. You don't know how badly I needed that. It was the only way I could get out. After fifteen years all I had was a bad stomach, and a share of The Council's profits that I couldn't get at. Then, Sanderson came up with the idea to skim the currency exchange transactions. He'd gone through his own money, and he was desperate. It was his idea to get Regan to supply him with a systems analyst. He told Regan he wanted to do some studies for the legitimate side of the business."

"Regan?"

"Yeah." He paused, and then went on wearily. "McCormick's name on The Council."

Behind him, Quintain heard Chris' gasp of surprise.

"He's dead," Quintain said.

"I'm not surprised. He always was a hot-head."

"*Regan!*" Quintain said wonderingly, trying to stall. "And you were Diamond. It's like . . . like some kind of comic book world."

"Yeah, isn't it?" Burger said sadly.

"Who else? What other code names? How about Pendelton?"

"Atlas," Burger chuckled drily, "trying to compensate for his weakness." Burger paused. "I know what you're doing Quint—you're stalling. Don't waste your time. We'll go at my pace, because I'm the one with the gun. Right?"

"And you're the one with all the money. Did you arrange that too—Verna and Sanderson?"

"The Council wanted Verna and Sanderson burned. I went along . . . Oh, shit! I set it up. Do you realize what I'm talking about? I'm not talking about some petty theft. I am talking about a million dollars!"

"Terrific."

"I don't expect you to understand," Burger said with bitter weariness. "You don't know what it's like. It was like living in an insane asylum. All the phoney names, the games. When I first went into the business, I was young and patriotic. I thought I was doing it all for the preservation of the free world, and crap like that. And it was so goddam glamorous, I thought. Let me tell you, it's not glamorous at all. It's squalid drudgery; it's associating with twisted, sick people who feed on death and betrayal, and the more they feed the hungrier they get. It's being locked in so tight you can't get out. It's scheming and counter-scheming, until you don't know what's real any more, and what's some sick nightmare . . ."

"Why didn't you kill me when you had the chance? Why all that Office of Soil Conservation crap?"

Burger hesitated. "I didn't want to kill you, Quint."

"A little time," Quintain said angrily. "You were just going to buy a little time with my life, that's all?"

"No!" Burger said fiercely. "I was buying *my* life. Buying it back." He paused, and then said, more calmly, "It was a question of survival, Quint."

"Jesus," Quintain exclaimed. "The sheriff! How the hell did you get a county sheriff to go along?"

"He wasn't going along with me. He was following orders. The Council's been working on a case for the government."

"*Ours?*" Quintain asked sarcastically.

"If you'd been through what I have, you wouldn't have many illusions left, Quint."

"Believe me, I lost a few in that machine shop tonight."

"I really thought for a minute there you were going to get Felix. You've got a natural aptitude, Quint."

Quintain laughed humorlessly. "For survival, like you. Except I don't murder my friends."

Burger sighed wearily. "I've told you how it was with me. If you can't understand it, there's nothing more to talk about. Tell me what happened tonight."

"They blasted the place up, and took the survivors."

"What did they look like? Arabs?"

"Yes. They were led by a man they called Colonel."

"That's bad news, Quint," Burger said softly. "For you and for me."

"I told them where to find you."

Burger chuckled drily. "Nice try, Slick. No. You had to go all the way back to the office to convince yourself to come after me. Not that it matters, because by the time they finish with what's left of The Council, they'll know it all anyway. There are people on that Council who would sell out their mothers at the first sight of their own blood."

"What are you going to do?"

"That's a good question. What I'm not going to do is let

242

the Colonel take me. I know his methods, and I don't plan to go out begging someone to put the bullet through my head. I tell you what. I've got a little bet with myself. You get up very carefully, remembering who I've got this gun pointed at, and go to the window and tell me what you see."

Quintain got up and went to the window. As he passed Chris, he tried to give her an encouraging smile, but it felt pasted on his face. In the street across from the entrance to the building were two cars parked bumper-to-bumper. "Two cars."

"Anyone in them?"

Quintain saw the interior of one car lit briefly with a cigarette. "Yes."

Burger laughed drily. "I win my bet."

"It's them?"

"You can count on it. Now, you just come back over here and sit while I figure out some things."

Burger was silent for a long time. Finally, in a dry, low voice that was almost a whisper, Burger said, "It comes out one way."

Quintain felt an icy finger of fear touch his spine. "What?"

"You've got to understand, I'm not in operations," Burger said in the same arid voice. "Never have been. Oh, I've been trained." The gun barrel elevated slightly. "I can use this thing. It's just that I never have. Once. But that didn't count. More of an accident."

"Fight my way out?" Burger continued, as if reflecting a question he'd been asked. "They'd take me. Worse. They'd take me alive. Too many things to ask me. I won't go that way, Quint.

"I could use you two. But it wouldn't work. They wouldn't hesitate. You'd be in the way, and they'd get you out of the way."

Burger's tone was argumentative, as though he were defending in debate a position assaulted from various opponents. Quintain kept his eyes steadily fixed on the gun barrel, looking for a waver, a sign of inattention. He readied his mind and will for an attack.

Then it came. The gun barrel trembled, dipped, and disappeared into the shadows. Quintain was rising, his legs thrusting his body forward toward the shadowy outline of Burger's body, when Burger's head emerged from the shadows. His eyes were fixed on Quintain's face. There was a querulous vulnerability in those eyes, a silent plea to Quintain for an answer. In Quintain's ears the sound of the gun roared. Chris screamed.

Quintain stood transfixed, crouching, his legs still levering his body forward, his good hand curled at his side. The gunshot echoed on inside his head. Burger's arm lay on the floor, curved above his head, the gun still in his hand. The hole in his right temple was neat, circular, bloodless. He no longer had a left temple.

Quintain sank into the floor blindly. His hand clamped on Burger's shoulder, as he held his chin on his chest and let the vortex take him.

Chapter 21

THE COLONEL stood in the open doorway. His quick dark eyes took in Burger's body, the gun, Chris kneeling beside Quintain with her arm around his shoulders. Her head was thrown up so her eyes looked steadfastly into the Colonel's face.

"Mr. Quintain." Quintain slowly raised his head and met the Colonel's gaze. "My apologies for using you this way. But it was necessary. Unfortunately, we acted too late to get what we wanted." His eyes indicated Burger's body.

"He killed himself rather than be taken by you," Quintain said in a shaken voice.

The Colonel shrugged. "I would've done the same in his place. You have to understand that the issues involve the lives of thousands of people who have been deprived of their rightful home."

"Colonel," Quintain said slowly, "I hope you can live with that rationalization, because I couldn't."

The Colonel offered Quintain a tight smile. "I have to, Mr. Quintain." He looked over his shoulder and made a gesture. Two men pushed into the room. "The least we can do," the Colonel said, "is tidy up a bit." The men lifted Burger's body and disappeared out the door with it. The Colonel picked up Burger's gun and then he was gone.

They couldn't remain in the apartment. The memory of Burger's death hung in the room like smoke. They went down to the garage and Quintain backed the MG out. He drove clumsily, with one hand.

The sun was nearing its zenith. A low pall of smog and

mist hung over the city. The sun was a cold yellow ball. Quintain turned west on Wilshire. "The ocean," he said, vaguely. Chris seemed to understand. She nodded.

"We should tell someone," she said. "The authorities."

"Yes. But not now. I can't face it right now."

In Santa Monica he drove to the fishing pier and parked the MG in the municipal lot. They walked to the end of the deserted pier. Quintain leaned on the railing and took a long, long breath. A wave broke against the pilings beneath them with a roar. Chris moved close to him and slipped her arm around his waist. She studied the profile of his face, sharp against the grey sky.

"You know," she said. "I think you've lost it."

"What?"

"The boyish look."

He looked down at her. "Good riddance."

She tightened her hold on his waist and put her head on his shoulder. "Oh, no," she said. "I liked it. That was my look. I'll make it come back."

"How?"

"I have my ways. You'll see."

"It may take a while."

"I have the time."

"We'd have to be together?"

"Of course, darling. I can't work my magic long distance."

He smiled. She lifted her head and looked into his face.

"There," she said very gently. "You see. It's working already."